GAME MISCONDUCT

THE ATLANTA VIPERS

BOOK 1

ELIZA PEAKE

GAME MISCONDUCT

By Eliza Peake

Editor: Masque of the Red Pen

Cover by: Concepts by Canea, London

www.elizapeake.com

❀ Formatted with Vellum

NATIONAL ELITE HOCKEY LEAGUE

 **Atlanta Vipers**

Eastern Atlantic Division
Head Coach: William Holt

Centers

NO	PLAYER	POS	HT	AGE	PLAYER NOTES
19	Logan Beck	C1	6'2	32	Polished. Smooth talker. Fan favorite.
91	Riley Hunt	C2	6'1	27	Flashy playmaker. Charmer off ice.

Wingers

NO	PLAYER	POS	HT	AGE	PLAYER NOTES
17	Beau Holloway	LW1	6'3	37	Veteran. Single dad. All heart.
88	Finn McCade	RW2	6'2	31	Chaos gremlin. Fast hands, faster mouth.
12	Cal Reid	LW3	6'3	24	Quiet. Rising star. Maddox's shadow.

Defense

NO	PLAYER	POS	HT	AGE	PLAYER NOTES
4	Eli Ramsey	D	6'0	33	Steady. Loyal. Fallon's twin.
27	Jace Rourke	D	6'5	39	Team captain. Stoic. Legacy presence.

Goalies

NO	PLAYER	POS	HT	AGE	PLAYER NOTES
33	Maddox Lasker	G	6'4	39	Grumpy. Legendary. Wants redemption.

Front Office

NAME	TITLE	DEPT	NOTES
Sloane Carrington	Owner	Executive	Fierce, brilliant, and newly in charge.
Dean Ward	GM	Executive	Strategic. Resentful of Sloane's control.
Vivian Blake	Dir Player & Team Affairs	Team Operations	New to team. Loyal to Sloane.
Fallon Ramsey	Community Outreach	Communications	Grounded, local. Eli's twin.
Sierra Dane	PR/Media Manager	PR & Media	Polished, sharp. Stays on brand.

GAME MISCONDUCT PLAYLIST

Sabrina Carpenter – "Feather"
Taylor Swift – "I Can See You"
Keith Urban – "Blue Ain't Your Color"
Teddy Swims – "Lose Control"
Fleetwood Mac – "The Chain"
Kenny Chesney feat. Grace Potter – "You and Tequila"
Taylor Swift – "Don't Blame Me"
Luke Combs – "The Kind of Love We Make"
Bruce Springsteen – "I'm on Fire"
Teddy Swims – "911"
Adele – "Love in the Dark"
Chris Stapleton – "Cold"
Post Malone – "Circles"
Taylor Swift – "The Man"
Miranda Lambert – "Tin Man"
Taylor Swift – "King of My Heart"
Keith Urban – "Stupid Boy"
Hozier – "Too Sweet"
The Rolling Stones – "Beast of Burden"
Taylor Swift – "New Year's Day"

Find the playlist here on Spotify —> Game Misconduct Playlist

CHAPTER ONE

Sloane

IT TAKES a hell of a woman to run a hockey team, and headlines like this remind me the world still expects me to fail:

"Trending Hockey News: Is the Atlanta Vipers Second Season Doomed Before It Begins?"

It's clickbait. Lazy speculation wrapped in a question mark so they can pretend it's not slander.

But it still hits like a gut punch.

I minimize the tab and pull up the spreadsheet I've already combed through three times this morning.

And yep. The one column that matters the most is still using the P word.

Player Contract Status: Maddox Lasker – Pending.

My fingers curl tight around the edge of my desk. I reach for my coffee cup instead only to find it cold.

Again.

That makes three so far today.

And the sun has barely climbed over the Atlanta skyline.

The fact that I've left any coffee behind, much less multiple ones, is how I know I'm coming unglued.

If the cup isn't empty, I'm not in control—and right now, control is slipping between my fingers faster than this team's PR narrative.

My cell phone dances a jig on my desk and when I pick it up, I swallow hard when I see the agent's name on the screen.

Peter Dalton.

Also, when the hell did it become eight o'clock? I came in at six thinking I'd get a shit ton of work done.

Joke's on me. All I've managed to do is waste coffee and work my stomach into knots.

Time is a blur when your entire legacy hangs on a hockey player who gives new meaning to procrastination.

I swipe the screen, putting Peter on speaker. "Please tell me you have news I want to hear."

"Hey, Sloane. Good morning." His thick Boston accent fills my office with a tone that's too casual for my liking.

Then again, Maddox's agent is always too casual—like if he keeps his voice light enough, I won't notice he's full of shit.

Grinding my teeth together, I stand and walk to the window, my heels clicking softly against the polished floor of my office. "I don't have time for charm. Where's Maddox's signature?"

He laughs like we're on friendly terms. "You know Maddox. He's… processing."

"Is that what we're calling it these days?"

"He's not trying to be difficult."

I huff out a humorless laugh, watching the streets fill with traffic. "Maddox Lasker not difficult? We both know that's bullshit, Peter."

Another pause. "He's just used to Boston. That's a lot of years with the Freeze. A lot of routine. Your offer's solid. He's just not sure he wants to uproot."

"What's he actually doing? Because from where I sit, it looks a lot like hiding."

"He's not hiding. He's weighing his options."

"What options?" I snap, running out of patience for this fucking runaround Peter seems hell bent on giving me. "He's a free agent with no active offers except mine, and the clock is ticking."

"I wouldn't say no active offers—"

I close my eyes and silently count to ten. If I lose my shit, the next thing I'll read about is how *emotional* I am.

Fucking patriarchy.

"Don't play semantics with me. If he had a real offer, he'd have taken it. This is his shot. I gave him a lifeline, and all he's done is stall."

"Sloane, come on. He's just—he's been through a lot, okay? He needs time to make sure this is the right move."

I pause, tapping my nail against the phone screen, watching the seconds of the call tick by. "You told me three weeks ago it wasn't about the team."

"It's not."

"Then what the hell is it about?"

Peter exhales like I'm the difficult one. "He doesn't like change. He's quiet, methodical, set in his ways."

"So am I, but I still manage to get shit done."

"Sloane, he just needs more time."

"He doesn't get time," I say coldly. "He gets a choice. He either wants to play hockey or he doesn't. And if he wants to sit in Boston brooding over his past, fine. But not on my timeline."

Peter sighs. "You're putting a lot of pressure on him."

"Damn right I am. Because I'm not running a charity, Peter —I'm building a franchise. And right now your client is the only thing standing between me and the season opener without a goalie the team needs."

"I'll talk to him again—"

"You know what? Don't bother. I'll talk to him. In person. If Maddox has a problem, he can say it to my face. I'm not negotiating through his silence, and I'm not giving him another week to play hide and sulk."

Peter sighs. The kind of sigh I've heard a lot since my father died. The patronizing kind. "Sloane, I don't think that's a good idea."

"Well, lucky for me, I didn't ask for your opinion. And, Peter? Let your client know, I won't be coming to play nice."

I toss the phone onto my desk and drop into my chair. Pressing my fingers into my temples, my stomach twists with a mix of rage and something colder.

Something sharper.

Doubt.

I glance at the framed jersey on the wall. The one with my father's name stitched into it. With his signature scrawled across the fabric in black Sharpie—fading at the edges, like he's slipping out of reach even now.

"You asshole," I whisper. Not with venom. With something else. Something that coils tight and stings behind my eyes. "What were you thinking, Dad?"

The question lies heavy in the silence.

I push out of my chair before the ache can settle in too deep and walk over to the frame.

My fingertips hover over the glass, not quite touching; like maybe if I don't make contact, I won't fall apart.

"You started this expansion team to be *your* team. Your legacy. And you handed it to me like I'd know what the hell to do with it. Like I'd know how to finish building it."

I stare at the name, the number. My throat works around the grief I can't swallow.

"Was I your backup plan? Or was this always the play?"

Involuntarily, I hold my breath as though waiting for his powerful, deep voice to answer me.

I *need* him to answer me.

My heart clenches knowing this is one need that'll never be met.

The glass reflects my face back at me—tired eyes, a tight jaw, lipstick that should be smudged but wouldn't dare.

I look like I know what I'm doing. Like the woman who stands behind a podium and smiles while the media circled like sharks.

But inside…

Inside, it's chaos.

"What would you do?" I ask him, softer this time. My voice cracks halfway through, but I let it break.

Would he see the way they look at me now? Would he hear the doubt, feel the weight? Would he have known how to handle a player like Maddox Lasker—ice in his veins, fire under his skin?

Of course, he would have.

But would he have trusted me to figure it out?

I breathe out hard, like I can expel the ache with air. My hand finally touches the glass. Cold. Smooth. Impenetrable.

Just like him.

"I'm not you," I murmur. "But I'm all that's left."

God, I hope that's enough.

The office is quiet except for the hum of tension vibrating behind my ribs.

Three taps is the only warning I get before the glass door opens.

"You looked like you were about to throw something," my assistant, Tessa, says, stepping in with her usual quiet authority and a fresh cup of coffee. "I brought reinforcements."

With one last glance at the jersey, I step away and let the armor fall back into place. "You're a lifesaver; thanks. How bad is it out there?" I ask, crossing back to my desk.

"Depends…" She trades out one of the mugs with cold

coffee with the fresh cup. "If you mean the media—circling. If you mean Dean—he'll call momentarily."

She grins. "If you mean me—I still believe in you, even when you look like a Bond villain about to detonate your desk."

That earns her a weak smile.

As I sit down and sip the fresh coffee–sighing when it hits my tongue–she perches on the edge of my desk, perfectly at ease in a crisis. "Want to talk about it?"

I drum my fingers on my desk with my free hand. "Lasker's still stalling. Peter gave me another non-answer. I told him to warn his client I'm coming to Boston and I'm not going to be nice."

Her brows lift. "That'll go over well."

"I don't care if it does. I've kissed every ring, massaged every ego, fought off every old-school owner who said I was too young or too green or too female. I refuse to let Maddox fucking Lasker be the reason they write my obituary."

Tessa nods. "Then we go get him."

Before I can reply, the desk phone buzzes and Dean's name flashes on the screen.

Dean Ward. The GM of the Atlanta Vipers.

He's a former pro center turned front-office whiz. Pragmatic, calculating, hard to read.

And he uses silence like a weapon. His hockey mind is as sharp as they come, and he's known for talent spotting and aggressive trades.

My father handpicked him to be the general manager of the Vipers, having known Dean since he was a rookie in the NEHL.

And from what I gathered after my father passed unexpectedly, Dean thought he would be the one calling the shots.

The shots my father left for me to call.

Needless to say, Dean isn't my biggest fan, which is fine with me.

I'm not his biggest cheerleader either.

I press the speaker button. "What's up, Dean?"

His voice crackles, already annoyed. "Still nothing?"

"Still nothing."

"Then we cut him. Call up the G2. Make it look intentional, and get the press off your back."

"No. I'm headed to Boston now to talk to him."

"Are you kidding me? He's not worth chasing."

"He's a cornerstone and worth confronting."

He snorts. "You want the league's most volatile goalie anchoring your crease because…?"

"Because he's still the best shot we've got at launching the new season with credibility."

"You've got the whole team except him."

"I've got a perfect launch—except one glaring hole the media is already picking at. This isn't about chasing a man. This is about not letting silence write my story."

"You sure this isn't about proving something?"

I glance over at the framed jersey again, biting back a sigh.

Fuck me if legacy doesn't feel like a noose some days.

"I'm sure."

Dean pauses, the silence stretching.

"If there's nothing else–"

"You're letting your pride get in the way, Sloane."

Pride.

It's always the word they use when a woman won't yield.

Never strategy. Never guts. Just pride.

"I'm not proud," I say tightly. "I'm strategic. I know what optics matter right now. And if I let the only unsigned contract slide, I send a message I can't take back."

Dean sighs. "Then handle it, *boss*."

The line goes dead.

My hand curls into a fist that I'd use on his throat if he were standing in front of me.

I jab the button harder than necessary, my blood boiling.

"Find out how long it'll take the jet to get ready for a trip to Boston."

Tessa's already tapping on her phone. "Done. Want me to book a driver too?"

I nod. "And a room. Somewhere quiet."

"Quiet might be hard in Boston," she says, already on the move. "But I'll find you somewhere with thick walls."

She pauses at the door, tilting her head. "You going to punch Lasker when you get there?"

"I might."

"Just make sure the cameras are rolling. We need the coverage."

She flashes a grin and disappears.

I blow out a breath and lean back in my chair. Staring at the ceiling, I breath in for three and out for three. Once, twice, three times before my blood pressure lowers.

Minutes later, with my laptop, phone, and a file folder with the name Maddox Lasker in my tote bag, I'm heading out the door.

I stop at Tessa's desk. "I'm going home to pack. You know how to find me."

"Yep. The usual flight crew is on standby and said they'd be ready to leave in an hour and a half, flying out of PDK."

"Perfect."

"And Richard's waiting with the car downstairs. He has the itinerary."

"Thanks for throwing that together, Tess. I'm so grateful I could cry right now."

The smile she gives me is genuine. "I'm rooting for you, girl."

"Glad to know someone is."

"Call me when you land. And maybe try not to strangle anyone before then."

"No promises."

Her laughter follows me down the hall, leading to the elevators.

Thankfully, I'm alone in the elevator when I pull up his profile again.

Maddox Lasker. G1. Age 39. Four-time All-Star. Plays like a weapon. Unrestricted free agent. Played his last full season like the ice owed him something.

The Boston Freeze colors still frame his headshot—blue and silver with that glint of contempt in his eyes.

His photo glares up at me from the screen. Stone-faced. Cut jaw. That faint scar above his eyebrow is like punctuation for a sentence he never says out loud.

There's no denying it. The man is smoking hot. Always has been.

The kind of man who looks like a warning label and tastes like regret.

The kind of man who'll fuck you up and make you thank him for the wreckage, which you would do willingly.

The kind of man I've always avoided.

But damn if my pulse doesn't kick just looking at him. Even when I'm ready to wring his neck for tanking my launch momentum.

He's trouble with a capital T.

Unfortunately, he's still my best bet.

The elevator dings and I straighten, slipping my phone into my purse. In the few moments before the steel doors open, I see my reflection.

On the outside, I look like what I am. Composed CEO. Franchise owner. Woman on a mission.

But underneath?

Underneath, I'm already bracing for the collision.

Let Maddox Lasker glare all he wants. Let him brood in his fortress of Boston solitude.

If he won't come to Atlanta, then I'll bring Atlanta to him.

CHAPTER TWO

Maddox

"Is Maddox Lasker being traded from Boston? Reports from The Freeze front office won't confirm or deny, but sources close to the team say Lasker's days are numbered."

The perfectly coiffed blonde continues as I stare at the TV screen—sports highlights flashing by, each replay twisting the knife of my career.

My pulse pounds with each commentator's dissection of my stats.

Alone, perched on the edge of the sleek gray couch in my Boston apartment, I usually find a certain peace in being by myself. In my minimalistic sanctuary.

Minimalism means less baggage, fewer ways for the world to get its hooks in me.

It's supposed to feel liberating.

Spoiler alert: right now, it doesn't.

My gaze sweeps around my condo, taking in the smooth surfaces, where not even dust dares to hang around. With a gut punch, I realize just how much it reflects me—empty, controlled, almost aggressively uncluttered.

Restlessness rises in my chest, pushing me to stand and cross to the large window looking out over the city.

Down below on the street, the city hums—horns blare, people walk fast, eyes down, because eye contact only invites inane conversation.

And who's got time for that?

I catch a glimpse of my reflection in the window. Hard eyes stare back, rimmed with shadows and edged in bitterness.

I barely recognize the man in the glass. And I have no idea what the hell to do about it.

But the team knew what to do, didn't they?

Boston to Atlanta. Traded like broken furniture—shuffled off, too volatile to keep. A liability, a PR nightmare they weren't willing to handle anymore.

Never mind the championship trophies I helped them win over the years.

I run a hand roughly over my face, irritation flaring. At thirty-nine, it was easy for them to rationalize the trade.

Not only would I make the team's spin doctors earn their keep, but they think I'm washed-up—a veteran presence only useful for ticket sales.

And according to them, I'm not great at that anymore.

My agent, Peter, insisted it's a fresh start—new city, new team. But he doesn't get it. How could he?

His words were calm, logical, rationalizing every bruising blow to my pride. "It's best for everyone, Maddox," he'd murmured.

Best for everyone but me.

I run my thumb along my jaw, where the bruise from the fight has faded. Too bad the memory and the fall out from it all hasn't.

Defending a rookie had cost me everything.

My phone buzzes insistently from the coffee table, Peter's name at the top of multiple text boxes.

Grinding my jaw, I stomp over to the table and snatch up the phone, swiping the screen open.

Peter: You there?

Peter: Contract's solid. You know that.

Peter: I know Atlanta's not Boston, but this is your only real chance. Dallas passed. Tampa passed. Don't throw away the opportunity, Maddox.

Peter: Unless, of course, you ARE ready to retire

Fucker. He knows exactly what buttons to push.

Frustration boils beneath my skin, a raw heat that scorches my throat. I thumb a terse reply.

Me: I'm not retiring. I'm thinking.

His reply is instantaneous, as if he's poised, waiting, knowing what I was going to say before I even knew what I was going to say.

Peter: You mean sulking. Don't make me cut my vacation short and fly to Boston. Sign. The. Fucking. Contract.

I snort.

Me: Since when do you go on vacation?

Peter: Since the wife forced me to. But we're not talking about me.

Peter: Look, M. I get where you're coming from. I'd be pissed too. But we went over this already. You gotta let Boston go. They promised to keep the details quiet and waive your fines if you promised to go away quietly.

Me: I have been quiet. I haven't said shit.

Peter: I know. But we both know the media will catch wind of this sooner than later, and the longer you wait to give Atlanta an answer, the worse this will be. In other words, if you want to continue to play, get your shit together.

I toss the phone aside, knuckles white, my jaw clenched so tight it aches.

Peter's right, but that doesn't make it sting any less.

I built something in Boston. A legacy. Respect. Roots. Something I never had growing up.

Trading it all for a city where I'm just another expendable player twists sharply in my gut.

I pace like a caged lion, thoughts spiraling.

Like I've got a fight coming and no place to throw the first punch. Heat builds low in my spine, pressure pulsing like a war drum in my chest.

My jaw aches from how hard I'm clenching it, breath hot and fast, but my fingers are ice.

I'm wired and numb at the same time—like my body can't pick a lane.

Atlanta's just another city. Another stadium. Another jersey. But it doesn't feel that way.

It feels like exile.

A sharp knock jolts me from the simmering anger. I glance at the clock, hunger gnawing low in my gut. Expecting food delivery, I ignore it.

My face is known in this city. It only took once to make the mistake of opening the door to a delivery guy who ended up being a rabid fan.

He tried to get into my condo, and my food was stone cold by the time he left.

Lesson learned.

But another knock comes, more insistent this time.

Why the fuck is the Dasher knocking? Don't they read the instructions?

Then a voice cuts through—female, firm, undeniably familiar.

"Maddox. Open up."

Fuck my life. Did she actually fly her fancy ass up to Boston?

I press fingers to my temples, irritation spiraling. This is so much worse than a rabid hockey fan wanting to talk about all my stats and tell me his life story.

This is a hockey owner who doesn't like the fact I'm not asking how high when she says jump.

Sloane fucking Carrington.

I will say this for the woman. Her kind of persistence could make stone walls crumble.

Which, admittedly, makes licks of anxiety churn in my gut.

Three more sharp knocks, rapid, relentless. Each strike reverberates in my chest, agitation coiling tighter. Her voice slices through again, harder and edged with steel.

"Open the door, Lasker. Or I'll keep knocking."

"Go away," I grumble softly. She can't hear me, but even if she could, she wouldn't listen.

As promised, she continues to knock, not letting up. If I weren't so pissed off, I'd admire the set of brass balls on her. She's bold enough to invade my territory and doesn't sound the least bit sorry for it.

With an exhausted groan, I stalk to the door, each step punctuated by resentment.

I yank the door open, shirtless, using bare skin as armor, an attempt to unsettle her.

But the instant she fills my vision, framed by muted hallway lights, every nerve ending fires.

And I'm the one who's unsettled.

Sloane Carrington in the flesh puts Sloane Carrington on the screen to shame.

Dark blonde hair tumbles around her shoulders in waves, and her eyes flash sharp green fire. In her skirt and tailored coat, she looks like she was engineered to make men underestimate her before she cuts their legs out from under them.

And those fuck me heels make her legs go on for days.

I should not be noticing any of that.

And yet, here I am with a chubbie.

Her stare flicks down, slow, deliberate. Skimming my tattoos and lingering a heartbeat too long on my exposed chest.

When her eyes meet mine again, she doesn't look the least bit apologetic.

"How the hell did you even get in?"

She shrugs, unbothered. "Your doorman likes ambitious women in heels."

I make a mental note to have a talk with Carlos.

Leaning against the doorframe, I cross my arms, feigning indifference I don't feel. Pulse hammering, I mask my reaction beneath carefully crafted sarcasm.

One elegant brow raises. "Are you going to let me in?"

She holds up a manila folder that I know contains my contract. "I'm delivering your future."

I huff out a laugh. "Dramatic much, princess?"

Her eyes narrow but her voice is velvet-soft, razor-sharp beneath. "We need to talk."

"Do we?" My tone drips mockery, defiance. "Don't recall inviting you."

"I wouldn't be at your door uninvited if you'd answer your phone."

"There's a reason for that."

"Oh, I'm sure there is, but that doesn't stop me." Her chin lifts, defiance blazing brighter as she steps past me, her coat brushing my bare chest.

The residual heat that momentary contact leaves behind can fuck all the way off.

Her perfume lingers—a clean, expensive scent at odds with the turmoil inside me. It's a sharp contrast to my stark apartment.

"You've got thirty seconds." I shove the door shut with unnecessary force, sound vibrating through my spine. She doesn't flinch, unperturbed as she tosses a contract onto the coffee table. The paper lands with a soft slap, like a gauntlet.

She turns to face me. "You've got forty-eight hours." Her voice remains unwavering, as if stating the obvious.

"You came all the way here just to deliver a contract I didn't ask for?"

"I came here because you matter."

I blink. The words hit in a place I thought I'd boarded up a long time ago.

For a second, we just stare. The air between us tightens, shifts. Something electric moves through it.

Not just tension—a *charge*.

"And if I don't sign?" I snap, contempt masking the vulnerability causing my muscles to tense up.

She doesn't say anything, just continues to study me curiously with those forest green eyes.

I smirk, an irresistible urge to press her buttons. To rattle that unshakeable composure. "Maybe I'll retire. Coach high school hockey."

She steps forward, boldness radiating with each decisive move. I brace against the heated flush her proximity brings, my pulse traitorously quickening.

"You won't retire," she murmurs, conviction heavy in her tone. "You're not ready to fade into obscurity."

I lean closer, jaw clenched, challenging her head-on. Her scent invades my senses, and heat crackles between us, electric, unwanted.

"You think you know me." Low, harsh words escape, a veiled threat beneath them. "Princess, you know nothing."

She meets my glare, unflinching, stunningly composed. "I know enough. Enough to see you have something left to prove. Mostly to yourself."

A slow, hot breath fills my lungs. My jaw flexes as I fight a rising tide of discomfort. I step closer again, forcing her chin upward.

Her breath hitches softly, causing a dark glee to race through my veins at that tiny victory.

"You have no idea what I want, Sloane."

She holds her ground, that stubborn mouth curving slowly, dangerously. "Then enlighten me."

Why the fuck do I find her so tempting, terrifying, impossible?

Sloane watches me closely, eyes flickering briefly to my clenched jaw before returning resolutely to my eyes.

"You delivered your message. You can leave the same way you came in."

My shoulders tighten, awareness coiling sharply as she pauses, refusing to retreat. Instead, her voice comes soft, whisper-close, searing through my defenses.

"You'll sign." Her voice barely above a whisper. "I won't let pride cost you your career."

She picks up the envelope, walks over, and places it in my hands. Her fingers brush mine—barely.

But the contact of our skin hums between us.

"You've got two days. After that, the offer's gone."

She turns to leave, her heels clicking sharply, echoing in the silence.

"You always this pushy with your players?"

She spins on one of her spiky heels, a sharp feline smile curving her lips. "Only the ones worth the trouble."

Her words are a sucker punch to my gut. I stand frozen, my breath tight, my pulse erratic.

The front door closes quietly, the scent of her perfume lingering in the air, making my knees weak.

What the fuck is wrong with me?

I drop down on the sofa with a heavy sigh just as the vibration of my phone shatters the silence.

A message from Peter lights up the screen and after reading it, I bite back a growl. His words are a reminder I don't need.

> Peter: Atlanta's a good market. Don't screw this up.

Leaning back, I stare up at the ceiling as though it will give me all the answers. I sit in the heavy, suffocating silence long after Sloane walked out.

Deep within, beneath the layers of anger and pride, a flicker ignites. A reckless hope I'd nearly extinguished.

Maybe Sloane Carrington is right.

Maybe I'm not finished yet.

Maybe I can still prove them all wrong.

My heart pounds, erratic with sudden, unwanted possibilities.

The fight in the locker room wasn't only about defending a rookie. I can't escape the cold, hard truth.

I want redemption.

I fucking crave it.

Maybe Atlanta isn't exile.

Maybe it's a chance.

But I'm not going to lie.

Leaving Boston feels like severing limbs. Atlanta is unknown, uncertain. And hot as the surface of the sun in the summer.

I've never been good with uncertainty or any type of change.

The thought tightens my throat, clenches my gut as the reality sinks in—I'm leaving Boston, the place I thought I'd retire. Trading familiar ice for unknown territory. Leaving comfort behind.

At my age, it's a terrifying fucking thought.

But I can't ignore the frustration and fragile hope battling it out deep within my belly.

Sloane was right about one thing. I'm not done fighting, no matter how much it hurts. No matter how risky it is to open myself up to the possibility again.

Forty-eight hours.

Just enough time to make Sloane Carrington sweat a little.

I rub rough hands down my face, pulse thudding unevenly.

The phone buzzes once more. A glance at the screen shows it's fucking Peter again.

He's nothing if not persistent.

> Peter: I know Sloane is a new owner, but she's impressive. She knows the game, on and off the ice. She learned the ropes from one of the best. Don't underestimate her.

I stare at the screen, irritation and reluctant admiration mingling uncomfortably.

He's right—damn him. Sloane Carrington might be younger, driven, challenging, but there's a strength in her I can't ignore.

"Only the ones worth the trouble."

It wasn't the answer I expected.

I push my hands through my hair, pulling the strands until my scalp stings.

Fuck me, I've let her get inside my head and that's the last place I need her to be.

She could destroy me. In more ways than one. Or she could be exactly what I need.

I can't read her. And worse? I want to. I need to. That kind of need isn't just dangerous—for a man like me, it's lethal.

Either way, I'm fucked.

Because it only took one meeting with her to know she's going to be the most dangerous thing I come across in Atlanta.

I blow out a hard breath of resignation.

If she's the test, I'm already flunking.

And the season hasn't even started.

CHAPTER THREE

Sloane

IT'S BEEN a couple of hours since I left Maddox's place, and my body is still on high alert.

I can still feel the vibration in the air.

I can still feel *him*.

He didn't physically touch me with those rough, player hands or with that full, smirking mouth that looked like they knew exactly how to make a woman beg.

And the fact that I'm thinking about his mouth at all is a problem.

Even more of a problem is that it isn't just the physical I'm feeling here.

It's more.

The imprint of Maddox Lasker is etched into every nerve ending like a bruise I can't stop pressing.

When I left his place, I came straight to the hotel Tessa booked for me, uncorked a vintage red someone had the forethought to leave me, and buried myself in work. I didn't even bother to kick off my shoes or shed my blazer.

With the way I feel, though? I might as well still be in his doorway, staring down the bare chest of a man built like a weapon, and looking at me like I'm the enemy.

An enemy he wanted to kiss or kill but wasn't sure which just yet.

Blowing out a hard breath, I put my laptop on the coffee table and stand to stretch the kinks that assault my neck.

I slip off my blazer, letting it fall onto the sofa like it weighs ten pounds. The rest of my armor follows—heels, earrings, watch.

Every piece that says: "I'm a Carrington. I'm an in control CEO."

One by one, I strip them away until it's just me in this hotel suite that costs a small fortune and yet feels like a cage.

Crossing to the bathroom, I flip on the light and brace my hands on the marble vanity, staring into the mirror.

I look the same, with the same sleek, dark blonde hair and serious expression. The same woman who doesn't flinch, at least not on the outside.

But I see the difference in my eyes. The green irises won't lie to me tonight. If the eyes are the window to the soul, my soul is tired, confused, and haunted.

I press a hand to my sternum, like I can settle the buzz still alive beneath my skin.

My heart won't slow down and the burn he left behind isn't on my body.

It's in my bloodstream.

Jesus. Get it together, Sloane.

I flick the light off and move through the suite, bare feet silent against the thick carpet. I hit the remote, and the TV blares to life—some overly tanned couple shouting about trust issues while a pop remix screeches behind them.

Love Island.

God help me, but I love this shit.

Normally, I let this kind of chaos numb me out. Other people's disasters, served up with a side of abs and accent drama.

But tonight it doesn't land. I'm too keyed up. Too raw. My whole body hums with that scene, that apartment, that man.

Maddox didn't back down. Not when I pushed, not when I stepped into his space, not even when I delivered the damn contract like a challenge.

He looked at me like I was fire.

And he looked like he wanted to burn.

I drop back onto the couch, stare blindly at the screen, and try to drown in the nonsense playing out in some island paradise.

But my pulse still races, my skin still tight.

Clenching my thighs together, I try to shove aside what this really is: me, not getting laid in far too long.

No one's ever looked at me the way Maddox looked at me. Not with so much intensity that made me want to have angry sex against the door of his condo.

I rub my temples, pushing aside all thoughts of fucking one of my players.

Lord, my father is rolling in his grave right now if he knew where my thoughts were.

Well, that's one way to cool down. Just think about dear old Dad and all the ways I can disappoint him.

"No, no, no. Not tonight, Satan."

But as usual, Satan has other plans, and the memory of the first time I truly felt my father's disappointment slithers through the cracks.

I'd made it to Nationals when I was sixteen in the senior division, which should've been a celebrated accomplishment.

My father didn't sit with the other parents. Oh no, Victor Carrington made sure to stand behind the glass, arms crossed tight, wearing his expressionless owner's face.

There was no clapping, no shouting, no telling me I had it in the bag.

Just those eyes that looked like mine, watchful.

Waiting.

I'd skated clean—technical, controlled, nearly flawless—and when I landed the final jump, I knew I'd scored high.

I gave the applauding crowd my best camera ready smile, but inside dread snaked its way into my chest.

Even though I'd skated better than my competitors, I knew it wouldn't be enough for him.

When I skated over to where my coach stood, telling me what a great job I did, I looked around for my father, but he was already gone.

By the time I got back to the locker room, he'd texted one line:

You should've gone for the quad.

No good job. No pride for his daughter who was the youngest in her division at the time and well on her way to the Olympics.

Just a reminder that clean and perfect wasn't enough unless it broke boundaries too.

That moment never left me.

I never made it to the Olympics because I'd stopped skating competitively the next year.

Instead, I thought if I learned his business, I'd earn his approval.

I chased that validation until the day he died.

With all of this ridiculous waiting around for Maddox to get his head out of his ass, I can practically feel my father's disappointment from the grave.

The weight of all the uncertainty settles in my chest again, sharp and familiar. I sit with it.

Let it fester. Let it fuel me.

I reach for my laptop, dragging it onto my lap like it'll anchor me. The Vipers roster is already open on the screen.

Scrolling through the names, I make notes—cap space, penalty minutes, performance ratings. Words blur. Numbers mean nothing.

Because the one name I need to see on the roster as active is the only yellow highlight at the top of the spreadsheet.

Contract: pending.

I stare at the words until they look like they're no longer spelled correctly.

He's the last piece. The one they all said I wouldn't get.

I scroll again and again. Type. Delete. Re-type.

But my brain keeps replaying the moment in his doorway— him shirtless, arrogant, unreadable.

And then the flicker behind his eyes. The part he didn't mean to show me. The part that made my heart catch and my stomach turn over.

I wanted to reach for him. Not to soothe. Not to control. But to feel the heat and the spark of electricity I saw in his gaze for a split second before he contained it.

My phone lights up with an email notification and the three text notifications I ignored earlier catch my eye.

They're all stacked like bricks on my chest.

Two are from Dean, because of course he needs to remind me he's watching.

Or to insinuate that he should have my job.

Dean: Status? Tell me he signed.

Dean: I want confirmation Lasker's in. He's not the only option.

"Oh yeah, Dean? Well, I want to rip your head off, but we can't always get what we want."

I angry tap out the lie he wants to hear.

> Me: Negotiations ongoing. Will update you by tomorrow.

I don't wait for his response. I already know what he'll say. Some cold variation of *don't screw this up*.

He won't say *please*. He never does.

Tessa's message, while still wanting to know about Maddox, didn't tighten my muscles like Dean's.

> Tessa: Was it bad?

I hesitate. But I don't want to lie to her.

> Me: No signature. But he didn't kick me out.

> Tessa: So… progress. Do you need tequila or a punching bag?

A tiny laugh escapes, barely there, but it's there. And it's not the curated kind I use in press rooms.

This one's real. Weak, wobbly. Human.

> Me: I can only choose one?

> Tessa: I'll have both waiting when you get back.

> Me: And this is why you're stuck with me.

> Tessa: I think I can handle that.

> Tessa: Close the laptop and go get some sleep.

The TV screeches into another commercial break, bright colors and bodies too shiny to be real.

I follow Tessa's advice and close the laptop, setting it aside and numb out on reality TV for a while.

After I watch two episodes back to back, it's nearly midnight, and while I'm tired as fuck, I'm still wired.

I walk over to the wall of glass overlooking Boston as the city sparkles outside the window.

Pressing my forehead to the cold pane of glass, I think that somewhere out there, Maddox is still awake. He strikes me as the kind of man who doesn't sleep easy.

He's pacing. Thinking. Stewing.

Maybe still shirtless.

God, get a grip.

My phone rattles on the coffee table and my stomach somersaults.

For some reason I know who it is before I check the screen.

Maddox.

When I grab my phone, I see his text on my lock screen.

There's no hello, no lead-in.

My stomach drops. Then clenches. Then flips over completely.

I read it again. And again.

Like some lovesick teenager instead of a twenty-eight year old CEO of a hockey team.

And I need to start thinking like one.

I read it one more time from the lens of what I am. The owner in negotiations with a stubborn ass mule of a man.

He's not surrendering. He's pulling me into his world. Onto the ice. Out of my comfort zone and into his.

The businesswoman in me is annoyed at him barking orders at me. But the woman in me?

Well, I shouldn't like it.

But I do.

My thumb hovers over the screen. I could say *Fine*. I could say *I'll be there*.

I could say *Fuck you*.

But I don't type anything.

Instead, I let the message glow against my skin like a dare. A warning.

Or a promise.

I step back from the window, heart hammering. I don't know if I want to fight him or follow him into the dark.

Maybe both.

Tomorrow night, I'll meet him at the rink.

And whatever happens next…

I know one thing for sure.

I won't come out unchanged.

CHAPTER FOUR

Maddox

THE ICE DOESN'T ASK who I am. Doesn't care what I lost. It just waits—clean, cold, honest. Out here, everything else falls away.

My lungs burn, and my quads scream. My skin is slick with sweat under my hoodie as it clings to my spine, and collects at the small of my back.

But I keep going.

I skate like I'm chasing something. Maybe I am. I want to skate whatever this fucking tightness in my chest is that makes breathing difficult.

It's been here nearly an hour already. I don't have a clue how many laps I've skated so far. All I know is that I'll keep moving until punishment becomes clarity. Until breath is the only sound and pain's the only thing louder than her voice in my head.

Only when it matters.

Her words won't let go of me. Not even after a dozen hard laps.

I dig my blades into the ice and push harder.

Common Ice is empty. Just the hiss of my skates carving into the frozen surface and the rasp of my breath echoing through the rafters.

The overhead lights buzz like they're judging me, and the chill cuts deeper than usual. Not that I care. I didn't come here to be warm.

I came to remind myself I still belong somewhere. Even if that somewhere is foreign and not where I planned to end my career.

The last year of my life here in Boston plays like a movie reel in my head. All of the media bullshit, the rumors and whispers, the closed door meetings, and then the final blow.

Why the fuck am I holding on to this place? It's treated me like shit for the last year. Even though I've given this team, this city, this community the best years of my life.

Years I can't get back.

Blowing out a breath, I push my body harder, faster until it feels like punishment. Even though each lap is better than any therapist I've seen.

The ice is the only therapist I've ever needed.

My legs shake, my hands go numb, but I still don't stop skating.

I don't want easy. I want blood. I want to remember who I am, not who the whole world thinks I am.

The door creaks open, and I don't have to look to know who it is.

I knew she'd show the second I sent the text last night.

Not a question. Not a request. Just a line I drew in frost.

And she crossed it just like we both knew she would. Because control looks good on her, but challenge looks better.

Power in motion. Precision in silk.

The sharp click of heels on concrete isn't just an announcement. It's a declaration.

There's no hesitation in her stride. No apology for taking up space.

Sloane Carrington doesn't knock because she doesn't have to. She walks into rooms like they were built for her.

I don't look directly at her, but I *feel* her. Like static before a storm. Like gravity shifting under my skates.

Skating a slow loop, controlling my breath, bleeding tension with each stride.

My body aches in a good way—worn out, emptied out—but my head? My head's a goddamn war zone.

And it's all because of the woman who I feel watching me from the other side of the glass.

I circle wide. Let her watch. Let her see I'm still here. Still skating. Still *me*, even if the league tried to write a different story.

I coast to a stop at center ice, chest heaving. I don't move. Just close my eyes for one long second, trying to slow the riot inside me.

I turn and raise my gaze just in time for her eyes to meet mine.

And grind my molars so that my jaw doesn't drop to the floor.

I thought the only thing the woman owned were crisp blouses and those skirts that hug her covers in a way that's really not safe for the workplace.

But not tonight.

Tonight she's in a slim black leather jacket that stops at her waist and black jeans. The black heeled boots make those already long legs look endless.

Those lush lips are set in a perfect, unreadable line.

Even though she doesn't look made for ice rinks—especially local, gritty rinks like this one—she doesn't look out of place either.

She looks expensive and hot as fucking hell.

And completely and utterly out of my league.

Yeah, like you had any chance with her anyway, Lasker. She's not a puck bunny or a Hollywood starlet, jackass.

I glide toward her, slow, controlled. I let the silence stretch. I want to see what she does with it.

She doesn't blink. Doesn't flinch. Her eyes track me like I'm a threat and a challenge all at once.

I lean my forearms on the boards, sweat running down the side of my face. "You always show up to random places this late at night? Or am I just lucky?"

She raises one brow. "You're not lucky. I want my signature." She pauses, tilting her head. "And I think you're smart enough to know this is your only shot."

I huff out a laugh, bitterness hot in my veins. "Oh, you think so?"

She steps closer, unfazed. "You called me, Lasker. If you really had other options, we wouldn't be standing here."

"I called you because I'm not ready to hang up my skates and pretend I'm fine with fading out."

"You could've just said that."

"Didn't feel like explaining myself to someone who came into my apartment like she was delivering a goddamn subpoena."

Her mouth twitches. Almost a smile. "Would it have helped if I'd brought donuts?"

"No. But it would've confused the hell out of me."

Now, she smiles all the way. And fuck me, if I don't like the way her green eyes light up.

But just as quickly, the smile fades and she watches me like she's collecting data—reading body language and cataloging every scar.

I hate how good she is at reading me and we just met in person yesterday.

I also hate how much I want her to see something she likes.

I reach into my jacket and pull out the contract. The corners are curled from my hands. I slap it onto the top of the boards.

Her gaze drops. Lingers.

"I'll sign it," I say, quiet now. "But not because I believe in your pitch."

She lifts her eyes back to mine, unreadable. "Why then?"

"Because I don't know who I am without the game. And I'm not ready to figure that out."

I pull the pen from my jacket, flip to the final page, and scrawl my name in thick black ink. My hand trembles at the end. Just a little.

But enough that the edges of anger whip through me.

"There." I slide it toward her. "That's what you came for, right?"

She doesn't move. Just stares down at the signature like she's trying to decide if it's real. I watch her—jaw tight, shoulders square, fingers curling into the edge of the bench.

For a second, she looks like she's holding the weight of the whole fucking league.

"I didn't just come for the signature," she says, voice lower now. "I came to see you in your element."

I don't answer. Because if I do, I'll say too much. I'll tell her I feel like I just signed away the only part of me that still made sense.

That Boston wasn't just a team. It was a lifeline. A home I built from nothing.

A home that threw me away so easily.

And now?

Now I'm back at square one with fifteen years on my body, in a brand new city…

And with a woman who scares the shit out of me.

"You didn't ask for a bonus. No guarantees. No media clause." Her tone is careful, curious. "You're either reckless or serious."

I meet her eyes. "I'm going to play. Not to phone it in and cash a check."

Her pupils shift. Just slightly. Like I caught her off guard. Like she wasn't expecting plain honesty tonight.

She doesn't look away.

Neither do I.

I press my palm flat to the boards to steady myself. "This rink," I say, eyes sweeping the empty seats, "I used to sneak in at night. When I was fourteen. Lights off, no music, just me and the cold. I'd skate until my legs gave out."

A muscle shifts along her jaw. She doesn't speak, but something softens around her eyes.

"Because out there," I nod toward the doors, "everything was chaos. Home was a mess. School was worse. But here? Here I could disappear. Be something."

Sloane doesn't speak. She just listens. Like it matters. Like *I* matter.

I swallow hard. The burn in my throat isn't from skating anymore.

"I thought I'd retire here," I admit, voice barely audible. "Finish where I started. On my own terms."

"You still can," she says gently. "Different city. Different team. But still you."

"You don't know me."

"I'm starting to." Her eyes don't waver. "And I know you're not done."

That hits like a punch.

The air between us tightens, thickens until you could cut the tension with a knife.

There's no one else in the rink, but I still feel the weight of this moment pressing in like heat under all the cold.

I step back from the boards, crossing my arms to keep from doing something stupid—like reaching for her.

Her perfume drifts between us, clean and expensive, with something sharper underneath.

Something that reminds me of pressure and control and sex and power.

"You really believe that?" I ask.

"I wouldn't have flown to Boston if I didn't."

I nod once. "Then I guess we're both gambling."

She nods back. "High stakes make it interesting."

The corner of my mouth lifts despite myself. "You always talk like this? Like we're negotiating the fate of the universe?"

Her lips curve slightly. "Only when I am."

The weight of the silence is heavy as we hold the stare between us.

"I signed that contract for me. Not for you or the team."

She doesn't blink. But her chest rises just a little deeper.

"I wasn't sure if you would," she says softly.

"I didn't think I could." I pause. "Until you looked at me like I still counted."

Her breath catches. Not loud. Just enough that I feel it like a pull in my gut.

She swallows. Her throat moves just once.

The contract disappears into her bag. Her hands are steady now, but I don't miss the way she exhales—like she's been holding her breath all night.

Like my name on that page just gave her permission to breathe again.

She holds out her hand and gives me her best practiced smile.

"Welcome to the Atlanta Vipers, Maddox Lasker."

Her tone is clean, crisp.

All business.

But the second I take her hand, it stops being about business.

Her fingers curl around mine—firm, steady. Warm.

My thumb grazes the inside of her palm before I even think to stop it.

Her skin is soft there. Sensitive.

That smile falls and her lips part, letting out a strangled gasp, but she doesn't pull away.

Neither do I.

The silence thickens, and my pulse pounds hard at the base of my throat. She doesn't look at me, her stare staying on our joined hands.

Then she steps back, slowly, like she had to talk herself into it, and turns toward the tunnel, ready to leave.

The heat of her hand lingers on my skin like a ghost.

"Hey," I call out.

She pauses. Looks back.

"You said earlier you don't wait for odds. You make them."

Her chin lifts. "That's right."

"Then don't waste me."

That freezes her. Just for a second. And then she nods, once. Solid. Like a promise.

"I don't plan to," she says. "But don't waste yourself either."

With that, she's gone.

Her heels echo down the concrete hallway, fading fast, but I stay where I am—sweat drying on my skin, pulse still pounding, silence folding in around me like armor.

I stare out at the ice.

It's still the same.

Still cold.

Still mine.

For the first time in a long damn time, it feels like something *might* be waiting on the other side of this.

I push off the boards and skate another lap.

Not for Boston.

Not even for her.

Just for me.

I told myself I didn't care who I played for. Didn't care where I landed.

But she looked at me like I might be more than what I've lost.

And *fuck me* if I don't want to earn it.

CHAPTER FIVE

Sloane

TWO DAYS.

That's how long it's been since Maddox Lasker signed his name on the dotted line.

Two days since I stood in an empty rink in Boston and watched a man unravel in front of me—and still choose to stay in the fight.

Two days since I flew home with his signature on my contract and something far more dangerous lodged behind my ribs.

He's under my skin.

And I hate how much I feel it.

A low hum of anticipation threads through my bones as I move through the dark, empty tunnel leading out to the arena, my heels echoing—sharp, deliberate, louder than they should be. The air smells faintly of concrete dust and last night's resin.

I slow at the tunnel's mouth, where Dean is already waiting.

He leans against the wall like he owns it, posture relaxed, tie loosened just enough to feign ease. His phone is in hand, attention elsewhere.

Smoothing my jacket, I square my shoulders and let the mask settle into place.

Sloane Carrington, CEO of the Atlanta Vipers NEHL Hockey Team.

Untouchable.

The second I step into his periphery, I feel his gaze shift. A flicker of satisfaction there. He likes being ahead of me. Likes the idea of me chasing him, even though I'm technically his boss.

I don't give him the pleasure.

"Punctual, as always," Dean says, still not looking up.

"You called this meeting. I showed."

He pushes off the wall and walks away, expecting me to follow. The shitty part is, I have to.

We head to the conference suite. At the door, he gestures for me to enter.

Raising my chin, I don't pause, don't flinch. I walk past him like he doesn't matter, even though his eyes linger a beat too long as I pass.

Inside, the air is stale and cold. Deliberately so.

The table between us is bare except for one folder dead center, like a landmine. Two leather chairs. No drinks. No pretense. Just a war waiting to be waged.

I sit, crossing one leg over the other, waiting for him to close the door.

He doesn't sit. Just leans on the edge of the table, wedding band glinting under the fluorescents. Objectively, Dean is a handsome man. But if he's anything like he is at the office, I pity the poor woman wearing the matching band.

His expression is smooth, his eyes calculating.

"You've made quite the splash. Bold move to go to Boston." The corner of his mouth lifts. "Congratulations."

"We needed a goalie. I got us one."

"Lasker's a risk."

I match his gaze, refusing to blink. "He'll win games. He commands respect on the ice."

"You didn't run it by the board."

"No. I didn't." My voice stays even. "And before you start, I know exactly what Section Four says. I also know what Section Three says about competitive benchmarks, and Lasker gives us the best shot at hitting them."

"Which means you also know you triggered the Legacy Clause."

"I ran the numbers," I say. "I knew it would trigger oversight. I also knew we'd make the playoffs with him on the roster."

He slides the folder toward me. The sound is soft, but it lands like a gavel. Inside, I already know what's waiting—the words *Legacy Oversight Provision*, Section 6, staring back in neat black font.

"You broke both the dollar cap and the term limit," Dean says. "And Lasker's disciplinary history? That's reputational risk. Two violations in one move."

My stomach knots, not from surprise but from the reminder of what a second trigger in the next eighteen months would mean—reduced control, maybe even forced sale.

I knew all that when I signed him. I just didn't expect them to start sharpening the knives this fast.

"The Oversight Committee will want a full review," he says. "You'll present your rationale next week. If the acquisition doesn't meet our return metrics, your role as controlling owner becomes…conditional."

My spine goes rigid. I don't move. "Is that a threat?"

"It's governance," he says, smiling faintly. "Exactly the kind your father wanted in place."

"It's sabotage."

Dean doesn't flinch. "It's policy."

My stomach turns, a slow, heavy roll. I grip my knees under the table so hard my nails leave half-moons in my skin.

"You think I didn't run the numbers?" I ask, voice even.

"I think you're making emotional decisions." His tone is mild. Patronizing. "And emotional decisions get people fired."

I bite the inside of my cheek to keep from exploding.

He wants a reaction. A crack. Something he can take back to the board to paint me as reckless.

Too young. Too green. Too female.

I give him nothing.

"I vetted him. Thoroughly."

Dean tilts his head. "That's what worries me, Sloane. You think research is the same as risk management."

My cheeks flush, heat prickling under my skin. I imagine my father's watchful eyes behind Dean's. The pressure at my temples builds—like if I let myself blink too long, the veneer will crack.

"The city wanted a cornerstone," I say. "I gave them one. I'm not afraid of risk to get what we need."

His mouth curves, not a smile but something colder. "You should be. The board is, at least. They don't like surprises. Especially not from you."

There it is. The thing he's been circling all along. Not from me.

Dean crosses behind me, slow and deliberate, circling like he smells blood. His cologne hits like bleach—too sharp, too clean.

"Tell me," he says softly, "is this really about building the franchise? Or is it about proving you're more than your father's shadow?"

I stiffen. That line isn't just strategy—it's personal. And it lands like a blade.

The image of Maddox flashes—sweat slicking his skin, eyes daring me to flinch.

You ever feel like you're not enough?

I grit my teeth.

"If you have a concern about my leadership," I say, turning the chair to face him, head held high, "take it to the board."

Dean meets my gaze, satisfied he's pushed my buttons. "They're already watching."

He walks out without another word, leaving the room colder than when he entered.

The door clicks shut behind him, soft as a threat.

I don't move. Not at first.

With my hands shaking, I just sit there, staring at the folder like it might bite.

Then I exhale. Once. Twice. Three times.

When I finally stand, my legs are unsteady. I gather the folder and force my spine straight, letting the soles of my shoes ring sharp against the hardwood as I leave.

I will not be seen unraveling.

Not by Dean. Not by anyone.

The elevator ride is quiet. My reflection stares back from the mirrored walls—perfect hair, flawless makeup, face locked down. But my stomach churns, my chest tight with something too big to contain.

I make it to my office before the first tear threatens. Once inside my sanctuary, I shut the door with more force than necessary and lean against it, eyes closed.

The ache in my chest is a live wire. I want to scream. Or cry. Or break something, anything, just to feel the aftermath.

I sink into my chair like my bones forgot how to hold me. The darkness and all its friends presses in, thick and heavy.

Turning on the desk lamp, low and warm, I boot up my laptop with hands that still tremble.

There's too much to do. Too much to prove. Too much riding on one signature I forced out of a man who looks at me like I'm both a threat and a promise.

Opening a fresh PowerPoint, I get down to work, the anxiety ebbing from my body as I type.

Asset Analysis: Lasker, M.

The cursor blinks at me for half a second before I start typing headers with ruthless precision:

- Strengths.
- Weaknesses.
- Statistical Impact.
- Integration Risk.
- Reputation Risk.

I pull up his player profile.

Maddox Lasker.

His headshot first comes up first, and I can't deny the hit to my bloodstream when I see him.

Much to my utter dismay, if this is how addicts feel with their drug of choice, I can see why it's so hard to stop.

Jaw like a blade, eyes so electric blue and mysterious at the same time, they seem unreal. If I hadn't seen them first-hand, I'd think there was some doctoring of his photo.

His hair is damp and tousled as if he's just come off the ice and the sight of him on my screen is a physical thing that I can't control.

My chest contracts, lungs fluttering against the cage of my ribs, and there's a heaviness at the base of my throat.

All of which only serves to piss me off.

These *feelings* are raw and mighty fucking inconvenient.

I scroll through his stats, searching for solace in numbers—goals per game, face-off percentage, penalty minutes, power play conversions.

The data is clean, almost reassuring in its objectivity. But every note I type brings him closer, until I'm no longer analyzing a player but the tremor he set loose in me.

I add another bullet:

- Unknown variable: Potential for disruption.

My finger hovers over the delete key, but I leave it. I have to name what I can't control.

A photo lingers in the preview—him in a corridor after practice, sweat-dark hair, mouth set in a line, eyes full of everything he never says.

I drag it into the presentation, just for reference, but my hand shakes.

Staring at the image, I try to reduce him to a file, a risk, an asset. It's what a good owner does.

That's what my father would have done.

But all I can feel is the pounding in my chest, the electric burn under my skin, and the certainty that I've let something wild through the gates.

This was supposed to be a solution. Not a complication.

And still, I can't look away.

The buzz of my phone breaks the staring contest I'm having with my monitor.

Griffin.

I smile faintly. Of course.

How the hell my cousin knows I'm unraveling, I'll never know but he always seems to know.

I stare at his name on the phone screen, letting it ring until it goes dark.

If I answer right now, I'll break.

And if I break, I'll lose this round.

I don't have the luxury of losing any round at this point.

Instead, I open a new blank PowerPoint. I fill in slide after slide with numbers, charts, graphs. Projections. Market impact. Growth potential.

It's all my armor.

I type faster, harder to the point my fingertips become sore. But I'm trying to drown the thoughts pressing in from every side.

Maddox.

Dean.

My father.

The contract is signed, but nothing's settled.

Maddox is a fuse waiting to be lit.

Dean's circling like a shark.

And my father, who has the talent of controlling everything I do from the fancy ass casket I put him in.

"You wanted a legacy, Dad? I'm going to give you a fucking legacy despite your rules."

I wish that declaration echoing off the silent walls made me feel better.

But it doesn't.

My eyes burn. My chest aches.

I close the laptop before I throw it out the window.

I'm sure Dean and the board would have all kinds of things to say if someone found my laptop on the immaculate lawn outside.

Blowing out a breath, I give myself a mental pat on the back.

I'm still here. And so is my laptop.

I'm alone. Angry. Afraid.

But unbroken.

For now.

CHAPTER SIX

Maddox

THE VIPERS' locker room, also called the Hiss Room, is loud.

Obnoxiously loud.

There's no reverence, no order.

Just bodies and chaos and too many scents fighting for dominance—sweat, detergent, cedar planks, and cologne that smells like a tequila hangover in Vegas.

It's a far cry from the reverent stillness I left behind. Boston was mahogany benches and history on the walls. You didn't speak unless you had something worth saying.

Here, it's slick, modern, and new with the walls vibrating from a Post Malone track blasting from a hidden speaker.

Half the guys are yelling over one another, and someone's drawn a massive cartoon dick over the penalty kill setup on the whiteboard.

What the fuck did I sign up for?

I step in, gear bag over my shoulder, every sense stretched tight. No one rushes to greet me, not that I expected it. But every head turns, just for a beat.

Long enough to size me up.

"Hey, boys, look alive. Boston's bad boy just wandered in—hope the penalty box here is reinforced."

And the first barb is thrown.

By Riley Hunt no less, which doesn't surprise me.

He's all grin and ego, hair styled like he didn't sweat through a warmup. Skates unlaced, posture loose, but his eyes are sharp—the kind of sharp that cuts just for the sake of it.

A peacock in hockey gear. All showy feathers and noise, waiting for an audience.

Laughter hits in a wave. Testing. Measuring.

"Should we bow? Or just roll out a walker and save the paramedics the trip?"

I keep my expression neutral. Let them bark. Let him flex. I've seen a dozen Rileys flame out by Christmas.

The room doesn't stop, but it hums differently. A few guys laugh. A couple glance at each other.

Logan Beck whistles under his breath as he continues lacing up. Calm, composed, like he's already in mid-season form while the rest of them posture. He's polished as hell—one of those guys who belongs in every room, and he knows it.

Captain Jace Rourke—silent, solid, spine straight—doesn't look away from his stick as he tapes the blade with military precision.

Eli Ramsey sits a few stalls down, tape winding methodically around his own stick. He doesn't join the noise—from what I know of the man, he never does—but the hard edges in his silence carry weight.

The kind of guy who grinds until you forget he's there, right up until he knocks you flat.

Beau Radford hangs back near the rookies, steady hum in the chaos. He leans over to help one of them sort out tangled straps, voice low, calm, like the caretaker role fits him even while he's lacing up to break bodies.

They're all ignoring Riley and his posturing, so I know what he wants from me.

He wants a reaction.

Hell, he's fishing for it.

All confident swagger and gleaming teeth and that twitchy little gleam in his eye like he's waiting to poke a bear and then duck.

But I don't flinch. Just stare back at Riley.

"You need something, Hunt?" My voice is low. Controlled.

"Just making sure your pacemaker didn't glitch on the walk down. Wouldn't want the season to start with a eulogy."

A ripple of laughter follows. Muted, but not insignificant.

I'm not put off by Riley or any of the other guys in this locker room. That's how this works. Day one, someone always has to challenge the new alpha.

Finn McCade strides out of the showers like he owns the place, towel wrapped around his waist, steam clinging to his shoulders, tattoos dripping.

"Give it a rest, Hunt," he says, shaking his head, flinging water everywhere. "If he wanted to drop gloves, you'd already be on your back. You forget how to read a room, or just like the sound of your own voice?"

The tension cracks just enough for the rookies to breathe again.

Riley turns away, temporarily shutting the fuck up.

Thank God.

Finn's the chaos gremlin of the bunch. He stalks across the room half-naked like he's on stage, slapping a rookie on the shoulder, and whistling off key to Post.

He winks at me on his way past. "Welcome to the snake pit, Lasker. You want whiskey or a blindfold?"

I don't smile, but my shoulders settle by half a degree.

Glancing around, I find my stall on the far side. The name-plate still smells like new paint.

The number's right, thirty-three, but it doesn't feel like mine. It's not the one I earned.

I stare at the stick and jersey hanging in my locker. It's shiny and new, and when I touch it, stiff and unfamiliar.

Not mine.

I drop my gear bag and start unpacking in silence. It's the same ritual I've done a thousand times, but every movement now feels like I'm putting on someone else's gear.

Gloves, pads, shin guards, skates.

I glance over to the far edge of the room, where it's quiet in the midst of all the noise.

Cal Reid, the newest rookie to the league.

He's got good stats for a young player, better than I saw out of Peacock in his rookie year.

But judging by the way he's in the corner like he's trying to disappear into it, he's got confidence issues.

Which will get him clearing waivers sooner than later.

His hoodie nearly hides his face while he laces and re-laces his skates over and over, the way nervous rookies do when they need their fingers to outrun their thoughts.

It hits too close.

He reminds me of—

Nope. Not going there.

I turn back to my stall, strip down to compression shorts and a sweat-warmed undershirt.

My body runs hot, and I'm way too aware of every scar under the skin. The left shoulder pulls tight from the old rotator cuff tear and my right knee clicks when I shift.

It's the kind of damage that doesn't show up on game stat sheet but lives in your bones.

"You always this quiet, or just biding your time?"

Jace's voice cuts through the low buzz, calm and unreadable.

I glance his way. "Ask me after practice."

His nod is barely perceptible, but I catch it.

Respect, maybe. Or a warning.

Hard to tell.

Peacock Hunt isn't done.

"Boston finally trade you in for a newer model? Can't imagine they'll miss the penalty minutes."

I let the silence stretch until I feel him start to squirm. Then I turn just enough for him to see the look in my eyes.

"Careful, kid. Keep chirping like that, and I'll start treating you like the newer model. And you won't last a shift."

Finn hoots from across the room. "Damn, Hunt. You just got buried in the locker room. Wear a helmet next time."

Riley's smirk falters—just a flicker—but enough to make it worth it. He leans back like he's unbothered, but the tight set of his jaw says otherwise.

Coach Holt barrels in, voice like a war drum. "Five minutes! Move your asses or I'll move them for you."

That's the cue. The room erupts into organized chaos—helmets snapped on, sticks grabbed, skates thudding against rubber flooring.

I slow my pace on purpose. Let the pack surge ahead.

Cal fumbles with his jersey, shaking hands missing the head hole on the first try. No one helps.

No one ever does.

He finally gets it on, but he's trembling.

And it's not the cold.

I look away again.

He's not mine to save.

I lace up last, boots tight enough to cut off circulation. I like the pressure. Like the silence of it.

Lace. Loop. Knot. Repeat.

As I rise, the overhead lights flicker slightly, humming against the thump of blood in my ears.

My feet carry me toward the tunnel like they remember something my brain's trying to forget.

It's just practice. Just drills.

But my spine is a loaded spring. My hands won't unclench, my chest too tight to fully breathe.

Sloane's name flashes across the back of my eyes like a warning label.

The curve of her lip when she handed me that contract. The frost in her voice when she walked away.

The fire she left behind.

I bury it. I have to.

This is the only place I'm still mine.

I step out onto the rubber mat, shoulder to shoulder with the rook.

Cal doesn't look at me. But his knuckles are white around his stick.

"Keep your head down," I mutter, voice too low for anyone else to hear. "And skate like you mean it."

His head jerks up. Just for a second.

Then he nods. One quick, sharp movement. Like it costs him something.

The first edge of my blade hits the ice, and every noise dies.

Cold rushes up my legs. Familiar. Brutal. Perfect.

The rink is a blank slate. But it remembers everything.

I take a breath that feels like a blade down my throat.

Let them watch. Let them doubt.

Riley wants a show? He's gonna get it.

Jace wants answers? I'll write them in fucking blood.

Finn wants chaos?

I'll give him fire.

Out here, I don't owe anyone a word.

Just the game.

And that's the only language I've ever spoken fluently.

CHAPTER SEVEN

Sloane

THERE'S A MOMENT, every season, when the ice goes quiet.

That hush between drills—skates stilled, sticks braced on knees, chests rising and falling in steam-laced clouds. It's like the eye of a hurricane, all quiet waiting for the storm.

The moment hangs heavy above the rink while Maddox's gaze locks with mine through three inches of glass and the echoing silence of empty seats.

Just me.

Just him.

My pulse drums in my throat, so loud I worry he can hear it from the ice. I drop my hand from the lapel of my blazer when I realize I'm fidgeting.

I can't give away the fact that when he looks at me, the skin at the back of my neck prickles the way dry ice burns—slow, certain, and unforgettable.

Imperceptibly, he tips his chin. A move no one else seems to notice but me.

It's becoming clear to me—much to my utter shame—I notice everything when it comes Maddox Lasker.

The curl of black tape at the end of his stick handle.

The shape of his mouth, unsmiling under the cage.

The way he holds still as if stillness is a weapon he learned how to sharpen.

I'm here to evaluate an asset. All of my assets. That is the official story.

Unofficially, I can't stop looking at only one of them. The one wearing number thirty-three.

Spoiler alert: that's not a good thing.

Maddox drops into his stance.

He's not the fastest to move. He doesn't need to be. He holds the crease like it belongs to him, weight balanced, glove relaxed, stick flat against the ice. Every shuffle is efficient.

Three sharp pushes and he's square to the first shot, pads sealing the ice. The puck smacks into him and dies at his feet. He angles it away with a clean flick to the corner, already resetting for the next play.

The next time it's a glove save, snatched so fast the shooter barely finishes his follow-through.

Then, a blocker deflection—puck steered harmlessly into the glass. He absorbs the slapshot to the chest like it's nothing, the sound of impact echoing like a gunshot, and he doesn't so much as flinch.

Why do I find that so fucking hot?

I blow out a breath to make myself remember to breathe.

Riley Hunt cruises through the crease, trying to screen him.

Maddox doesn't give him the satisfaction of a look. He holds his ground, shoulders squared, eyes locked on the puck.

A player zips in from the blue line, tips off Riley's stick at the last second, but Maddox snaps his pad down and swallows it whole.

He rises without hurry, drops the puck for his defense, and Riley might as well be invisible.

Controlled. Professional. Precise like a surgeon.

I should be taking the notes I need to defend my decision of signing Maddox so they don't take the team away from me.

Especially given that he's a veteran nearing the end of his career.

He looks good in conditioning. Reads plays early and stabilizes presence in chaos.

Instead, the heat sparking low in my belly is coiled tight, feeling anything but professional.

I grip the railing and let the cold steel bite into my palm in order to ground me. Inhaling deeply, I drag my focus back to the job I'm supposed to be doing.

Holt rotates them into rush drills. Two-on-ones. Three-on-twos.

Maddox reads each play like a map he's already memorized. He challenges high, cuts angles early, drops into the butterfly when the shot comes and explodes back to his feet before the rebound can become a threat.

The puck clangs off his blocker, sails high off his shoulder, and sticks to his glove like a magnet.

He controls the play with an ease that makes my throat go dry.

The board wants numbers on Maddox. And not ones like what the rate of my pulse must be watching him play in the flesh.

We have his stats from the Boston years and as legendary as he is, they come with all the caveats and baggage from the last few years.

What we don't have—and what I need to bring—is what it feels like when he's on the ice with our guys.

The way the air shifts. The way the rookies sneak glances at him when they think no one's watching.

The way Riley, all teeth and swagger, keeps drifting too close to the blue paint like a moth daring itself toward flame.

Speaking of Riley, he takes a breakaway, coming in fast, shoulder dropped, telegraphing top shelf.

Maddox waits, patient, then robs him with a glove snap so arrogant it borders on cruel.

I take a breath through my nose and smell cold, rubber, and a citrus cleaner that never quite kills the sweat.

Holt blows long and sharp. "Net-front battles!"

Assistants dump pucks into the corners, two at a time. Defense crashes back, forwards crash the crease. Screens, tips, rebounds…it's pure madness on the ice.

Riley plants himself square in front, hacking for sight lines. Maddox slams his right pad flat to the ice, leaning hard into the post, the other leg braced up to block high. It's a stance that eats pucks alive if done right—no daylight, no room, no mercy.

The puck rockets toward the net, but Maddox kicks it out with his pad and uses his hips to lever Riley just far enough off balance that the kid hacks air.

Not dirty, just surgical precision.

Riley stumbles, recovers, and spits out something I can't hear.

But as much as he's trying to rile him up, Maddox doesn't bite.

He's already reset, eyes following the next pass.

The man's got leadership qualities in spades. There's no wasted motions or violence. He keeps it all contained until the exact second it needs to be used.

Something loosens inside my chest and then tightens again. I uncurl my fingers from the rail and rub the indentations with my thumb.

"Control," my father used to say. "Talent is for show. Control wins the room."

That was his gospel, and I believed it.

Still do.

But after watching Maddox, I'm beginning to think control can also be something else—it can be lethal, hot, and with a promise waiting for a trigger.

Holt shifts them into a half-ice scrimmage. It's full of quick changes, and the tempo is nasty.

It's the kind of session that looks like chaos to civilians but is pure math in motion. Maddox is the constant that keeps the equation balanced.

He calls short, sharp cues—pointing, tapping his stick, steering traffic with a twitch of his glove.

Our defense collapses tighter, lanes close. He gets three shots in five seconds, chest, pad, glove, then freezes the puck like he's ending an argument.

I can sell that to the board.

I can also feel my pulse in places I shouldn't.

As practice continues, players shout and slam. Coaches bark out orders and tips. Trainers shuttle water and Gatorade.

Maddox peels a glove off, flexes his hand, scar flashing. He looks up again. Not long. Just enough.

My breath hitches, my body answering in ways that make me want to step back and give myself a lecture.

You have to remain professional, polished, untouchable.

I adjust the cuff of my shirt so the French seam lines perfectly with the hem of my skirt. I imagine I can smooth the thrum under my skin into a flatline.

I imagine I can smooth out anything that keeps me from being anything but the owner of the Atlanta Vipers.

Holt's final whistle cuts the air, indicating the end of practice. Helmets lift and players laugh, shoving at each other as they head into the locker room.

Maddox doesn't celebrate. He pulls his mask free and collects his gear like a soldier expecting the war to go on without him.

But just before he leaves the ice, he looks up.

For a second, I swear the glass isn't there. The distance collapses into a line of heat that runs from his eyes to my sternum and all the way down between my legs, where my thighs clench of their own volition.

It feels like a dare.

It feels like an answer to a question I don't let myself ask.

I force my hand to release the railing. The dents in my palm mirror the place between my ribs that hurts when I breathe too hard.

My phone buzzes. I tug it free, still watching the ice.

Tessa: Sierra's looking for you. She needs you in the tunnel in five. You've got interviews in ten. Where are you?

I swallow the instinct to text back hiding in plain sight.

Me: On my way.

Shoving my phone into my blazer pocket, I take one last look, but Maddox is gone.

While disappointment hits the pit of my stomach, I smooth my hair like my Aunt Sara used to do before she pushed me into a room full of people who would be delighted to see me fail.

Smile, shoulders back, and remember they can smell fear, darling.

I straighten my spine and head out of the observation deck to face the hell known as Media Day.

Sierra meets me at the mouth of the press room, her bun tight with not a hair out of place.

But licks of panic shine in her eyes.

"They moved the locals up," she whispers, shoving a schedule at me. "Fox 5 is already setting up, and Channel 2 is short a mic, and—" She swallows, resets. "Where do you want Jace first?"

"Jace goes last," I say. "Start with Finn. Give Channel 2 his special brand of charm so they feel special. Keep Riley moving

—if he stalls, pair him with Logan. Keep Cal with you. He needs a handhold."

"And Lasker?"

My tongue touches my teeth. Heat flares low. "He's with me."

She crosses his name off her list. "Copy."

My phone buzzes again.

> Tessa: Board liaison in the hall. Wants a word before you hit the podium. Dean wants a revised quote for the release. Where do you want the hit to land?

> Me: Tell Dean we hold the quote 'til after the first interviews. I want real tape to pull language from. And tell the liaison he gets five minutes in the green hall after Finn's spot. If he wants more, he can schedule it like everyone else.

I angle myself into the press room doorway. There's heat from all the lights and hungry cameras.

Dean slides up beside me. "You ready for it?"

A glance over at him and lift my chin. "I'm a Carrington, Dean. I was born ready."

He purses his lips as I step up to the podium where my notes are stacked.

The weight of eyes on me is stifling, but I straighten my spine and let the mask drop.

"Good afternoon," I say, and the room hushes.

Bring it on, vultures.

CHAPTER EIGHT

Maddox

THE LOCKER ROOM stinks of sweat and wet fabric—normal after practice, but heavier today, like the air knows we're about to be paraded around.

The kind of smell that clings, no matter how much body wash the team leaves in the stalls.

Guys peel off gear fast, the scrape of Velcro, the slap of pads hitting the floor. Steam's already curling from the showers at the back.

Nobody wants to look like they just crawled out of a drill line when the cameras start flashing.

I tug my mask free, drop it hard on the bench, and strip down slow. My shoulders ache from the morning skate, the kind of burn I welcome.

Out there I'm in control. In here?

It's a fucking circus.

Riley's voice cuts through the noise, loud enough to carry over the hiss of showers and the clang of lockers.

He's already half-wrapped in a towel, talking big like he's the captain instead of just a kid with a dangerous smile.

Finn eggs him on, pulling rookie Cal into their orbit like it's some goddamn comedy act.

Laughter echoes off the tile. Cameras aren't even in the room yet, and Riley's performing.

I shower fast, just hot enough to loosen my neck. No lingering. No small talk.

By the time I step out, the handlers are setting up lights and banners in the hallway. Jerseys are laid out clean, crisp, like we're mannequins instead of men.

Riley's first to throw his on, hair still damp but styled with his hands like he's about to do a cologne ad. Finn follows, tugging his jersey over his head and winking at one of the assistants, earning a giggle.

I pull mine on slow, every movement deliberate, the weight of the Vipers logo sitting heavy on my chest.

It's supposed to mean something. For me, it's a reminder of how fast a logo can turn into a target.

The photo station is just outside, all blinding lights and cameras clicking nonstop. Riley struts into the spotlight like he owns it, flashing that smirk he probably practices in the mirror.

When its Finn's turn, he hams it up—stick raised like a sword, a flex that makes the handlers laugh.

When they wave me forward, my jaw's already tight. They want intensity. They want something they can plaster on a billboard.

I give them flat eyes. Nothing else.

"Little more energy, Mr. Lasker," the photographer quips.

I bare my teeth—but not in a smile. More like a wolf giving a warning before he bites. The flash goes off, and for a second I see them flinch.

That's all they get.

The next station has video rolling. "Say your name, position, and something fun about yourself."

Fun about myself?

Jesus Christ.

"Maddox Lasker. Goalie. Fun's not part of the job."

The videographers exchange a look and then shuffle me quickly down the line like I'm radioactive.

Which is fine by me if it gets me out of this shit show faster.

I've always hated media day. The cameras and platitudes they want aren't my stage, the crease on the ice rink is.

Out here, it's all just a bunch of bullshit.

In the large ballroom where the interviews take place, the lights are hotter here than on the ice. White, unrelenting, like they're designed to bake answers out of you.

Reporters crowd in, microphones thrust like weapons.

"Thirty-nine now, Maddox—how much gas you think you've got left in the tank?"

"Big contract for a guy your age. Last paycheck?"

"Atlanta's banking their first season on you. Think you've still got it?"

The words slide in sharp, designed to draw blood. I keep my answers clipped, neutral, just this side of polite.

"Ask me in April. I'm here to play, not talk."

I level my stare with the guy who brought up my age. "And we'll see what's left in the tank when the games matter."

"Boston ended messy, didn't it? Care to comment?"

"Is it true about the—"

The word *incident* floats between two of them, hushed, barbed. My pulse spikes, and heat licks up the back of my neck. I lock down my jaw so tight my teeth ache.

I won't give them anything. Not a twitch, not a flinch. My face stays stone, my voice flat. "Next question."

The urge to shove past them thrums in my chest, sharp and dangerous. But walking out would hand them the story they want.

And I've given enough headlines to the league already.

So I lean back into the posture I know best—stillness, patience, control.

Just like in the crease.

Let them fire shot after shot. Let them burn themselves out against the wall I've built.

I won't back down from what I did in Boston, but in order to keep my career intact, I have to move on from it.

I wish these fuckers would move on too.

Behind me, Riley's laugh cuts through the noise. Bright, cocky, smooth. He's working the cameras like it's his job, grinning for every mic shoved his way.

Yep, Peacock is the perfect name for him.

Finn cracks a joke nearby, and the room ripples with laughter.

The rookies love it. The media eats it up.

I grit my teeth harder, because the contrast is too loud to ignore. Guys like Riley and Finn shine under the spotlight.

I survive it.

And survival is all I've got left to give.

The questions taper off, and handlers shuffle the herd. Players rotate in and out, cameras swinging to catch every angle, every sound bite they can milk.

When it's Finn's turn, he takes center stage and leans into the mic, eyes wide, cracking a one-liner about his hair being "game-ready, even if the rest of me isn't."

The room bursts out laughing. Reporters lap it up like he's the golden retriever of hockey—chaotic, impossible to stay mad at.

Good for the team, even if it makes me look like the asshole.

I don't give a shit. I've never been the guy to make the team look good in the media.

The only time the media loves me is when I'm helping the team rack up playoff cups.

And that's fine by me.

Well, most of the time it's fine. Every so often though, there's a dull weight in my chest, and I wish things were different for me.

But they never have been and—at this point—they never will be.

The rookies shuffle in behind him, and I catch Cal's voice falter.

He stumbles over a stat, his face reddens, and his shoulders fold inward like he's about to implode under the lights.

I drift just close enough to be in the frame, but not enough to draw notice.

"Breathe, rookie" I murmur under my breath, low enough only he hears.

His chest expands, shaky but deeper. He resets and answers the next question cleaner. No one notices the way his spine straightens, but I do.

This is the part no one tells you about when you're working your way up to the pros.

Not only do you protect the net, but you steady the kid. You make sure the cracks don't spread.

That's the job, even if no one calls it that.

Even if it gets you fired.

Finn claps Cal on the back with a grin, pulling the spotlight away, and the tension breaks. The cameras eat it up—chaos and charm playing better than silence and steel ever will.

I shift my gaze across the chaos and find her.

Sloane Carrington.

Not on camera, not taking questions. Just there in the background, directing traffic like a general disguised in a tailored blazer.

Controlled steel, every movement precise. She tilts her head, sends one rookie right, waves another forward, corrals Finn without raising her voice.

She never looks my way, but I feel it anyway.

The gravity of her being in my orbit, pulling without even getting close to touching.

A presence that makes the room move sharper, cleaner.

I drag my eyes away before anyone catches me staring.

Cameras flash again, and the circus rolls on.

The stage lights hit like a cross-check. Too hot, too blinding. Rows of microphones lean forward like weapons, reporters stacked shoulder to shoulder, their pens and cameras twitching for blood.

I drop into the chair, suit jacket stiff across my shoulders. The name placard in front of me reads like a challenge: *Maddox Lasker Goaltender.*

The first question cracks out.

"Thirty-nine. That's ancient in this league. You think you got what it takes to last all season?"

My jaw tightens. "Ask me in April."

Laughter ripples, sharp-edged. Another voice jumps in.

"Last season was your worst statistically since your rookie year. Why would Atlanta take a risk?"

The murmurs sharpen. More questions slam down—Boston, the suspension, the "incident" no one will drop.

My pulse spikes, heat climbing my throat. Every instinct screams to stand, to walk, to leave them with nothing but the scrape of my chair.

And then she's there.

Sloane Carrington slides into the seat beside me like she owns the oxygen.

She's calm, precise, and doesn't flinch at the barrage of questions that are judging both my worth and her decisions.

"What Atlanta gains," she says, voice cutting clean as a skate blade, "is one of the most experienced goaltenders in the league. A man who knows pressure, who's stood in the crease when the odds were stacked, and who still came out swinging. This city doesn't need safe. It needs strong."

The room stills. Reporters pivot, pens flying to catch her words.

She redirects the next question before I can open my mouth, slices the angle on another, and reframes every strike until it sounds like strategy instead of damage control.

It should piss me off.

And it does.

Every muscle in me bristles at being handled, leashed. I don't need her smoothing edges I sharpened on purpose. But watching her work—unflinching, unbreakable—forces something else out of me.

Respect.

The press pushes harder, trying to wedge daylight between us.

"Are you worried, Ms. Carrington, about managing a player with…temperament issues?"

Her smile is a blade. "The only folks who should be worried are the opponents underestimating him."

Heat coils low in my chest.

Not pride. Not exactly.

Something sharper, messier.

Because the whole time she's steadying this ship, her presence pins me harder than the questions ever could.

Control against control.

And under it,—sparks neither of us will name.

The press conference ends in a blur of flashes and questions I don't bother remembering. My jaw aches from clenching, my palms damp inside the cuffs of my suit.

I shove back from the table, cutting through the bodies, and slip down a side corridor just to breathe.

Thank fuck it's empty out here.

Pacing back and forth in the hallway, I blow out a series of short breaths to battle back the anxiety nipping at my throat.

A couple moments later, my heartbeat returns to normal, and

I let the stoic mask slide back into place just before opening the door…

And slamming straight into Sloane.

A muffled "oof" comes from her, and my hands shoot out to grip her elbows to keep her upright.

But touching her is a bad, bad idea.

She's cool steel. Untouchable with her crisp lines, sharp heels, and not a hair out of place.

She looks like the lights don't touch her,—like she eats fire for breakfast and calls it protein.

I'm all sweat-slick under my jacket, heat crawling down my spine.

And I feel about a million years old standing next to her.

"Watch where you're going, Sloane."

My tone is sharp, even condescending, but I can't let her see any of my cracks.

Her eyes narrow when they meet mine, and she pulls out of my grasp.

"Me? You opened the door like you were trying to pull it off the hinges."

She smooths down her blazer and lifts her chin, somehow staring down at me even though I've got several inches on her.

And that little defiant move makes me want to shove her against the wall and kiss that red war paint off her full lips.

"You enjoy pulling my strings up there?" The words scrape low, half snarl, half something else.

Her eyes flash, quick as a whip. "Someone has to keep you from strangling yourself with them."

I step closer, not even meaning to, until the space between us is measured in heartbeats.

The faint edge of her perfume threads the air, and it's like it was custom made for her. Clean, sharp, and nothing soft about it.

My chest tightens against the heat rolling off her, the way she stands her ground instead of backing down.

"You think you've got me leashed?" I murmur. "Careful, old dogs like me bite."

Her chin tips up, mouth curving in a blade of a smile. "Good thing I don't scare easy."

The air snaps, charged enough to burn. My pulse drums in my ears, her gaze locked on mine like neither of us is willing to give the first inch.

Footsteps echo down the hall, and the spell fractures.

With one last look, she turns on her heels and walks away, each step deliberate, leaving me strung tight.

Her heels fade, but the scent of her lingers, sharp as ozone after a storm.

My hands flex at my sides, restless, like I need something to hold onto.

She thinks she's the one pulling strings. Maybe she is.

But the fire under my ribs says otherwise.

I drag in a breath that doesn't cool a damn thing.

Practice didn't drain me. The cameras didn't either.

She did.

And I hate that I want more.

CHAPTER NINE

Sloane

THE GLASS DOORS to my office click shut behind me, the hush almost too heavy after the chaos of media day.

I drop my bag on the desk and flop down into my chair, kicking off my heels in the process.

The relief is immediate but dangerous.

Because without them, without the polish, it feels like armor slipping away.

The room smells faintly of paper and coffee gone cold. My body hums with leftover adrenaline from hours of smiling, nodding, and spinning stories for the press.

And all of my key players showed the press who they are today. Some of that good, some bad.

Riley thrived like a show pony, every grin landing with the cameras like he'd been born under a spotlight.

Finn cracked jokes loud enough to echo, half the reporters eating it up, the other half already wondering what trouble he'll cause by Christmas.

Eli, quieter at the edge of the scrum and steady as stone, gave nothing flashy but rolled his eyes at the Riley and Finn comedy show.

I sigh, closing my eyes for a moment. Riley and Finn could be a media nightmare if I don't watch them closely.

Especially Finn. He's loud and reckless, but talented.

And he knows it.

One of them who doesn't know it, though, is my rookie. Cal stumbling through his first microphone gauntlet, wide-eyed and raw, but earnest enough to make them forgive him.

Maybe I should pair him up with Logan. A buddy system so to speak. Logan's my most polished PR guy on the team. Every answer he gives is clean, measured, and rehearsed.

I tap my finger on my chin. Eh, maybe Logan is too polished for the rookie right now.

What am I thinking? Beau is the perfect mentor for Cal, since they're both wingers. And Beau's got that easy, approachable warmth.

Single dad to a little girl, the cameras soft around him because they see it too—that quiet, dependable gravity that makes people lean in.

Beau's also one of my older players, kind of a co-captain so to speak to Jace.

I smile thinking of the way Jace looms like the anchor he is, older, grimmer with his presence alone and commanding respect even without a word.

Reminds me of another older, grimmer presence.

Maddox.

Just saying his name in my head makes me…well…stupid.

He stonewalled most of the reporters questions, his jaw looking like it was carved from granite.

It's like he didn't realize that the less he gave, the more they wanted. Every camera was hungry for more because he gave them nothing at all.

And that didn't help my case with the board.

I press my palms to the desk, trying to frame it as a win. It was controlled chaos, but the key word is "controlled."

Except there's nothing controlled about the way my body betrays me, every nerve firing hot at the memory of our collision in the corridor.

I can still feel the steady weight of Maddox's hands when he caught me. The heat of his body bled through the thin fabric of my sleeve.

His voice low and sharp as the blades he skates on: *You enjoy pulling my strings up there?*

The worst part of it all? How much I had enjoyed being pressed against that rock-hard body that vibrated under his suit.

I shake my head, hard, even while my breath stutters.

Nope. No, no, no.

I'm the owner. His boss.

Not some random puck bunny in his orbit.

Not someone's risk.

But my pulse still trips over itself, proof that control is an illusion I can't quite grip tonight.

I square my shoulders. "Time to get back to work, Carrington," I say to the room before picking up my phone and opening the note app.

"Have chat with Holt and Beau about mentoring Cal," I recite out loud while I type.

And just as I start to type more, my phone buzzes in my hand.

Griff calling…

I groan and mock banging my head on my desk.

"Don't tell me you actually watched the circus," I say as I answer.

He laughs, the sound warm, too knowing. "Watched? Cousin, I've got the clips on repeat. Your goalie looks like he wanted to strangle every reporter in the room. Great optics, by the way."

I pinch the bridge of my nose. "Maddox isn't here to charm reporters. He's here to win games."

"Mmhmm." Griffin stretches the sound out like he's winding

me up. "You sure about that? Looked a lot like a man cashing one last paycheck to me."

The words prick, sharper than I want them to. "He's worth it," I say, too fast. "He's exactly what this team needs."

"Whoa. Defensive much?"

"I made a choice. I'll stand by it." My voice is clipped steel, but it wavers underneath.

He doesn't rush to fill the silence, but lets it sit, lets me squirm against it. "Hey. I'm just saying—eyes are on you, Sloane. They're waiting for you to slip. And you know as well as I do, one stumble and they'll tear you apart."

I lean back, eyes on the stretch of trees shrouded in night. No movement, no mercy—just a weight that settles over me the way expectation always does. "Tell me something I don't know, oh sage one."

He chuckles, but it's softer now. "Okay, how about this. I've got your back, always. Even if you decide to gamble on broody goalies who look like they eat reporters for breakfast."

My throat tightens. "I know you do. And I appreciate it."

But even in his reassurance, there's something else—an edge he can't hide.

Like he suspects more is brewing under the surface than I'll ever admit.

And the worst part?

He's not wrong.

I clear my throat, forcing my voice lighter. "Enough about my goalie. How did *your* media day go?"

He groans. "Don't remind me. Half the questions were about last season, the other half about whether I plan to shave my beard. Riveting stuff."

A smile tugs at my mouth before I can stop it. "Better you than me."

"Debatable," he mutters. Then his voice softens. "Mom asked about you today. She worries, you know."

My chest tightens in a different way. Aunt Sara—always carrying more than her share, always steady when the rest of us splintered. "Tell her I'm fine," I say. "And that I'll call soon."

"You'd better." Griffin's tone carries the weight of both a tease and a warning. "Mom's been on my ass about you calling her."

"Why doesn't she just call me herself?"

He scoffs, "Two reasons, Lo. One, we're talking about Sara Ashford here. She doesn't do the calling. And two, if you do her like you do me, it'd take eleven billion times to call before you answer."

Griffin's use of the nickname he gave me when we were kids and he couldn't say my whole name causes a thickness in my throat.

I miss those times.

"Geez, drama much? How do you get any hockey played if you're calling me eleven billion times?"

He chuckles. "Smartass."

"Learned from the best."

"Damn right you did."

I sigh. "But okay, you have a point. And I will call her. I promise."

We say our love yous and goodbyes and when the call ends, silence swallows the office again.

I straighten in my chair and pull the keyboard closer to me. My fingers hover over the keyboard, but the ping of my inbox stops me from typing.

Subject line: Debrief: Media Day Performance – Tomorrow 9AM.

Dean.

Of course.

The wording is clinical, polite on the surface, but I know better.

It's a power play. His way of reminding me he's still in the game, still watching for cracks.

My stomach knots. My jaw locks. "Predictable," I mutter, voice sharp in the quiet.

He'll frame it as strategy, as accountability. But what it is— what it always is—is a test.

And tomorrow morning, I'll have to walk into his office and remind him who actually runs this team.

And that in spite of the leash my father put on me from the grave, I'm the one making the decisions here.

The dread coils low in my gut anyway.

I lean back and close my eyes against the light of the monitors.

Unbidden, Maddox's face fills the darkness behind my lids.

But it's not his press conference glare or the goalie's mask of indifference.

It's the man in the hallway, heat and shadow, closing the space between us until I could barely breathe.

My chest tightens. I hate that it felt good.

This is dangerous. Attraction is risk.

And risk gets exploited.

I bite the inside of my cheek, hard, chasing pain to push the thought away.

I am not that woman. I am the owner of this franchise. I don't blur lines.

But the memory clings, stubborn and electric as static under my skin.

And the truth, the one I won't say out loud…

Maddox unsettles me.

Not because he's a mistake I can't afford,—but because some traitorous part of me doesn't want to shove the mistake aside.

When I open my eyes, I pull up the PowerPoint I've started called "The Lasker Dossier."

I click through the slides, crisp bullet points summarizing the day.

- Riley: Chaotic, media gold.
- Finn: Unpredictable, likable, but could possibly be media nightmare. Keep eye on.
- Cal: Green but salvageable with the right mentorship.
- Logan: Prince of PR
- Beau: Warm, approachable, possible mentor for Cal?
- Eli: Quiet protector
- Jace: Stoic, anchor of team.
- Maddox: Volatile, magnetic.

My chest tightens, a pulse of something I don't want to name.

I click to a blank slide, fingers hovering over the keys. Then I type.

Internal Risk Assessment – Sloane Carrington

- Boundary slippage.
- Emotional distraction.
- Loss of control = unacceptable risk.

The cursor blinks at me, an accusation in a flashing vertical line.

I'm not supposed to be on the list.

I'm not supposed to be a variable.

But here I am, typing myself into the problem like I'm just another player who might crack under pressure.

My pulse jumps so hard I press a hand flat against my sternum.

Control masquerading as strategy. That's all this is.

If I write it down, maybe it'll stay in the box. You're suppose to journal and all that, right? To get all of this out of your head?

Isn't that what they say?

But the box already feels too small.

I snap the laptop shut. The sound echoes, too loud in the empty office.

Internal Risk: Sloane Carrington.

The words loop in my head, sharper than any headline, sharper than Dean's condescension.

I lean back, exhaustion pressing me into the chair, but my pulse won't slow.

It's still there, the memory of Maddox's hand steadying me, the way he didn't back down.

The heat I can't seem to shake.

Control, I remind myself. Always control.

But the echo is louder.

Boundary slippage.

Emotional distraction.

Loss of control.

I laugh, low and humorless. "This can't be good."

The office doesn't argue. Just shadows pooling deeper, the hum of the city pressing against the glass.

I rise, heels dangling from my hand, and walk toward the door. Each step measured, hard enough to sound like steel.

But the words follow me anyway, stitched into my skin.

Internal Risk: Sloane Carrington.

I glance over at the framed jersey on the wall and for a split second, I swear I smell leather like my father's standing right here.

For the first time in a long time, I don't know if I'm the one holding the leash—or if it's already slipped from my hand.

CHAPTER TEN

Maddox

THE WHISTLE BLOWS, and the scrimmage snaps to life.

I lock my knees and square my frame, tracking the first rush coming down the ice.

Riley cuts in fast, slick hands moving like he's performing for a highlight reel instead of a practice. Showboating, peacock that he is.

He drags the puck across the slot, fakes one way, and goes the other. I stretch, glove snapping out in time to shut him down.

"Fuck!"

He's loud enough for the bench to hear, and Finn laughs so hard he nearly drops his stick.

As usual, Finn's busting balls as much as playing. He doesn't shut up the whole practice—giving me shit about my age, about Riley's missed chance, about anything that'll get under some-one's skin.

If you're in his orbit, you're a target.

Logan runs the next play clean and efficient, settling the chaos with one perfectly placed pass that lands tape-to-tape.

The guy doesn't waste movement, doesn't waste words

either. He's already running mid-season form while the rest of them are still shaking off summer rust.

Eli grinds it out along the boards, a hard check here, a stripped puck there. Nothing flashy, but there's an edge to him—controlled violence in every shift.

Beau slides into a defensive read, body angled not just to cut off Riley but to keep Cal from getting flattened in the process. Always the caretaker, even when he's breaking plays apart.

Jace watches it all calmly. He's a helluva captain. The man doesn't need to yell to be heard.

His presence does it for him. We all read off him without realizing it.

Cal's the only one still tripping over his own eagerness. Kid nearly face plants chasing down a loose puck, but he scrambles up quick, skating harder like he can make up for it with hustle.

I watch him and can't help but see myself twenty years ago —raw, reckless, and desperate to prove I belonged.

The play turns and Finn fires one from the top of the circle, and I drop down, block it, then send the rebound flying.

Fuck me.

Pain knifes through my shoulder with the motion. Sharp, sudden, blinding.

I mask it and push up like nothing happened.

Nobody notices, and that's the whole point.

I can play through it.

I *will* play through it.

Because the second I show weakness, it's over.

We cycle through several more scrimmages before the whistle's called, indicating the end of practice.

"Hit the showers. Team meeting in ten," Coach Holt calls out.

We shuffle into the locker room, which soon stinks of sweat and adrenaline, steam rising off the showers as guys strip out of their gear.

Letting the rest of the guys get to the showers first, I strip down to my compression gear and sit on the bench, moving gingerly to hide the pain in my shoulder.

I need ice, but there's no way I'm doing it in front of the whole team or even a PT if I can get away with it.

True to his word, Coach Holt walks into the locker room, calling us into a quick huddle, voice carrying over the chatter.

He goes over some specific areas of improvement, thankful "goal tending" was left off the list.

"Energy was sharp today," he says, gaze sweeping the room. "Conditioning's still got room to improve before the regular season starts. Don't get sloppy—preseason isn't a tune-up; it's an audition. You want your spot, then earn it now."

Heads nod. Nobody jokes back.

We all know he's right.

His eyes land on me a beat longer than the others. I keep my face neutral. Whatever he's looking for, he won't see it with me.

After the group breaks, Holt jerks his chin at me. "Coach Hartwell wants a word in the film room."

I nod and head down the hall to see what the goalie coach has to say about my performance.

Coach doesn't waste time. Clips flash across the screen, my saves, my misses, angles I know by heart.

He points out a drop in my stance, a half-second delay on a slide. "Stay sharp," he says, like it's that simple.

Like it doesn't burn every time I push that shoulder the wrong way.

I nod. No excuses. No explanations.

But every note he gives me lands heavier than it should, like a reminder the younger guys are right there, faster, fresher, and waiting to take my spot.

And if I slip? They'll hand it over without blinking.

When I return to the locker room, it hums with that low, fluorescent buzz, too bright, too empty. Everyone else cleared out a while ago, and that's exactly how I like it.

No eyes on me. No one watching the old man ice his busted shoulder.

I tug my compression sleeve down, teeth clenched against the stab of movement. The joint feels like ground glass, grinding every time I shift.

I grab an ice pack from the cooler, slap it against my shoulder, and fumble with the plastic wrap to hold it in place. One-handed, it's sloppy—slips halfway down my bicep before I even get it tight.

"Son of a bitch," I mutter, jerking the wrap, pain spiking sharper.

That's when I hear it—the click of high heels.

Sharp, deliberate, wrong in this space that smells like sweat, rubber, and disinfectant.

I don't even look up. "Locker room's closed. Holt's gone."

Silence. Then, that voice. The one that makes my blood run hot, even when it's low and cutting and scolding me. "You're wrapping that wrong."

My head snaps up to find Sloane standing just inside the doorway, arms folded, eyes locked on me like she owns the damn place.

Which—technically—she does.

"Not your business," I bite back. Ice shifts, water seeping cold down my chest.

Perfect.

Just perfect.

She doesn't leave. Of course she doesn't.

Instead, she crosses the room, every step echoing in my ribs, until she's standing right in front of me. "Give me that."

I should tell her to go to hell. I should grab the roll of wrap out of her reach and prove I don't need anyone's help.

But my fingers let go before my pride can catch up, and

suddenly she's bracing the pack against my shoulder, moving with quick, sure hands.

Her scent hits first—something clean, sharp, and threaded with expensive perfume that doesn't belong in a men's locker room, no matter how state of the art it is.

Then the heat of her palms against my skin through the thin layer of compression fabric.

The brush of her wrist against my chest.

My body goes rigid, breath stalling as she winds the tape smooth and tight, no wasted motion.

I can't stop watching her. The way her brow furrows, the way she doesn't hesitate.

Like she's done this before. Like she knows exactly where it hurts.

Finally I rasp, "How the hell do you know how to do that?"

She ties it off with a neat snap, steps back just enough that the warmth of her touch fades, and meets my eyes.

Calm. Steady. "I used to be an Olympic-contending figure skater. Injuries were part of the deal."

The words hang between us, heavier than the ice on my shoulder.

I study her—really study her. The steel under the polish, the edge under the silk.

It shouldn't surprise me, but it does.

And it makes something tighten in my chest that has nothing to do with pain.

She turns before I can say anything, heels clicking on the tile as she walks away like she didn't just strip me bare in the most dangerous way possible.

"Actually…" she says, coming back over to where I sit. "You're the one I was looking for. We need to talk. Come to my office before you leave."

There's an edge in her tone making it clear this isn't optional.

My pulse spikes for an entirely different reason. The ice

burns cold, but it's nothing compared to the heat curling low in my gut.

But I can't let her see what she does to me, even if she wasn't the woman who signs my paychecks.

I narrow my eyes on her. "And if I don't?"

Her lips curve in a feline smile that has nothing to do with humor, but doesn't respond before turning on that spiked heel and walking away.

Her heels echo down the hall, sharp and steady, leaving me with nothing but melting ice and the echo of her touch burning through my skin.

I sit there longer than I should, jaw locked, trying to smother the fire she lit with her hands on me and the command in her voice.

She doesn't get to do this—walk in, strip me bare without touching skin, then order me upstairs like I'm one of her rookies.

But the truth? My body's already decided.

I strip the wrap off, shoving the ice into the trash, and sling my bag over my shoulder like I've still got a choice.

Heading for the elevator, the burn in my shoulder feels like nothing compared to the one low in my gut.

When I get to the top floor and exit the elevator, every step to her office feels like giving in, but I don't stop.

I can't.

Not when part of me wants to see what she does next almost as much as I want to tell her no.

The hallway stretches out in front of me, sleek and silent, a world away from the sweat and chaos downstairs.

My boots sound too loud against the polished floor, every step dragging me deeper into her territory.

By the time her assistant comes into view, I already know I've crossed a line I swore I wouldn't.

Tessa looks up from behind her desk as I step in, every inch of her composed, not a detail out of place.

"She's expecting you." Smooth, neutral. No judgment. But I catch the faintest twitch at her mouth, like she knows more than she lets on.

My jaw tightens. My hand fists around the strap of my bag. I shouldn't be here. Shouldn't be giving in to her pull.

But I walk forward anyway.

The office door looms, wood and glass polished to a shine. One step, and I'm in. One step, and I'm back where I swore I wouldn't be.

My hand hesitates on the handle, breath catching against my will.

I turn it. Push through.

And there she is—Sloane Carrington, seated behind her desk, calm as a storm's eye, looking like she owns the whole damn world.

The door clicks shut behind me.

Just the two of us.

Again.

CHAPTER ELEVEN

Sloane

THE DOOR CLOSES SHUT behind him, and the air changes shape. It gets heavier, denser, like the room remembers him before I do.

Maddox crosses the threshold without hurry, shoulders squared, jaw locked, that contained kind of force he wears like armor.

My pulse jumps in a way it has no business jumping, and I smooth my fingers over the edge of my desk to keep from giving myself away.

He eyes the space around him—floor-to-ceiling glass, sharp lines, walnut, and order. While he doesn't normally hang out in these types of rooms, he manages to command it and make it feel smaller anyway.

"Take a seat, please," I say, voice steady and flat enough to skate on.

He doesn't, not at first. He stands there like a challenge, like the silence between us has a clock in it.

He's testing me.

I let the beat stretch, matching his stare, spine tall, breath measured, not so much as a blink I don't own.

The trick with men like him—men like my father, men like

every investor who's ever thought "young" meant "easy"—is to let them think they're winning the second before they decide to give ground.

Then you set the line.

Maddox finally moves. He drops into the chair with a sprawl that reads as deliberate disrespect. Long legs open, shoulders heavy into the back, one big hand curls on the armrest like a warning.

I feel the rip of heat in my chest anyway. It irritates me that I feel it, and the irritation irritates me more.

He smells like cold air and clean soap and the ghost of rubber from the rink. It pulls at a thread I should have cut downstairs—my palms on his shoulder, the heat of him through the thin compression fabric, and the way he went very still under my hands when I wrapped the ice tight.

He didn't say thank you. He didn't have to. I felt the bite of his breath. I felt my own.

I lace my fingers together and lock my elbows, the posture my old etiquette coach would call "composed readiness."

"Dean and the board want a different story out of you," I say, clean and clinical. "On the ice, you're doing what we brought you here to do. Off the ice, yesterday was… not what we need."

His jaw tics. A small movement. A warning. He lifts his gaze to mine without lifting his head, like a man sighting along the barrel. "I'm a goalie. Not a circus act."

His voice is sharp enough to cut glass.

"You're a goalie and a face," I answer, not unkindly. "And the city is watching our second season as hard if not harder than our first year."

I drum my fingers on my desk. "Media day is designed to feed them. You looked like you wanted to break every microphone in the room."

"I wanted to leave the room. That part wasn't a secret."

Tension snaps through me so fast it almost makes me laugh.

Not because he's wrong, but because he's honest. I respect honest.

But respecting his honesty only complicates things.

"Perception is louder than truth. You know that, even if you hate it."

He leans back farther, like he's testing how much space he can take. "You want me to smile on command and pretend I like being poked."

"I want you to look like you're part of something, because you are."

We stare at each other across twenty-eight inches of walnut. I could tap the desk once and call this done with an edict. I could play the owner card so hard it cracks his teeth.

But power only works once if you wield it like a hammer. The second time, men like him break the hammer.

"There's a way to fix it," I slide a folder across the desk with a tab that reads COMMUNITY INITIATIVE in Sierra's precise handwriting. "Saturday morning at Atlanta Children's hospital. Photo window is ninety minutes. We're reading to two rooms, signing jerseys in the atrium, and doing a small meet-and-greet with the oncology floor for those who are up for it. Cameras will be there at the beginning and the end. Middle is just you and the kids."

There's a flicker of something in his eyes at the mention of kids. But it's fleeting, and I almost wonder if I imagined it.

"A dog-and-pony show."

"A show of decency. They need it. We need it. It's the right play."

"Sloane, I don't have a soft side."

I meet his eyes and don't blink. "Yes, you do."

He doesn't move, but there's that flicker of something again. I didn't imagine it because it takes him a little longer to shut it down this time.

"I've seen it, Maddox."

As soon as I say it, I want to claw the words back.

Not only does he know for sure now that I watch him, but what I've seen is dangerous for me.

The way he holds himself still when rookies flail, the way he doesn't humiliate weakness even when the room would cheer him for it.

The way he let me touch him, for a breath and no more, wrapped him tight and close and didn't shrug me off.

The way my own body feels traitorous even now.

"You don't know me," he says, quiet enough to make my skin prickle.

"Maybe not, but I know what I saw. And I know what it will do for this team if people see it."

He looks away, huffing out a breath that isn't quite a laugh. After a moment, his gaze comes back to the folder. He flips it open with two fingers like it might bite him.

His eyes skim the schedule, the talking points Dean insisted we include, the photo thumbnails Sierra curated to look candid. His mouth hardens.

"This is nothing but theater."

"Be that as it may, it's good for the community. And for this franchise. One that you agreed to be a a part of when you signed the contract."

His gaze meets mine, the intensity pinning me to my seat. "I signed the contract to do my job, which is to stop pucks."

"It's the core of the job," I concede. "But this isn't your first rodeo, and you know as well as I do, that isn't the whole of it."

I cross my arms and lean back in my chair. "We may not be storied in all the history you're used to like in Boston, but we're a professional organization. We do the same kind of community outreach here you did there."

He lifts a brow. "I didn't come here to be liked."

I wish I could tell him I didn't hire him to be liked. That I hired him to anchor us when the ice turns ugly and the city gets hungry for blood.

That I hired him because control that violent and clean is rare, and when he's on the ice the team breathes easier even if they pretend otherwise.

But we're not that kind of honest with each other.

"You came here to win," I say. "Winning requires oxygen. Optics are oxygen. Those kids will gladly give it to us for free if you don't choke on your pride."

He leans forward, forearms braced on his thighs. The chair creaks, just a little, a sound that shouldn't feel intimate but does. "You think this is about pride."

"I think this is about choice," I say. "You can choose to make my job harder, or you can choose to make it easier. Either way, my job gets done. Yours goes better if you don't pick a fight with a camera."

"That what this is? You and your job?"

"That's what all of this is. My name is on the deed. Every misstep hits my desk first. Every win and every loss lands on my back. So, yes. It's my job. It's also your job. We do them or we watch other people do them for us."

He studies me for a long moment, and the weight of it is almost physical.

I feel it at the base of my throat. Along the inside of my wrists. Behind my knees.

Other places no one can see, but I can sure as hell feel.

"Listen, media day wasn't all your fault," I say, because it's true and because I need one moment of truth between us that isn't a weapon. "They came for you. You protected yourself. I don't blame you for that."

Surprise registers subtly in those icy blue eyes, shifting the heat from fury to focus.

"You don't blame me," he says, not quite a question.

"No. But I do need you to course-correct. And I need you to do it quickly."

He looks back down at the folder, his thumb dragging along the edge, and I almost feel the scrape against my skin.

He's thinking about the cameras, the kids, the way the world turns fast when you invite it to watch.

"The hospital…you'll be there."

I nod. "Yes."

"With me."

"Yes."

"Reading," he adds, like he can make it sound ridiculous enough to end the conversation.

I roll my lips inward to keep from smiling. "A book called 'The Hockey Sweater.' And if you complain about the translation I'll let the eight-year-olds correct your French on live local television."

For the first time since he walked in, his mouth moves in something that could almost be a smile if you glossed it in fiction and put it under soft lighting.

"You've thought this through," he says.

"I make a living thinking things through.

He tilts his head, that stare on me once more. "Do you make a living doing it for me?"

"That depends on whether you insist on making it necessary."

He sits back again with a sigh.

"I'm not a celebrity. I'm not polished. I'm not pretty. I'm thirty-nine, and I creak when I get out of bed. Half the guys in that room want my job because they should. Cameras make me feel like I'm supposed to lie. I don't like who I have to be to make you happy in front of a lens."

The truth of it hits hard. Not because I want him polished. Not because I want him to lie.

Because there's something indecent about asking a man who

has built his life on control to hand a piece of that control to strangers with tripods.

"This isn't about pretty," I say. "It's about letting people see that who they're pouring their hope into is a person. It's about the kids who will sleep better because the guy they see on billboards looked them in the eye and made them laugh. It's about the rookie who breathes easier because the cameras caught you doing what you already do—standing still when other people wobble."

His gaze hooks on mine and holds. Heat moves through my chest like whiskey.

"I see everything," I say.

"And you wrapped my shoulder," he adds after a beat, and now it's like there's no desk between us.

There's only the memory of my hands on him. His skin hot, my fingers confident because confidence was safer than feeling anything else.

"Yes, I did."

"Why?"

I shrug a shoulder. "I knew how and because no one was there to help you. Because it would hurt less if it was tight."

He studies me the same way he studied the folder, like he could pry the edges up and see what is underneath if he decided he has time for it.

"You didn't have to," he says.

"I don't do 'have to' very often. It makes me interesting company or terrible company, depending on the day."

He snorts. The sound is a rough cut of amusement that does unforgivable things to the base of my spine.

"Saturday," I say, before the room slides any closer to the edge. "Ten a.m. Call time at the hospital is nine-forty. Sierra will email the talking points; ignore the ones that feel like lies. Dean will coordinate the outlets for the top and the bottom of the shoot."

I level him with my best "don't fuck with me stare." "You will not stonewall. You will not snarl. You will stand still for photos and make one kind of joke that reads as human, not hostile. I'll be there. If you need a lifeline, I'm there."

"I don't take lifelines," he says.

"I know; you take wins. This is one of them, so take it, Maddox."

He taps the folder again, slow and deliberate. Once. Twice. "I'll think about it."

I try not to roll my eyes.

There it is. The non-answer that men give when they want to keep you in the air over the net and call it mercy.

My father used to do it all the time.

I don't take the bait and keep my voice cool. "This isn't an ask. It's mandatory."

A long moment slides by, thin as a blade.

He holds my stare like a man holding the line in a tide. I don't look away.

The chair scrapes when he stands, towering over my desk once again.

Heat rushes to my core seeing him like that. The woman in me responds before the rest of me can body-check her.

And I hate it.

I hate the heat.

I hate the wanting.

I hate that the wanting makes me feel alive when I'm supposed to be steel.

Maddox turns for the door. He pauses with his hand on the knob, then looks back over his shoulder.

The look lands like a physical thing—a palm at the base of my neck.

And doesn't that just make me think all kinds of inappropriate things.

"Mandatory," he says, like he's trying the word on.

"Mandatory."

Something unreadable passes across his face. Not mockery. Not surrender. A private calculation I'm not invited into. Then the mask slides into place. He opens the door and steps out, closing it behind him with a soft click that still feels like a slam.

I take several deep breaths, giving myself a pep talk with each one.

I am steel.

I am Sloane fucking Carrington.

I own this damn team.

I belong here even if they think I don't.

Time to get back to work.

I have eight emails from Dean, three calendar holds from the league office, a text from Tessa asking for the updated sponsor deck, and Sierra's draft schedule for Saturday waiting in my inbox.

The work won't do itself while I sit here vibrating, thinking about how Maddox's skin felt under my hand.

How I want to feel it again. The muscle, the heat, the control lying just beneath.

And just how much I hate myself for wanting it.

Just one more time.

CHAPTER TWELVE

Maddox

THE PIT HUMS like a live wire.

Fans pressed to the glass, faces painted venom green, every seat filled like it's the playoffs instead of a meaningless preseason.

But there's nothing meaningless about tonight.

New city. New logo on my chest.

A first impression I can't afford to fuck up.

The ice smells fresh—paint still sharp under the sweat and rubber. My pads creak as I shift in the crease, settling into the cage.

Every nerve's lit. Every sound's magnified—the slap of pucks on boards, the scrape of blades, the Barracudas shit talking during warm-ups like their mouths can win them the game.

A winger brushes too close on a skate-by, mutters something about "old man legs." I don't bite.

Not yet.

My shoulder twinges when I roll it, a reminder I'm not firing clean yet. My body feels slow under the weight of gear that feels heavier than it should. Like it's lagging a second behind my brain.

I clamp my glove tighter around the stick, force my breath steady. Focus and lock in.

It doesn't matter how my shoulder feels tonight. What matters is stopping the damn puck.

The puck drops and chaos explodes.

Tampa's center wins the face off clean, shoves it back, and they come charging, driving hard.

Their winger cuts wide and fires a low blocker. My pad's there, but the rebound spits out hotter than I like. Their forward pounces, whacking for daylight.

I sprawl, glove snapping, stick jabbing, body sprawling over the crease. Whistle blows late, pileup pressing heavy over my ribs. Thirty seconds in, and they're already testing whether I can survive the storm.

It was a decent save, but I can feel it. My edges aren't crisp. My legs aren't snapping the way they should.

Fans roar anyway, feeding me energy I don't trust. My lungs burn already, chest tight.

The Barracudas keep pressing, like hungry sharks circling. I make two clean stops, but the third slips.

It's a low wrister, a weak shot, and one I should eat alive. It skitters through the gap between pad and post before I can clamp down.

Fuck me.

It's the ugly kind of goal that makes the crowd groan like they've just watched a car wreck.

The noise shifts, and the energy in The Pit tilts.

It feels a lot like doubt.

Heat crawls under my gear, sweat sticking at the back of my neck.

Fuck. You can't afford to be that guy. Not here. Not now. Not in front of her.

Because yeah, I know exactly where *she* is. High box, perfect view of every mistake.

My eyes flick up without meaning to, and I catch her.

Leaning forward, elbows on her knees, lips pressed tight like she's got steel sewn into them.

Eyes locked on me, sharp and steady.

It should feel like pressure, but it feels like heat.

The wrong kind of heat.

It's like she's got me pinned here in my own crease, stripped down under all this gear.

My chest tightens, pulse racing harder than the play in front of me.

For God's sake, Lasker. Fucking focus!

The whistle blows, and the game resets. I drag my focus back, but it sticks on her, even when it shouldn't.

Riley decides he'll play hero. He toe-drags through two guys like he knows he's on television.

Flashy stick work, diving blocks. He's all swagger, all noise, but he leaves holes big enough to drive a truck through.

He loses the puck at the blue line, and Tampa counters fast. I read the pass, slide across, chest stinging when I take the shot square.

Riley's skating back with that grin like it's all part of the plan. My teeth grind so hard my mask rattles and my irritation spikes.

I don't need him grandstanding. I need him to stay in his lane.

Logan cleans the next sequence with a tape-to-tape pass that settles the chaos.

Jace keeps his calm, barking one command and pulling the team back into shape.

But me? I'm scrambling, chasing the play instead of commanding it. That's not me.

That's never been me.

I glance up once and find her watching with that unreadable expression that digs under my skin worse than a blade.

Doesn't matter if she's judging or waiting—I can't stop seeing her.

And it's costing me.

As the game wears on, it turns mean. Barracudas finish every check, and shoving matches break out after nearly every play.

Riley's in the middle of most of them, along with Finn, who's stirring shit like he was born for it.

Tampa smells blood, and they're pressing.

Their forward winds up and rips one high. My glove flashes, snagging it clean.

I hold on to it long enough for the cameras to see it before I drop it with a thud. Finn skates past, grinning, and winks like he set it up just for me.

I barely keep from rolling my eyes.

Cal gets burned next—pinched too deep and caught flat-footed. Three-on-one.

My gut drops.

I square, force the shooter wide, and save it with a kick. It rebounds to the trailer—snap shot. I stretch, glove open, and snag it by a thread.

The whistle blows and Cal looks like he's about to implode.

I tap his shin pad as I skate by, low enough no one notices. "Breathe."

His nod is jerky, desperate.

After that, something shifts. My legs catch. My reads sharpen.

Save by save, I claw myself back. A glove snatch here, a kick save there, stringing together moments that keep us alive.

By the third attempt, I'm dialed enough to shut the door when it matters.

Big stops, heavy traffic, chaos in the crease—I hold it down.

We scrape out a one-goal lead, and somehow, we hang onto it.

The horn blares and The Pit explodes.

We win 3-2.

Relief rips through me, but it's laced with something colder. Frustration.

Because it's a win that doesn't feel like a win.

It feels like we survived, not conquered. It feels like we were one shift away from crumbling.

And the first face I look for when I rip my mask up?

Hers.

Sloane's already on her feet in the box. Hands folded in front of her, expression unreadable. No cheer. No relief.

Just cool, measured eyes locked on mine, cutting through the chaos like she's the only one in the building.

And God help me, my chest pulls tighter. It's want tangled with resentment, heat laced with shame.

We file into the locker room, where it's thick with silence. Pads clatter to the floor, showers hiss, nobody says much. We all know what that was.

Not good enough.

We didn't earn it.

The silence grows thicker when the sound of heels hit the tile sharply. Sharper than the smell of sweat and disinfectant. Every head snaps up, and movement stops.

Sloane walks in like she owns the room. Like she owns *us*.

She doesn't waste time, doesn't soften, doesn't give us any phony platitudes.

Just lays it down for us, voice crisp and cold enough to sting.

"A win's a win. But it won't be next time if you keep playing like that."

No names. No fingers pointed. But it lands.

Hard.

Right on me.

My jaw grinds as I strip the tape off my pads. Sweat burns down my spine.

She doesn't even look directly at me, but I feel her words like a blade pressed to my throat.

That's when Riley decides it's time to talk.

"Maybe if someone back there wasn't asleep the first ten minutes, we wouldn't have been chasing all night."

His eyes cut to me and his stick clatters as he tosses it, voice sharp, dripping venom.

Everyone sees it.

Feels it.

And I'm on my feet before I know what I'm doing, fists clenched, blood roaring. "Say that again, Peacock."

My shoulder throbs, and my teeth ache from clenching. One more word, and I'll take a fucking swing.

He doesn't back down. Instead, he steps closer, smirk razor-sharp. "Maybe you should retire before you bury us."

Before I know what I'm doing, I lunge—heat, fury, all of it ready to break.

Jace steps in, hand flat on Riley's chest. "Enough."

Eli's there too, solid as stone at my side.

The room holds its breath.

Riley glares. I glare harder. The heat between us is wildfire, barely contained.

Finally, he leans back, smirk faltering. "Whatever." He rips off his jersey, and stalks to his stall.

My pulse hammers as Eli lets go of me slow, his eyes warning me without words.

The tension simmers, but it doesn't fade.

And through it all, Sloane is there.

She doesn't move, doesn't say a word during the scuffle.

But I feel her eyes, cold as glass, hot as fire, locking me down harder than any captain ever has.

Her silence is louder than Riley's shout. Louder than the heartbeat in my ears.

She doesn't need to cut in—because she knows I already feel it. The failure. The weight. The responsibility.

"Blame doesn't win games either, gentlemen. Get it together before the next game."

With that parting shot, she turns on her heel and leaves us chastised and in a silence that feels like Florida in July.

I drop onto the bench in front of my stall, letting the room clear out until I'm alone.

I sit thinking about the game, the near fight with Riley, and even though I'm the only one in the room, my stall feels too small and the air still feels too heavy.

I don't bother to shower, knowing the media outside the door has left by now.

As I pack my gear, sweat drying sticky on my skin, my phone buzzes in my bag.

My heart rate picks up as I drag it out of my bag.

Shit, I hope it isn't Sloane.

With my thumb, I swipe to brighten the screen.

Peter.

Shit, shit, shit.

> Peter: Saw the game tonight. Rough start, but you pulled through.

> Peter: Got your message about the community shit as you called it.

> Peter: Play nice. Keep your nose clean. Don't make this harder than it already is.

Pulled through. Play nice. His words scrape over my skin like salt in an open wound.

And those words may as well be a leash around my throat.

Like I didn't just fumble through a game we could've lost by five.

Like none of it matters unless I smile pretty and play along.

My jaw locks, my thumb hovering before I hit delete.

The text is physically gone, but it's burned into my brain, and carved under my skin with every other scar I've carried.

I shove the phone deep in the bag, zipper sharp in the silence. But it doesn't matter how deep I bury it.

The weight of it stays on my mind.

CHAPTER THIRTEEN

Sloane

THE ELEVATOR HUMS as it glides down from the top floor, my phone glowing in my palm.

Emails stack faster than I can swipe them away—Dean with his clipped reminders, Sierra with color-coded itineraries, and Tessa juggling interview requests.

My thumb hovers over the reply button when the car slows to a stop too soon to be the garage.

The doors slide open, and I make the grave error of glancing up.

Maddox.

And he looks like sex on a stick.

His broad shoulders perfectly fill out the dark suit with its sharp lines. He's decided against a tie—typical Maddox—leaving his stark white button down shirt open at the collar.

My pulse jumps so hard I nearly fumble my phone.

Crystal blue eyes meet mine, and it's like I've had the air knocked out of me when I see a spark of heat in his gaze.

I straighten, my back against the wall, letting my professional armor drop into place.

At least on the outside.

On the inside, I'm more like a cat in heat.

Without a word, he steps in, jaw tight. He doesn't look at me right away, just presses the garage button with a deliberate hand.

Then his gaze cuts sideways, slow and deliberate, and heat crawls up my neck.

We stand in silence as the doors seal us in together. Seven floors of polished steel and suffocating tension.

His reflection in the brushed metal catches my eye before I can stop myself. The jacket strains across his chest when he shifts his stance. His cufflinks catch the low light.

He smells faintly of clean soap and something darker, sharper—aftershave maybe. It's infuriating that I notice any of it.

I force my attention back to my phone, like the tiny glowing screen holds the keys to the universe. As though the man standing close enough that the air seems to tilt doesn't bother me at all.

It's a damn good thing pants don't literally catch on fire when you lie.

Unable to focus, I drop the phone into my handbag and clear my throat.

If he isn't going to acknowledge the coincidence we live in the same place, I guess I'll do it.

But before I can say anything, he speaks in a low, gravelly voice.

"Didn't know you lived here."

"Penthouse."

As if that explains everything.

His mouth twists in mix of a smile and grimace. "Figures."

The car hums lower, floors ticking past. My chest tightens with every number. I hate the way my body betrays me—too aware of the heat radiating off him, too aware of how the tailored suit makes him look like he belongs at a board meeting instead of a crease.

The silence stretches, and his cologne is making me crazy. I just want to find the source of it and inhale it.

The elevator dings, doors parting onto the garage. The tension follows us out, our footsteps echoing sharp against the concrete.

I should let him walk out to his car, drive alone, keep the distance we both pretend we want. Instead, I hear myself say, "We're going to the same place. Ride with me."

His eyes narrow, like he's debating whether to refuse just to spite me. Then his mouth twists. "Fine. But I call shotgun."

I arch a brow, unlocking the car with a tap. "You're lucky I don't make you sit in the back."

The corner of his mouth twitches like he almost smiles, but it's gone before I can breathe it in.

My keys feel too small in my hand. And when he slides into the passenger seat, the cabin of my SUV is too confined for how close this already feels.

The first few blocks are silent. And while my hands are steady on the wheel, my pulse is anything but.

Finally, he mutters, "This PR stunt—kids and cameras—it's a waste of time."

I don't look at him. "We've talked about this, Maddox. Optics matter. Especially yours."

"Optics," he repeats, like it tastes bad. "I hate that fucking word." He looks out the side window. "I just want to do my job. And that's playing hockey."

"You're more than your stats," I fire back, heat slipping in. "Sponsors, the board—they want a man they can sell. And the fans want someone they can believe in. They all want more than just a wall in the net."

He slants me a look, jaw flexing. "Newsflash, Carrington. Walls don't smile for cameras."

I grip the wheel harder. "Then try being human instead."

His laugh is low, rough, and it slides under my skin like sandpaper. "Not sure that's in the job description either."

He glances at the console, the playlist still queued from last night.

Pearl Jam - Alive

He smirks. "Didn't peg you for nineties alternative."

Heat flashes across my cheeks before I can stop it. "I like what I like."

"I pictured classical, something like Mozart or Chopin. Something stiff enough to match the suits."

"Wouldn't do much good to be lulled to sleep when I'm driving. Besides, I like music that cuts and makes me feel something."

"Didn't think you knew that."

I glance over. "I'm surprised you do."

His eyes linger on me a beat too long, something unreadable flickering in them. "There's a lot you don't know about me."

I swallow, throat tight. "Same goes."

Danger hums in the car, louder than the bass line. We shouldn't be here—talking about music, letting the edges soften.

This isn't what owners and players do.

But when the next red light hits and I feel his gaze on me, my pulse spikes so hard it rattles my ribs.

Too close. Too human.

Too wrong.

At the same time, the car ride ends too soon.

We pull up to the curb where balloons bob in the late-morning breeze, bright colors strung along the hospital entrance. Banners hang from the awning—*VIPERS CARE DAY*—and cameras already crowd the walkway.

Valet parkers greet us to whisk the cars away, and handlers wait in a neat little row along the sidewalk, clipboards ready.

The players and their assistants for the day are paired up, and I hang back to watch how each of them start the day.

Jace and Logan head in first, all calm confidence and PR smiles as the staff directs him toward the double doors.

Maddox follows, stalking toward his assistant like he's walking into enemy territory. His shoulders roll under the black of his suit, jaw set hard enough to break teeth.

Every inch of him reads: *don't come near me.*

The young woman who approaches him with an outstretched hand looks slightly scared but pushes through.

"Carrington."

Dean's voice slices from behind me, clipped and controlled.

I pivot and find him closing the distance with that smooth stride that makes my skin prickle. Tie knotted with lawyerly precision, smile polished within an inch of its life.

"Your guy doesn't look any friendlier today than he did on media day," he murmurs, eyes tracking Maddox like a hawk. "The man can barely string together a soundbite."

I inhale through my nose, steadying the heat at the base of my spine. "He's going to be fine."

He has to be.

"Do you really think parading him into a children's ward is the best play?"

I lift my chin and meet his gaze head-on. I'm getting tired of Dean always questioning my decisions.

"Yes, I do think it's the best play. They're sick children for God's sake, not wild animals."

Dean's laugh is a low scoff, meant to sound reasonable. "Optics are fragile, Sloane. One wrong look, one wrong word— and the whole narrative burns. He's not built for this kind of spotlight."

Maddox is right. "Optics" is getting on my last nerve.

So is Dean with his patriarchal high handedness.

I step just close enough that the cameras won't pick up my

reply. My tone is quiet but sharp enough to cut. "Then he learns. And you remember who makes those calls. This is my team, Dean. Not yours."

His eyes sharpen, assessing, like he's weighing how far to push. "We're supposed to protect the brand, not gamble it on a man who doesn't know how to smile."

My voice doesn't rise, but the steel in it hums. "I'm not gambling. I know exactly what I'm doing. And so will the board, when they see the tape."

A pause. His lips curve into that smooth politician's smile, brittle at the edges. "Of course. Your team."

I don't move until he does. Don't blink until he turns toward the cameras, charm plastered back in place.

Dean smiles, but I don't trust him to protect anything but his own interests.

And when I finally follow the others inside, my pulse is still pounding in my throat, hot and fast.

***

The pediatric ward is painted like a storybook—trees curling up the walls, stars scattered across the ceiling—but the scent betrays it.

Disinfectant. Bleach. The too-clean tang that clings to the back of your throat.

Cameras hover at the edges like vultures waiting for scraps, handlers dividing players into groups before the kids are overwhelmed.

Sierra sweeps up Riley, Finn, Eli, and Cal into her orbit. The volume spikes instantly.

Riley tilts his head toward a cameraman, grin sharp and bright, like he's auditioning for a toothpaste ad. A little girl giggles when he winks at her, and the reporter beside her beams like they just captured gold.

Finn drapes himself across the back of a chair, plucks the stethoscope hanging around a pretty nurse's neck, and presses it to his chest. "Am I dying?" he asks, eyes wide.

The nurse blushes with a laugh, then swats at him; the cameras flash. The man is complete chaos, contained only because he wants it that way.

Eli crouches by a boy in a wheelchair, his big frame folding down small. His voice carries just enough for me to catch the gentleness in it, nothing like the sharp edges he wears on the ice.

The boy's shoulders straighten under his quiet attention, and I see Sierra's relief in the way she exhales.

Cal hovers close, fumbling a bit as he pulls hats from his bag. His hands shake, but when he presses one into a little girl's lap, he does it like he's handing her a crown.

Her whole face lights up, and she giggles. Cal flushes scarlet, ducking his head as the cameras snap the moment.

The press eats it up.

Of course they do.

I stay with Maddox, Logan, and Jace. Safer.

Or maybe riskier, depending on how you measure it.

Jace is the picture of composure, squatting in the middle of a cluster of kids, stick in hand as he sketches a play across the linoleum floor.

His voice is low, steady, a coach in miniature, and the kids lean in as though he's teaching them secrets instead of hockey. Calm radiates off him like heat.

Beside him, Logan slides easily into the circle, suit jacket tugged open, tie gone. He lets one of the kids balance his phone on a tiny knee, showing off a highlight reel like it's contraband.

His tone is smooth, practiced—PR polished without losing warmth—and the laughter he earns is effortless.

He's the bridge, steady but approachable, a player who knows exactly how to give just enough of himself to make people feel like they matter.

And Maddox…

Maddox stands like a man on trial. Shoulders locked, jaw cut from stone. His hands hang useless at his sides, twitching once like he wants to shove them in his pockets and thinks better of it.

His eyes keep flicking to the cameras instead of the kids, tracking them the way he'd track a puck.

The contrast is brutal—Jace the calm anchor, Logan the polished face, Maddox the wall of ice and silence.

Dean would see liability.

The board would see a mistake.

But me?

I can't stop seeing the weight under his stillness. The storm wound tight in the cage of his body, begging for a crack.

And God help me, I want to see what happens when it does.

One brave little boy tugs on Maddox's sleeve, holding up a bright crayon. "Can you draw something?" he asks, hopeful.

The cameras pivot, hungry.

Maddox blinks down at him, huge and awkward, hand flexing once. For a heartbeat, I think he'll kneel. I think he'll take the damn crayon.

Instead, he clears his throat and gives the boy a stiff nod—more like acknowledging a teammate on the bench than responding to a child.

The boy's smile falters.

My stomach twists.

Damn it, Lasker.

Jace, smooth as ever, leans in and picks up the crayon, sketching a stick figure goalie on the corner of the play diagram. The kids laugh, tension broken.

But Maddox…

He still looks like a man being marched to his execution.

The reporters sense it, smell it, and circle closer. Waiting for the stumble, the grimace, the proof that he doesn't belong here.

My chest knots so tight it aches. I can't tell if I should cringe or pray.

The crayon slips out of the boy's fingers and rolls across the floor, rescued neatly by Jace's calm hand. The kids laugh, tension easing, but Maddox still looks like a statue braced for a firing squad.

Before I can redirect, a nurse with kind eyes and quick instincts presses a book into Maddox's massive hands. "Here, read this," she says in a low, kind voice before stepping away.

The cover is bright with cartoon animals splashed across it. And I swear—he stares at it like it's written in another language.

My stomach dips. Oh God. This is going to implode.

Then a small voice pipes up. "Mr. Lasker, will you read it? It's my favorite."

The sound comes from a boy in a knit cap too big for his head, pale skin waxy under the fluorescent lights.

He beams up at Maddox like the man just skated out of the TV and into his hospital room.

Hope, pure and unfiltered, shines in his eyes.

For a beat, Maddox doesn't move. Then, with a rough exhale, he lowers into a crouch.

The movement is stiff, awkward, like he's wearing his goalie pads instead of a suit.

He holds the book gingerly, as if the thin paper might split under his calloused fingers.

"Well, if it's your favorite, I need to read it, don't I?" His voice is rough but pitched low like a secret.

The boy nods so hard his cap slips sideways, and Maddox catches it with one big hand, tugging it back into place with surprising gentleness.

"What's your name?"

The boy smiles shyly. "Connor."

"It's nice to meet you. You can call me Maddox."

Then he opens the book.

The first lines stumble out of him, halting, like he's testing how the words fit in his mouth.

The boy leans closer anyway, eyes locked on every syllable. Maddox clears his throat and keeps going, voice rough but steadying.

When he hits the villain's dialogue, something unexpected happens. Maddox drops his voice lower, growling, giving the words weight.

The boy giggles, delighted, and Maddox's brow flicks up in something like surprise before he rolls with it, doubling down on the act.

The kid laughs harder.

Another page, and Maddox softens his tone for the hero, slower, careful.

The boy's hand creeps out, resting on Maddox's, tracing the knuckles of the larger hand like it's treasure.

Maddox doesn't pull away.

He flexes his fingers once under the small hand, as though giving a piece of himself costs nothing at all.

And then—God help me—the man smiles.

Not the bitter curl I've seen when he cuts down a reporter.

Not the sharp, practiced smirk that says he knows exactly how to piss someone off.

A real smile. Raw, genuine, unguarded. It transforms his whole face, breaking something open inside my chest.

Heat surges through my body, hot and fierce, so sharp I grip my notebook tighter to keep from trembling.

The owner in me catalogs it instantly: perfect PR, the kind of clip the board will salivate over, the kind of moment that sells tickets and cements legacies.

Gold.

But the woman in me…well, she aches.

Because I can't stop watching the way his shoulders ease

when the boy laughs. The way that smile—unpracticed and so damn rare—changes everything about him.

It's dangerous how much I feel just by seeing him smile.

This—this is what I knew was there. What Dean swore didn't exist.

Cameras flash like lightning, catching it all, but for once it doesn't feel staged. Doesn't feel like PR.

It feels real.

And it undoes me.

CHAPTER FOURTEEN

Maddox

CONNOR'S HAND IS SMALL, light as paper, resting against mine.

He's still grinning from the story, pale cheeks flushed like he's already halfway to the rink I just promised him existed.

Eight years old, hooked up to tubes and monitors, and he's got more fight in him than most rookies I've ever seen.

"Do you really play goalie?" he asks, eyes wide. "Like, stop the pucks and everything?"

"Every night," I say, voice low, a little rougher than I mean it to be.

His laugh is soft but real, chest shaking under his hospital gown. Then he flips open a sketchbook from his tray table, pencil lines crisscrossing the page.

Superheroes, all blocky shoulders and capes, battling across city skylines.

"Did you draw these?" I ask, leaning closer before I think better of it.

He nods, a little shy this time. "I'm making my own comic. I wanna be like Stan Lee. Or—" His eyes flicker up. "Or maybe make a hockey one. You could be in it."

Something shifts in my chest, hard and sharp.

I haven't told anyone about the stacks of comics shoved in boxes in my storage unit, the sketchbook I used to carry on buses between games in high school and college.

That part of me has been buried, dust on dust.

"Not sure I'm much of a hero," I mutter, but the words snag on my tongue when his grin grows wider.

"Yeah, you are. You just saved the city." He points at the goalie sketched into his page—a hulking figure in pads, stick like a weapon, net glowing behind him.

My throat tightens.

I reach for the pencil he's holding, careful not to crowd him. "Mind if I add something?"

He nods fast, shoving the notebook closer. My fingers feel too big, clumsy, but I draw anyway. A comic bubble over the goalie's head: *Not today.*

Connor bursts out laughing, and I can't help it—I laugh too. It rips out of me raw and unexpected.

For a second, it feels like I'm not sitting in a hospital ward, cameras watching, and handlers waiting.

For a second, I'm just a man sharing comics with a kid who believes I'm something more than I am.

And then I feel *her*.

Sloane's eyes on me, heavier than the press lights, hotter than the cameras.

I don't have to look to know she's watching. It coils in my gut, warning me of danger.

The board will call this "optics." She'll probably spin it that way too.

But the way her gaze crawls over me, the way my body tightens under it—it's not professional. Not PR.

It's something else.

I turn another page in the sketchbook, steadying my voice. "You're good, kid. Better than I was at your age."

He beams, pencil scratching as he adds another cape. And I

don't dare look up at her, because if I do, I'll forget the cameras and the crowd and the fact that she's my boss.

And I'll give away too much.

I double down my focus on Connor, as he works on the stick-figure goalie we've made up together. He laughs when I give the hero a scar. "So he looks tough, like you."

His words sink deeper than I want to admit.

Then I hear it—soft laughter from across the room.

I glance over before I can stop myself.

Sloane crouches beside a little girl, same pale skin, same sharp cheekbones as the boy beside me. Twins, no doubt.

The girl has a ballet book clutched in her lap, edges frayed, corners bent from love. The cover's worn thin like she's read it a hundred times.

Sloane leans in, dark blonde hair sliding forward, eyes warm in a way I've never seen in a boardroom. "You want to skate?" she asks, voice gentler than I thought she could be.

The girl nods, shy smile flickering. "Like the girls in the Olympics."

Sloane's smile curves slow and soft, and it sucker punches me. "Then you can. Next time I'll bring my skates. You'll try it with me."

The girl's eyes go wide, the kind of wide that swallows light. She believes her.

Just like that.

My chest pulls tight, a deep ache I can't shift.

Because that's not the Sloane Carrington the board sees, or the one who slices me down with clipped words.

That's the woman who wrapped my shoulder with her own two hands just the other night.

And damn if I don't feel it again now. That ghost pressure of her palm pressing ice against me, her scent cutting through sweat and disinfectant.

The brush of her wrist against my chest, the scent of her hair cutting through the stink of the locker room. She taped me like she'd done it a hundred times before, and for a second I wasn't the broken goalie or the PR liability.

I was just a man letting a woman touch the part of me that hurt.

The same way her hand now smooths over the little girl's hair, tucking a stray strand behind her ear. Gentle. Steady.

Like she was born knowing how to ease hurt.

Now I watch her do the same thing with that little girl. No hesitation. No armor. Just giving a piece of herself away like it's nothing.

Connor tugs my sleeve, pencil waving. "Draw another one, with fire powers this time!"

I chuckle, rough, dragging the pencil across the page. The lead smudges on my fingers, grounding me, but my gaze slides up again, traitorous, to where Sloane kneels on the linoleum next to the girl.

Her hand skims over the small of the little girl's back, tender in a way that twists me up inside.

And then, her eyes lift.

They find mine across the room and hold. Heat arcs across the space, hot and fast, like a live wire stripped bare.

I shouldn't be staring. She shouldn't either. But neither of us moves.

For one dangerous heartbeat, I let it stand. The connection. The reminder of how her touch felt on me.

Then I rip my gaze back down to the crooked lines I'm sketching and, force my voice rough to keep the boy laughing.

But my grip is tight on the pencil, knuckles white.

Because if I let myself keep looking at her, I'll forget the cameras.

Forget the kids.

Forget the job.

I'll remember only her touch.

And I'll want more than I can ever have.

A few minutes later, the handlers start wrapping things up, gathering cameras and clipboards, thanking staff.

Kids wave, clutching autographs like they're treasure.

I hang back, watching the people work around me, trying to keep my focus off Sloane.

Dean and Jace chat with the doctors, while PR prince Logan charms a couple of reporters by the doorway.

Riley and Finn are flirting with a couple of the young nurses, and Eli's standing with Cal like he's coaching the kid even now.

It doesn't take long, though, for my focus to be pulled back to the woman across the room.

And while everyone else appears occupied, I let my attention stay on her.

Sloane lingers with the girl, touching her little cheek before she stands, promising again about the skates.

The girl beams like she's just been handed the world.

Something deep inside me shifts, a slow grind I don't like.

I felt it when her palm pressed ice against my shoulder.

And now I've seen her give it to a child who believed her without hesitation.

The worst part?

I wanted to believe her too.

Soon, we say our goodbyes to the staff and make our way to the front of the hospital.

I keep my distance from everyone while we wait for the valet to bring up our vehicles.

Thankfully, Sloane's is the last to be pulled to the front, so there's no questions from anyone.

By the time we get into her SUV, the air feels heavier. There's too much silence stuffed into the cab as she pulls out of the hospital lot.

The radio's off, but I hear everything—the hum of the engine and, the faint sound of her breath change when the light turns red.

I sit angled toward the window, shoulder throbbing under my jacket, and try not to think about the fact that she smells like the little girl's shampoo and her own expensive perfume tangled together.

Warm and soft and not something I should even be thinking about at all.

My reflection stares back at me from the glass. Hair rumpled, collar tugged open. Old dog.

End of the line.

And yet, unbidden, a thought worms its way in—

What if there was a kid in the back seat? A boy with her dark green eyes and my jaw. A girl with her stubborn mouth and my sharp chin.

The image comes so fast, so clear, it punches the breath out of me. A family that never existed. Would never exist.

A life I never let myself want.

Jesus.

I clamp my jaw and, force it down. I can't go there.

She's too young. Too polished. Too…out of my league to be honest.

Not to mention she's my boss, for fuck's sake. The woman who signs my checks, who holds my career in her manicured hands.

Dragging a palm down my thigh, I ground myself in the coarse drag of fabric of my slacks.

I need to think about the crease, the ice, the saves I still have to prove I can make.

Anything but the way my chest pulled tight when I saw her hand on that girl's cheek.

The stoplight flips green. She doesn't look at me. Neither of us speaks.

By the time we get back to the parking garage of our condos, the silence is thick, suffocating, and alive with every thought I shouldn't be having.

I'm terrified that if I let myself break it, I'll say something I can't take back.

We continue to stay silent as we walk together to the garage elevator and step inside, her heels sharp against the marble, my loafers heavier than they should sound.

The doors close, sealing us in steel and silence.

I jam my thumb against seven. She presses nine a beat later, the penthouse button glowing like it mocks me.

She shifts beside me, posture perfect, spine steel. But I feel the crackle of nerves in her air. She clears her throat, and the sound is soft enough to slide under my skin.

"Well," she says finally, voice cool, and professional, too even. "Today went better than expected."

I almost laugh. The sound comes out low, rough, and nothing like amusement. "That your way of saying I didn't fuck it up?"

Her head snaps toward me. Her eyes—God, her eyes—flash sharp as cut glass. "You didn't. The kids loved you." A pause, softer. "More than you think."

My chest tightens. I should let it go, let the words hang.

Instead, I take a step closer, because I'm already at my wits' end. Her perfume threads the air—clean, sharp, expensive—and I'm drowning in it.

"Careful," I murmur. My voice is gravel dragged over stone. "Sounded almost like a compliment."

She doesn't back up. Doesn't flinch. Her chin lifts, lips curved in that dangerous line between smile and blade. "Maybe it was."

The floor hums under us, car sliding higher, too damn slow and too fast all at once. My pulse pounds hard enough that I can feel it in my throat.

I take another step, close enough now that the heat of her

body radiates against mine. My hand braces against the wall beside her head before I think better of it.

Her breath stutters. Just enough that I catch it.

Fuck.

I lean in, the space between us collapsing until her scent—like roses and amber—is all I can breathe, until her mouth is a whisper away from mine.

Her eyes partially close and her lips part, just slightly. "Maddox…"

The sight of her like this and my name on her lips wrecks me.

Everything inside me snarls to take, to taste, to finally break the leash we've both been yanking on since the day we met.

Then the elevator dings, and the doors whisk open.

Seventh floor.

My floor.

Sanity slams back, and I curse under my breath, pushing away from her and all her heat.

Her eyes are wide, chest rising quick against the silk of her blouse.

For one heartbeat, I want to say fuck it and close the gap anyway.

Instead, I step out, but turn to take one last look until the doors slide shut between us.

I'm left in the hall, pulse thundering, mouth dry, hating myself for walking away and hating worse that I wanted to stay.

CHAPTER FIFTEEN

Sloane

THE DOOR to my condo shuts with a quiet click that feels louder than the entire hospital had been.

For a moment, I just stand there in the foyer, heels still on, blazer still buttoned, handbag still slung heavy against my shoulder like I might have to run back out and face it all again.

But then my body reminds me I'm not made of steel, no matter how hard I pretend.

I drop my bag and kick off my shoes. The relief is instant and dangerous. Home is the only place I let the Carrington armor fall like a house of cards.

The silence wraps around me, but it doesn't soothe. My pulse is still too high, like my body hasn't caught up to the fact the cameras are gone.

Like it hasn't realized I'm alone.

What am I saying? It's not the cameras keeping me wired.

I lean back against the wall, close my eyes, and see him.

Maddox.

Not scowling. Not stonewalling. Not the man I've been fighting since the second he stepped into my orbit.

Smiling.

God, that smile. Raw, unguarded, like the boy with the book had cracked something open in him no one else could touch.

It should've been gold for PR, and it was. The press will spin it into the perfect redemption clip.

Dean will finally shut his smug mouth when he sees the tape. The board will see strategy paying off.

But for me?

It wasn't PR. It was something else entirely.

It was the way he crouched awkwardly in that black suit, knees bent like it cost him something to lower himself to their level, and still did it.

The way he let that boy touch his hand like it was something they did every single day.

The way his voice shifted—rough edges sanded just enough to coax laughter from a child who has every right not to remember what laughing feels like.

And when he smiled—really smiled—something hot and reckless twisted inside my chest.

And let's not even talk about the near kiss in the elevator.

I haven't been this fucking turned on in longer than I care to remember, and the man didn't even lay a finger on me.

Pushing off the wall, I cross into the living room, shedding my jacket as I go.

My skin still buzzes like I'm standing too close to a live wire.

This is not how I should feel about one of my players.

This is not how I should feel about anyone. I have a team to run and a board to please just to prove I can handle something that's already mine.

I sink onto the couch, hair tumbling loose when I tug out the pins. My reflection in the black screen of the TV catches me off guard—eyes wide, lips parted, chest still rising like I ran here instead of riding the elevator.

Then again, that elevator ride has my pulse dancing like it's my job.

My body knows it, even if my head denies it.

And worst of all, I can still smell him. Soap and heat and something darker that stuck to me in the car, in the elevator, in every breath we shared today.

I can still smell the faint mint of his breath when we were so close, I could see that his eyes weren't just one color of blue.

They'd gone from a crystal blue to navy in a heartbeat.

I bury my face in my hands.

This can't keep happening.

Because if it does, Maddox Lasker won't just ruin my season.

He'll ruin me.

My phone buzzes against the coffee table, a low vibration that makes my pulse jump like I've been caught doing something wrong.

I reach for it, half-expecting Dean with another sanctimonious "note" about today.

But it's Griffin.

Groaning, I drop my head back against the couch and mock-bang it once against the cushion.

I swipe to answer and barely get out a "Hello" before his voice fills the line, amused and too damn knowing. "Caught the highlights of your first preseason game, cuz. That was... something."

I roll my eyes, even though he can't see it. "It was a win."

"Sure," he drawls. "If you squint hard enough. Your golden goalie looked like he was skating in quicksand for the first period. Half the analysts are already debating if he's past it."

Heat sparks low in my chest. "He settled in. Pulled big saves in the third. That's what matters."

"Uh-huh." He lets the pause stretch. "And then Hunt trying to chew him out in the locker room? Yeah, not a great look."

I grip the counter tighter. "That's growing pains. Locker rooms sort themselves out."

"Unless they don't."

His tone isn't cruel, but close enough to make me bristle.

"Lo, I'm not saying you made the wrong call on Lasker, but you can't pretend there aren't cracks showing."

"I'm not pretending anything, Griffin." My tone is sharp.

I pace toward the window, staring out at the trees black against the night. "It's one game. Preseason. Do you really think I don't know the difference between a stumble and a collapse?"

Griff sighs, softer now. "Just asking if you're sure. Because you sound like you're carrying this one man on your back."

My pulse pounds in my ears. "I'm carrying the whole damn franchise on my back. Maddox is part of that. And for the record —he did fine at the hospital today."

That makes him pause. "Hospital?"

"Children's ward. PR lined up a charity visit. He read to the kids. Bonded with a little boy battling cancer. Even smiled."

Griffin chuckles, disbelieving. "Maddox Lasker. Smiling in public. Now that's a headline."

I bite back a smile, refusing to give him the satisfaction. "Point is—it worked. The press got their story, the board gets proof he's not a mistake, and the kids…well, the kids loved him."

There's a beat of silence, then Griff says, low and careful, "You liked it too, didn't you?"

The question slices too close. My throat tightens. "Don't start."

"I'm not starting anything." His tone softens, but the suspicion lingers. "I just know that sound in your voice. You're not just defending your player. You're defending something else."

I force my voice flat. "I'm defending my team. Period."

He hums like he doesn't buy it, but mercifully stays quiet.

For a moment, silence stretches—comfortable, complicated.

Then I seize it before it frays. "Actually, I'm glad you called. The gala's in two weeks. I need a plus-one."

"Oh?" His tone is instantly suspicious. "And this has nothing to do with keeping the gossip rags from pairing you with one of your players?"

I roll my eyes. "There's nothing for them to report. But you're perfect. Family, clean-cut, I know you own a tux, and not a liability."

He laughs. "High praise from a Carrington. Fine. I'll dust off a suit and play arm candy. But only if you promise to let me escape early when the speeches start."

"Deal."

There's a beat, then his voice shifts again, quiet but steady. "Just…don't let this guy burn you, Sloane."

Oh, great. He used my whole name for this one.

"No one is going to burn me, Griffin. I got this."

"Okay, if you say so."

"I do. So, I'll email you the details on the gala."

"Sounds good. Love you, Lo."

"Love you, Griff."

We hang up, and the silence that follows leaves my pulse rattling in my ribs.

I start to toss the phone back on the coffee table when an email notification pops up across the top of the screen.

Dean's name is waiting like a snake coiled in the grass.

Subject line: *Children's Hospital Recap – PR Outcome.*

Of course. He couldn't resist.

I click.

Attached are links to every major outlet that ran with the story—photos of Maddox crouched beside a boy in a knit cap, the rare smile that makes him look ten years younger.

Video clips of his gravel-rough voice reading, the boy's laugh ringing like music.

The captions are exactly what I predicted:

Vipers' Lasker Shows Heart Off the Ice. Carrington's Gamble Humanized. From Bad Boy to Big Softie?

It's gold. The kind of coverage we needed.

And then, Dean's note at the bottom: *Even a broken clock is right twice a day.*

Heat crawls up my throat as I stare at the infuriating words until they blur.

The asshole simply can't give me an inch. Always with the smug, calculated jabs.

The implication that Maddox is still a mistake and that I'm the fool propping him up.

I want to throw my phone, or better yet, punch Dean in his pompous face.

I want to march into Dean's office and remind him, in words sharp enough to leave scars, that I don't answer to him.

Instead, I breathe deep, jaw locked, because anger is exactly what he wants.

The truth is worse.

Because under the fury, dread coils low in my stomach.

He's right about one thing.

The board is watching.

Every article, every photo, every moment of Maddox's body language in front of those cameras will be dissected.

Not just by them, but by sponsors, by season-ticket holders, by every vulture waiting for me to slip.

And if Maddox cracks? If I crack with him?

I lean back, spine pressing into the softness of the sofa cushions, staring at the ceiling like it has answers.

This isn't just optics or perception or PR.

This is ammunition.

And if we crack, we'll be handing Dean the bullets to load the gun.

Dean's email glows on my phone screen like a taunt, but it isn't his words I feel burning me alive.

It's Maddox.

Always Maddox.

The way he cornered me in that elevator.

The way his body caged mine, broad chest blocking the air, eyes dark with something dangerous.

I wanted him to kiss me. No—I wanted him to kiss me and then take me. Hard and fast against the steel wall while I clawed at his shoulders.

The thought makes my pulse spike so sharp I can't sit still. I shove up off the sofa and storm down the hall toward my bedroom, shedding my armor as I go.

Jacket hits the chair. Blouse unbuttoned, sliding off my arms. Skirt unzipped and kicked away along with my heels.

By the time I reach the bed, I'm stripping off lace like it's strangling me.

I crawl onto the sheets bare skin hot, breath ragged. The drawer gives up my vibrator with a soft scrape.

Cold plastic in my hand, a poor substitute for the man who already owns too much of me.

The hum fills the room as I flick it on, low and steady. I part my thighs, the first press of vibration against my swollen clit ripping a gasp from my chest. My back arches, hips chasing more.

I see him—Maddox in that suit, tie gone, shirt undone just enough to tempt.

Maddox pinning me in the corner of the elevator, voice rough when he warned me he bites.

In my head, he snarls it against my ear: *"You want me to ruin you, princess? Want me to fuck you so hard you forget your own name?"*

"Fuck," I whisper, grinding harder, the vibrator slick with need already.

My free hand covers my breast, thumb circling until I moan, knees falling wider.

My pussy clenches around nothing, desperate for him to be here, for his thick cock to fill me instead of the buzzing plastic.

I imagine his hand around my throat, his mouth crushing mine, his other hand yanking up my skirt.

His filthy words spilling hot against my lips: *"Say you're mine. Say you want every filthy inch."*

"Maddox, please," I breathe, the words tearing out of me, broken and wanton.

The rhythm builds, spiraling me higher, every nerve lit like a fuse. My body begs for him, only him, even as I hate myself for wanting it this badly.

In my head, he's fucking me against that elevator wall, hips driving me up the steel, my heels digging into his ass, growling, *"Take it. Take every inch, sweetheart. You're not running from me now."*

The coil snaps. I shatter hard, pleasure tearing through me, white-hot and raw.

My cry echoes off the walls, muffled only when I bite my lip, tasting copper. My hips jerk, chasing every aftershock until I collapse into the sheets, panting, vibrator slipping from my grasp.

The room smells of sex and sweat and salt. My skin is damp, trembling, clit still twitching with the ghost of him.

There's no shame. Only the crushing ache of knowing I'll never have what I just imagined.

The first man who makes me burn like this—the only one who makes me *feel*—is the one man I can never touch.

I drag the sheets up over my nakedness, curling around the hollow ache in my chest. My throat tightens.

My body is spent, but the need hasn't left. It never does, not with him.

Maddox Lasker will ruin me. And I don't even care.

CHAPTER SIXTEEN

Maddox

THE HISS ROOM crackles like a storm waiting to break.

Not quiet, not reverent—alive.

Jerseys hang sharp and pressed, the Vipers logo glaring back at us from every surface. Gear clatters, sticks thump against the floor, the sharp scent of tape and sweat hanging heavy in the air.

Every guy's got his own ritual—music blasting, laces yanked tight, heads bowed in silence—but it all blends into the same hum that rides my nerves.

The bass from the arena filters through concrete, the muffled roar of fans pressing down like a freight train.

Opening night.

I've been here before, but never like this. Not with a new team, a new city, a new weight riding my shoulders.

Riley's the loudest. No surprise. He's strutting in the middle of the room, spinning his stick like a baton. The rookies laugh too hard, desperate to fall in step.

Finn's no better—shirt half off, tattoos gleaming, jawing about how he's already planning his celebration when he scores.

Logan's the opposite—hair slicked back, lacing his skates in calm, efficient movements like he's already a dozen games into the season.

He's the kind of guy you'd trust to sell a sponsor in a board-room or call a play in a war zone. Smooth, steady, untouchable.

Eli sits in the corner, head down, movements sharp. He doesn't waste energy, doesn't waste words, but there's an edge to him. Controlled violence coiled in quiet. When he hits the ice, it'll snap clean.

Beau is steady as hell, too—joking with Cal and showing him how to adjust his elbow pads so they don't slip. Patient, guiding.

The man's built like a wall but plays like a shield, always bracing, always protecting. Must be the single dad to a little girl thing.

Cal's the outlier. The rookie looks like he's vibrating out of his skin. He's fumbling his tape, hands shaking, eyes wide like the arena will swallow him whole.

I watch him for a second too long, because I know that feeling. Twenty-four years old, raw as hell, and praying no one sees the cracks in you.

And then there's Jace.

The captain, our anchor. Doesn't need to raise his voice to own the room.

He tapes his stick with surgical precision, shoulders squared like the weight of the team belongs exactly there. The rest of us take our cues from him, whether we mean to or not.

All in all, they're a formidable group of guys even Cal, who I can see has potential once he gets past the rookie nerves.

Even Riley the peacock. He's a helluva player, he's just too much of a showman for my liking.

I tug my laces tighter, hands moving slow and deliberate. I can't let my mind wander. Not to the shoulder that still throbs when I push it wrong.

Not to the whispers about my age.

And sure as hell not to her.

But she's there anyway.

Sloane.

Two weeks since the elevator incident as I've started calling it.

Two weeks since I had her pinned in a corner, her breath mingling with mine, one shift away from breaking every line I swore I wouldn't cross.

Two weeks of restless nights where I dream about kissing her, fucking her against the wall of that elevator.

Of waking up with her scent in my lungs and my sheets twisted like I'd been fighting ghosts.

She's too young. Too untouchable. Too much my boss. And yet...

My jaw flexes as I yank the last lace tight.

The locker room roars as Holt barks his call, players pounding sticks, energy spiking. The tunnel waits, the ice beyond it like a battlefield ready to be claimed.

The rookies are jittering, the vets steady, Riley flapping his damn gums.

And me?

I pull my mask into my hands, weight solid against my palms.

My body hums with the wrong kind of adrenaline, too sharp, too dirty. Because tonight isn't just about the crease.

It's about proving I'm not done, even if my bones scream otherwise.

It's about keeping my head down while the image of a woman I can't have keeps clawing through me.

The horn blasts outside, long and low, shaking the walls.

Game time.

And then The Pit goes dark.

For half a beat the place holds its breath, twenty thousand bodies packed into one arena, waiting for the spark. Then the fire cannons ignite, bass rattles the glass, and the crowd detonates.

Home opener. The circus in full swing.

"Ladies and gentlemen, let's welcome the visiting team, the Chicago Outlaws!"

Our opposition is met with a chorus of boos, but Atlanta's a melting pot city, so there's also a smattering of applause and cheers for Chicago.

Once each player on the Outlaws is introduced, The Pit goes dark once again and the tension is palpable.

The announcer's voice booms, rich and sharp, threading through the chaos.

"Atlanta… are you ready to feel the bite?"

A thunderous hiss rolls through the arena, thousands of voices joining the sound effect that pours from the speakers.

My skin prickles under my gear—it's eerie and electric, like standing inside the throat of a beast.

"Welcome your Vipers to The Pit!"

The crowd detonates. Spotlights sweep across the bench as names rip through the speakers one by one.

Riley Hunt struts out first, hair slicked back, grin sharp enough to blind. The place roars for him, the human highlight reel, and he eats it up—arms wide, tapping his chest like he's king of Atlanta already.

Finn's next. He makes a show of it, skating half a lap before even finding his spot, tossing pucks into the glass for the kids in the front row, blowing kisses to the cameras. The ovation swells, chaotic, perfect for him.

Logan slides out clean, efficient, nothing wasted even in a damn introduction. Eli follows, the crowd quieter for him, but he doesn't need noise.

Beau gets a wave of cheers, solid and steady, the kind of player who looks like he's been here forever. Jace, last before me, gets the captain's welcome—loud and reverent.

And then it's my turn.

"Number thirty-three. Goaltender. Maddox Lasker."

The sound that hits me isn't clean. It's jagged. Cheers crash into boos, the mix sharp enough to cut skin.

Boston baggage doesn't burn off easy, not even a thousand miles away.

My jaw locks. I don't flinch. I let it soak in, all of it—the love, the hate, and the noise.

If they want a villain, I'll wear the mask.

The ice reflects fire as I skate out, each push steady, shoulders squared. My body's already humming, the burn in my shoulder a steady throb under the pads.

Doesn't matter. The crease is waiting. That's mine.

But before I reach it, I make the mistake of glancing up.

The owner's box. High above the ice, lights catching on glass. And there she is.

In a red dress that would make me weak in the knees if I let it.

I'd bet my next paycheck she's wearing fuck me heels as well.

There's not a flicker of emotion on her face. To the crowd, she's untouchable.

But I know better. I've felt the heat under that control, the way her body answers even when her voice stays cold.

The sight of her spears a bolt of lust straight through me. Cuts past the noise, past the fire, past every bruise the crowd just hurled.

Heat floods low, wicked and reckless.

Under the lights, in front of everyone, I shouldn't feel this.

But my chest tightens, my gut coils, and all I can think about is her.

And then I don't have time to think of her anymore.

The puck drops and The Pit explodes, noise rolling like thunder down my spine. I lock in, knees bent, vision narrowed.

This isn't preseason anymore. This counts.

The first rush comes fast—too fast. Their winger cuts in off the left, snapping a shot high glove.

My shoulder screams when I reach, but the puck sticks to my webbing anyway. I freeze it, drop it, then clear it out with a smack of my stick.

The crowd roars like it's bloodsport.

Riley's next shift is a circus act—spinning off checks, dangling through traffic like the puck's magnetized to him.

He feeds Finn on the wing, and of course Finn turns it into theater, blowing a kiss at the Outlaws' bench before ripping one top shelf.

The place goes feral.

Logan takes the next face off, calm as stone, wins it clean, and it's surgical—two passes, Eli grinding down the wall, Beau backing him up, and the puck's in the net again.

Efficient. Ruthless.

I feel it in my bones—the shift, the chemistry. The storm that was missing in preseason?

It's here now.

But it's not all clean.

Their captain gets loose on a breakaway, and it's me and him, one-on-one. He fakes glove, goes blocker side.

My shoulder stabs as I push across, but I seal it off, puck hitting pad solidly, and the rebound dies under me.

He crashes the crease, stick jabbing, but I shove back, glove in his chest, my teeth bared behind the mask.

The ref whistles before I decide whether to drop him where he stands.

The roar that goes up isn't just relief—it's faith. The kind I thought I'd burned out years ago.

Shift after shift, the Vipers roll, even as the Outlaws get in some hard body checks and generally play just this side of dirty.

Cal stumbles a couple of times, nerves written all over his face, but he hustles back, stick down, eyes sharp.

I bark a cue—"Right side, Reid!"—and he actually hears it, resets, and clears a puck out of danger.

My chest tightens with something I don't want to name. He's raw as hell, but he's listening. That's more than most rookies ever give.

The goals pile up. Riley feeds Finn for another one, then Logan buries a rebound that ricochets off my pads and turns defense into instant offense.

Beau plays caretaker again, dragging Cal out of a scrum before he gets flattened. Eli throws a hit that rattles glass so hard I feel it buzz through my crease.

Jace? He's the spine. A steady heartbeat that makes everything else possible.

And me—I'm fire in the net, even with the shoulder grinding like a bad gear. Every shot that hits my pads feeds the blaze.

But every save is a message: I'm not done. Not even close.

When the horn finally sounds, it's 5–1, Vipers.

Decisive. Dominant. Not a scrap of doubt about it.

The crowd is on its feet, the kind of standing ovation that shakes walls. I pull my mask off slow, sweat dripping, lungs burning.

My name rolls down from the stands—some cheers, some boos, all of it loud.

All of it mine.

And then my gaze finds her.

Up in the owner's box, red dress standing out and cutting sharper than glass, hair pinned like armor, expression unreadable.

But I feel her eyes on me, heat through glass and distance and tens of thousands of screaming people.

Just looking at her is a gut punch.

Everything about the way I'm feeling is wrong.

Wrong place, wrong time, wrong woman.

And still, I skate off the ice with that pull branded in my veins, hotter than the win itself.

Luck continues to be on my side because somehow I manage to make it through the throng of reporters waiting in the tunnel without getting stopped for a soundbite.

The horn's still echoing in my skull by the time I hit the locker room, sweat running hot under my pads, the air sharp with victory. Five–one.

A statement win.

The locker room hums, louder than practice ever is—sticks clattering against stalls and towels snapping.

Finn singing something off-key just to make Riley groan. It smells like adrenaline and triumph, the kind of night that reminds you why you bleed for this game.

I strip off my gloves, shoulder aching, but the buzz of the win cuts deeper than the pain.

"Not bad for an old man," Riley calls across the room, towel slung over one shoulder, grin cutting bright. "Guess you've still got it…at least for now."

The room chuckles. A backhanded compliment, wrapped in that Hunt arrogance.

I meet his eyes for half a beat, sharp enough to make him shift, then let it roll off.

Tonight, the scoreboard says enough.

The room stills when heels strike the tile. Sharp, deliberate.

Sloane steps inside, Dean shadowing her like he's attached at the hip, but the room doesn't look at him.

It never does.

All eyes track her, red dress fitted like armor, composure crisp even here in the humid heat of sweat and steam.

God, she's fucking beautiful.

And I'm so fucked if that's what I'm thinking when I should be thinking about what she thought of my performance on the ice.

"Good game," she says, voice cutting through the haze. "A win like that sets the tone. You reminded this city tonight what hockey can be—fast, brutal, and unrelenting. Exactly what Atlanta deserves."

She scans the room, slow enough that every man feels it. "Wins like this aren't just numbers on a board. They're how we build something lasting. Keep it sharp, keep it ruthless, and keep it ours."

Energy ripples through the room, a tightening of spines, the hum of approval.

Dean claps once, politician-slick. "Strong start, gentlemen. Let's make sure it's not the peak."

Flat. Hollow. His words clang against the tile.

Sloane doesn't cut him off, but her eyes flick his way—one sharp glance, gone as fast as it comes. A warning without words.

She turns back to us, shoulders squared, voice smooth steel. "Tomorrow is the charity gala. That means every one of you shows up, suited up, polished, and on your best behavior."

Her gaze drifts deliberately across the room, locking on Finn just long enough to make him shift in his seat. "You are the face of this franchise. When people look at you, they see Atlanta. And I expect you to represent this team at the level of every other elite sport in this city."

The weight of her words hangs heavy, tighter than Holt's drills, sharper than Dean's clipped little notes.

The room doesn't erupt this time. It settles, quieter but charged.

Dean shifts beside her, plastered smile back in place. The guys don't look at him. They're still watching her.

When she leaves, the sharp staccato of her heels echo down the hall, and the silence holds.

Until Finn breaks it.

"Christ," he whistles low, dragging a towel across his chest. "Tell me I'm not the only one who thinks she's hot as fuck."

A couple guys chuckle, nervous, like they're not sure if they're supposed to agree.

My fists curl inside the tape still wound around them. Heat spikes, dark and instant, burning through the good mood of the win.

But I don't move. Don't say a word.

I can't.

Because the second I do, the whole damn room will know I think she's more than hot as fuck.

She's a woman who sees things in me she shouldn't, but I let her anyway.

Instead, I just sit there, shoulder throbbing.

The scoreboard says we won.

But the only thing I feel in my chest is the fire she leaves in her wake.

A fire I'd walk through to have more.

CHAPTER SEVENTEEN

Sloane

THE ZIPPER SLIDES into place with a whisper, green sequins catching the light like a thousand tiny daggers.

I smooth the fabric down my sides, palms pressing against my hips, as if I can force my pulse to steady by sheer will.

No such luck.

My reflection in the mirror stares back at me—steel spine and sharp jaw. And my dress?

Well, I picked it because it's a weapon dressed as a gown—glitter sharp, neckline dangerous, slit unapologetic.

My hair's twisted into a chignon so tight it feels like a crown, every dark blonde strand pinned exactly where I want it.

A Carrington never walks into a room half-finished. Not when the board will be there, not when Dean will be circling, not when the cameras are hungry for proof I don't belong in this role.

I slide diamond studs into my ears, their weight familiar, grounding. Aunt Sara's voice echoes in my head:

Never give them an inch. If you falter, they'll eat you alive.

But it's not Dean or the board making my chest feel tight. It's knowing Maddox will be there tonight.

God help me, the thought makes my skin flush hotter than a thousand suns.

I press my palms flat on the vanity, leaning closer. "Pull it together, Sloane."

The woman in the mirror doesn't look back with doubt. She looks back with ice.

Controlled. Perfect.

And maybe a little desperate under the surface, but no one will see that but me.

"Anyone home?"

I give one last glance in the mirror, checking my classic red lipstick, before grabbing my clutch and striding down the hall to where Griffin is standing in the living room.

Dark hair and trimmed beard, his tux a perfect fit.

My cousin smirks the second his eyes land on me. "Christ, Lo. Trying to kill half the room before they even pour champagne?"

I arch a brow. "If they drop, less small talk for me."

His laugh is low, warm, and familiar. He leans in to kiss my cheek, the scent of his cologne threading between us. "You look stunning."

I let the corner of my mouth tilt. "That's the point."

He offers his arm, all smooth charm and easy strength. Griffin's always been that—family and anchor, the reminder that someone in this city still sees me as a person, not just a headline.

For a flicker, I let myself breathe easier.

But when I glance once more at my reflection as we head out, I can't help the thought that cuts through everything else.

Maddox is going to see me like this.

And that thought…has my heart pounding and my stomach flipping.

I shouldn't care whether or not he thinks I look stunning, but the truth is I do.

The hotel entrance is a wall of light and noise—cameras flashing, velvet ropes straining, reporters calling names like it's blood in the water.

Griffin offers his hand after he steps out of the car, and I take it, steady, letting the shimmer of green sequins catch every bulb.

Flashbulbs pop. I angle my chin, smile just sharp enough to hold distance.

Griffin plays his role easily. He looks every inch the powerful plus-one. Safe. Handsome. A shield.

And then…

Maddox.

He steps from the black town car behind us like the air itself bends around him.

A black tux clings to every cut of his frame, broad shoulders swallowing the fabric, the sharp line of his jaw shadowed in the light.

No date. Just him.

All presence and heat, dragging every lens his way.

The crowd swells, shouting, and cameras detonate in bursts. He doesn't even try to smile. He doesn't need to. That scowl is magnetic, pulling focus until I feel it in my bones.

For one dizzying second, my body betrays me. I want to do nothing more than drink in the sight of him in that tux.

If I could just look at him, maybe I could make sense of the knot twisting in my stomach.

In the next instant, Maddox's gaze cuts over us, ice-blue and burning at the same time. It lands on Griffin's hand over mine and lingers just long enough that my throat goes tight.

His jaw clenches once, hard, like he's already decided what this looks like.

And he doesn't like it.

My lips part, instinct to explain rising like heat under my skin. Except he doesn't give me the chance.

He turns on his heel, shoulders squared, and strides straight into the ballroom with cameras snapping in his wake.

The photographers roar louder, chasing him, and just like that he's gone, leaving nothing but the hollow in my chest where his stare still burns.

Griffin watches him disappear inside, then glances down at me, his voice pitched for my ears alone. "He doesn't like me."

My breath hitches. "What do you mean? On the ice?"

"No, here. Right now."

"He doesn't even know you."

Griffin's mouth curves, knowing, dark hair catching the light. "Doesn't have to."

I laugh, but it scrapes my throat raw.

Something tells me this is going to be a long night.

Once inside, the ballroom hums like a hive, chandeliers dripping light across sequins and black ties, champagne bubbling in tall flutes.

I sit at a round table near the front, Griffin at my right, Dean at my left. Across from me, two board members and their wives chatter over the centerpiece—a spray of white orchids tall enough to feel like another barrier.

It doesn't take long for the conversation to shift.

"Griffin," one of the wives leans forward, eyes sparkling, "the media's saying you're in prime position this year. What do you think?"

Griffin smiles, polite, shoulders relaxed in his suit. He answers smoothly, the whole table leaning in.

And I'm invisible.

Every nod, every follow-up question aimed at him. Not the woman sitting here who owns the team hosting this gala, who signs their checks, who keeps the lights on in this room.

I sip champagne, slow, letting the bubbles coat the bite in my throat.

Griffin, to his credit, tries. "You should really ask Sloane about how things are shaping up here. She's the one running the show."

Dean clears his throat, smiling tightly. "Oh, she's modest. Griffin, how's your new captain handling the locker room?"

The pivot is sharp enough to cut. My hand curls in my lap.

I want to remind them whose logo is splashed across the stage backdrop.

I want to demand they look at me.

But I don't.

Carringtons don't demand. We remind.

I angle my chin, letting my gaze drift across the room like their dismissal doesn't sting.

And that's when I find him.

Maddox.

He's at the next table, posture coiled in the chair like he'd rather be anywhere else. He isn't laughing at the sponsor's jokes or schmoozing like Riley, who I can hear carrying on two tables over.

He's just sitting there, jaw tight, glass untouched.

But his eyes are on me.

Our gazes collide, and heat licks up my spine, dangerous and instant.

I should look away. Should fold back into the chatter at my table, the men who ignore me in favor of my cousin's stats.

But Maddox doesn't look away.

And I can't either.

It's a tether, thin and electric, strung tight between tables. My pulse trips, champagne fizz sharp in my veins.

Griffin leans closer, his breath warm at my ear. "Careful, cuz," he murmurs low enough no one else hears. "You're going to set his tux on fire with how hard you're staring."

Heat scorches my cheeks, but my face stays smooth and practiced. "Shut up, Griffin."

His voice is edged with quiet amusement. "Just observing."

Before I can answer, the emcee's voice booms over the speakers. "Ladies and gentlemen, please welcome the owner of your Atlanta Vipers, Ms. Sloane Carrington."

The table bursts into applause, chairs scraping back. Griffin rises with me, his hand brushing my elbow as I stand, glittering gown catching the chandelier light.

My spine is ramrod straight, my pulse pounding as I cross the room toward the stage.

But even as I climb the steps, even as the lights blind and the applause swells, I can feel him.

Maddox's stare.

Heavy. Hot.

Daring me to meet it.

And my body betrays me, every step sharper under the weight of wanting.

The applause swells as I reach the stage, heels clicking across polished wood.

Griffin stays one step behind, pausing at the podium's edge, his dark suit a shadow of quiet support. He doesn't try to wave, doesn't try to draw the cameras—he knows this is my stage.

I lift my chin, let the lights wash over me, and let the hush fall.

"Thank you," I begin, voice smooth and steady through the thunder of my pulse. "Tonight is about more than hockey. It's about community. About connection. About making sure that the youngest among us—the ones fighting battles most of us can't imagine—know they're not fighting alone."

A murmur runs through the crowd, approval soft and warm. I breathe it in, controlled, refusing to let my nerves show.

"We've partnered with Atlanta Children's Hospital to create programs that go beyond a single visit or a photo op. From equipment donations to long-term support for families in crisis, the Atlanta Vipers are committed to making a difference. Because this city deserves a team that fights as hard off the ice as it does on it."

Applause breaks out, strong and echoing. I let it rise and crest before leaning forward, gaze sweeping the room.

And there—front and center in the crowd—Maddox.

His broad frame is a dark slash against the glittering crowd. He doesn't clap. Doesn't smile.

He just watches me, unblinking, the force of his gaze dragging heat down my spine like a touch no one else can see.

My mouth goes dry, but I don't falter.

"This isn't just about wins or losses. It's about building a legacy together." I pause, breath even. "And with all of you here tonight, I know we will."

The applause roars back, bright and deafening. Cameras flash. Griffin nods faintly from the sidelines, quiet pride in his eyes.

But it's not his gaze that sears me.

It's Maddox. Still staring, still burning, like every word I said was meant for him alone.

I walk off the stage, and cameras descend the second I step down. Flash after flash, questions shouted over one another, handlers corralling bodies into neat little lines for the perfect shot.

Griffin slides to my side without needing to be asked, one hand at the small of my back as we pose. He knows how this works—angles, smiles, the practiced charm that makes the reporters eat out of his hand.

I smile for them too. Perfectly measured. Perfectly polished.

Maddox stands at the edge of the crowd, his height and broad frame cutting through the sea of tuxedos.

He doesn't push forward for the spotlight, doesn't offer anything to the cameras. He just watches.

Heat snakes up my spine every time my gaze catches on his. Every click of the camera feels like it's capturing something I shouldn't let bleed through.

"Closer," one of the photographers calls, motioning Griffin tighter against me. He obliges, grin flashing easy as ever, his arm sliding just a fraction firmer at my waist.

And that's when Maddox shifts—jaw locking, shoulders tight, a storm brewing behind his eyes.

It shouldn't thrill me the way it does.

But it does.

The bulbs keep firing, questions flying, Griffin leaning in to whisper something light in my ear that makes me laugh.

But all I can think about is the man at the edge of the frame —the one who doesn't belong to this part of my world, yet manages to own every breath I take anyway.

The camera bulbs finally dim, handlers ushering donors back toward the bar, the photos with Griffin still flashing across my eyes.

My cheeks ache from holding the same curated smile, my pulse raw from knowing exactly whose gaze burned into me the whole time.

When the floor opens and the band eases into something smooth, the first player at my elbow isn't Maddox.

It's Jace.

"Owner Carrington." He offers his hand with the calm weight of a captain who knows exactly what he's doing—making the first move before anyone else can. "May I?"

The corner of my mouth curves. He's impossible to say no to. "Of course, Captain."

The crowd parts as we step onto the floor. Jace doesn't speak much—he never does—but his steady presence is enough to make the donors murmur approval.

His hand is firm, his lead unshakable, his small talk clipped but respectful.

Safe.

When the song ends, he thanks me and releases me with the same precision he brought to the ice earlier this week.

I barely have time to exhale before Finn sweeps in, chaos personified in a tux.

"Boss lady," he grins, bowing low in mock chivalry, "you're too radiant to be wasted on the suits. Give a real guy a spin."

I roll my eyes but let him tug me back out.

He keeps it clean—for Finn—but his mischief is impossible to miss.

He twirls me a little too dramatically, cracks a joke loud enough for half the room to hear, and has the donors laughing along with us by the time the music shifts.

"Behave," I murmur under my breath.

He winks. "This is me behaving."

When he spins me out for the last time, Logan is there to catch me.

Smooth, polished, the perfect transition. His hand at my waist is respectful, his smile practiced but not empty.

He knows exactly how to make this look effortless, like the whole thing was planned.

"Donors are eating this up," he murmurs low, glancing toward the tables. "You're making us look like an organization that knows how to shine."

"That's the point."

He tilts his head, eyes glinting. "Not all of us need lessons."

I don't rise to the bait. I just hold his gaze and let the silence answer for me.

When Logan spins me out for the last time, Beau is there to catch me.

Smooth and solid, his palm steady at my waist, his movements confident without showboating.

"You're keeping the boys on their best behavior tonight," he says, keeping his voice low.

I smile, a quiet hum in my throat. "No easy feat let me assure you."

I've danced several songs in a row with nearly all of my players.

Except the one I really want to be held by.

My body hums with the press of too many hands, too many eyes.

Griffin stands near the edge of the floor, watching with arms crossed, a faint smirk curving his mouth like he knows exactly what game is being played.

Maddox sits in shadow, tie loosened, drink in hand.

He hasn't moved once—not to dance, not to smile, not to look anywhere but me.

His eyes brand me with every step I take, every polite laugh I give, every palm I let rest against my back.

And when I finally return to my seat, flushed and breathless, I swear I can still feel him watching.

CHAPTER EIGHTEEN

Maddox

I WATCH as she laughs at something Griffin says at the table, head tilted just enough to show off the line of her throat.

I clench my jaw and lift the glass of bourbon to my lips without tasting it.

Every fucking time I think I've gotten over it—over her—she does something else that pulls the rug out from under me.

I've watched her dance with my teammates and a couple of corporate donors too handsy for my liking.

Jace started it, leading her around the floor with a firm hand on her waist.

Finn twirled her and dipped her too low.

Beau kept his hand polite but lingered just long enough.

And Logan—*fuck*—Logan made her laugh.

That sound. Soft and full, like it was just for him.

It wasn't.

It's never just for them.

She's mine.

Even if I never get to touch her.

Even if I know better.

My glass hits the table harder than I mean it to.

The sound turns a few heads, but I don't care.

I push out of my chair and cross the ballroom without thinking—without giving myself time to talk myself out of it.

Every step feels like surrender.

Griffin says something to her, and she smiles politely—until she sees me.

Her smile falters. Her spine straightens.

I see the question in her eyes before I say a word.

I stop beside her, hand extended.

"Dance with me."

Her lashes lower just enough to give her time. One beat. Two.

Then she slides her hand into mine.

It's not hesitation.

It's surrender.

Her touch is cool from the glass of champagne she hasn't finished.

But her skin, her presence, is heat.

Undeniable. Unforgiving.

The crowd doesn't exist.

Neither does the damn gala.

Just the weight of her hand in mine as I guide her toward the dance floor.

The music slows—smooth jazz, silky and low. Something made for shadows and secrets.

I take her in my arms, one hand at her back, the other claiming hers.

She fits like I imagined. Like I remembered.

She's taller in those heels, but I still have to look down to meet her eyes.

"Been avoiding me, Carrington?" I murmur.

She arches a brow, smile faint. "You've been brooding from the shadows. I didn't want to get in the way of your aesthetic."

My mouth twitches.

God, she's good at this.

But not good enough to hide the tension humming beneath her skin.

"Wasn't sure you'd still be here tonight." I pause, eyes locking on hers. "Figured your *date* might've dragged you out early."

Her smile barely flickers. "He's not my date."

I arch a brow, pressure tightening in my grip. "No?"

"No." She draws in closer. "He's my cousin. Griffin Ashford."

The name lands like a puck to the sternum.

Griffin Ashford. Top-six forward in New Jersey. Makes headlines for charity work and model girlfriends.

And apparently? Related to the woman I've been trying not to want.

I drag my gaze over her—her bare shoulders, that neckline, the green glitter catching every ounce of light.

"Family lets you show up in a dress like this?"

Her lips curve. "If he knows what's good for him."

God, I love that fucking mouth, the sass.

It's a fucking turn on, and it shouldn't be.

"Well, he's had a front-row seat all night."

I lean in, my breath skating across her jaw.

"And so have half my teammates."

She doesn't flinch. Doesn't deny it.

Just lets the silence stretch between us like a wire strung too tight.

"They asked," she says finally, soft but steady.

"And it would've looked worse if I said no to everyone but you."

I press my palm more firmly to the small of her back, pulling her that final inch closer.

Her chest brushes mine. Her breath catches.

"Let 'em look," I murmur. "They won't see this."

"This?"

I lower my mouth to her ear.

"The way you're shaking in my hands."

She exhales sharply—barely a sound, but I feel it everywhere.

The song drags out longer than it should, and still I don't let go.

Because there's no going back now.

Not after this.

She doesn't pull away.

Even when the music slows further, wrapping around us like silk.

Even when my hand slides a fraction lower on her back.

Even when her fingers tighten slightly in mine, like she's holding on.

"You know," I murmur low, "you could've danced with me first."

Her eyes flick to mine, guarded. "You weren't exactly asking."

"Didn't think you'd say yes."

She tilts her head. "And now?"

I dip my mouth toward hers, just enough that my words graze her skin.

"Now I think you want to know what it feels like when I do more than ask."

Her breath stutters.

Her spine straightens.

But she doesn't let go.

I guide her through the next slow turn, and for a second—just one—we move like this is all we've ever done.

Like we know each other's rhythms.

Like the chaos we create outside this moment doesn't matter.

"I'm not some charity case you can fix," I say quietly. "And I'm not one of your rookies."

"I know."

"I'm not safe for you, Sloane."

Her eyes hold mine. Steady.

"No one ever changed the game by playing it safe."

That's it. That's the moment.

The one that slices through me like a blade and buries deep.

Because I've fought to keep her at a distance for weeks—told myself it was about the job, the team, the goddamn clause.

But the truth?

I just wanted to make sure she'd fight back.

The music fades.

But neither of us moves.

Not until someone brushes past us and the moment cracks just enough for her to step away.

Her fingers slip from mine like she's peeling off a layer of skin.

She gives a tight smile meant for anyone watching.

Then she turns and walks back into the crowd, spine straight, shoulders high, leaving behind only the scent of something sharp and devastating.

And I stand there, fists clenching and unclenching, jaw tight, knowing damn well I'm not going to make it through the night without her.

And I shouldn't still be watching her.

But I am.

She's back at her table, calm and composed, sipping champagne like her body wasn't just pressed against mine, like I didn't feel her ribs expand under my palm when I whispered in her ear.

I drag a hand through my hair and make my way toward the bar.

Need to cool off.

Need space.

Need a fucking lobotomy if I think I can get through another hour of this without touching her again.

"Lasker." A voice cuts through the noise behind me.

I turn, jaw tight, already bracing—another donor, another handshake, another conversation I don't want.

It's worse.

It's Griffin.

His jaw's set, smile professional, but his eyes aren't friendly.

"You and Sloane have an interesting rhythm."

I take a slow sip of my bourbon and let the burn settle. "If you've got something to say, say it."

He leans in slightly, voice low. "She's important to me. She's my family. Don't fuck with her head."

My jaw flexes.

Not because he's wrong.

But because he's right.

"I'm sure she appreciates the concern," I say evenly. "But she can handle herself."

"Yeah. She can. Don't forget it."

And then he walks off, back toward her table, sliding into the seat beside her like he's always belonged there.

I'm still watching when she turns her head just enough to glance my way.

It's brief.

Barely a second.

But it hits like a punch to the chest.

Because that look—sharp and soft and knowing—that's not the kind of look you give to someone who means nothing.

That's the kind you give to someone you don't want to mean everything.

Fuck the drink — I need air.

I head outside, drink in hand, and shit, I wish I smoked. It sounds like the kind of thing that would help right now.

Instead, I pace the sidewalk beside the front entrance like a caged panther. Gala attendees linger at the valet stand, their laughter looser now—glazed from champagne and ego.

I catch a flash of that green that's burned into my brain.

Sloane.

She stands near the front entrance, Griffin a step behind her, murmuring something too low for me to hear. She smiles—small, polite—but it doesn't reach her eyes.

The valet pulls her car up.

She thanks him with a nod, slipping into the back seat like she's done it a thousand times.

Like she didn't just light my whole fucking night on fire with a look.

Griffin doesn't get in. He stays behind, phone in hand, giving her space.

Good.

I stay half in shadow, jaw locked, watching her car ease down the drive and disappear into the dark.

I could've said something. Could've walked her out. Could've offered to take her home.

But I didn't.

Because she's my boss.

Because she's too young.

Because the line between us is already frayed to hell, and if I cross it now, I won't stop.

My grip tightens around the empty glass in my hand.

She doesn't need a man like me.

Doesn't need the baggage or the bruises I carry.

But Christ…

I want her anyway.

A shuffle of footsteps drags my attention to the side.

"Hey, Lasker."

I turn.

It's Cal. Jacket half-buttoned, tie crooked, face flushed and unsteady. He sways slightly, holding up his phone with a grin like we're drinking buddies instead of professional colleagues.

"You good?" I ask, voice rough.

He grins wider. "Totally. Just needed air. You?"

"Same."

A beat of silence.

Then he shrugs and sways again. "I need to go home. Gonna head out."

"How did you get here?"

"I drove."

That yanks me straight out of my spiral. "Fuck that; you're not driving now."

"Nah," he says too quickly, "I'm fine, man."

"Fine my ass." I step in, voice low but sharp. "You're drunk as hell, and you're not getting behind the wheel."

Cal stiffens, trying to puff up. "I'm good. I've driven worse—"

"I don't give a shit. That was fucking stupid anyway. You're not getting anywhere near the driver's seat of a car tonight."

He blinks at me, surprised.

I step closer to him, hands in my pockets. "Look, man. You got a team now. You're part of something. You don't fuck that up because you're too proud to call a ride."

He scowls, then shrugs again, all bravado melting. "Fine. I can't feel my damn knees, anyway."

I sigh, pulling out my phone. "Give me your address."

He hesitates.

"Cal."

"I don't know it."

What the actual fuck? "You don't know your address?"

"I can't remember it right now."

I sigh the long sigh of a man who wishes he was anywhere but here but knows he's right where he needs to be.

I hold out my hand. "Let me see your wallet."

A semblance of anger that only makes him look like a petulant boy crosses his face.

Damn, he's so young.

"Lasker, you got fucking money; you don't need mine!"

Jesus, is the whole world out to fuck with me tonight?

"I want to see your license. It has your address on it."

"Oh." He steps back. "That's true. Hold on."

He fumbles around, feeling all of his pockets except the back left one where I can see the outline of his wallet.

"Shit, I lost my wallet!" he slurs loudly.

"No, you didn't." I gesture to his pants. "Try that back pocket."

He feels it and pulls it out, drunken relief on his face. "Whew, thought I'd lost it."

Handing it over to me, he stumbles but manages to catch himself. "I'm cool, I'm cool."

I roll my eyes and open his wallet.

Well, hell. He lives on the opposite side of town from where I'm going.

This just isn't my night.

I text my driver and within moments, he's pulling up to the curb. Opening the back door, I gesture for Cal to get in. When he does, I nod to my driver.

"Take him home. Make sure he gets in the door. Text me when he's in."

I rattle off the address to the driver who—to his credit—only hesitates for half a second before nodding. "Yes, sir, Mr. Lasker."

"Wait," Cal says, eyes wide. "What about you?"

"I'll figure it out."

"But it's your car—"

"Don't worry about me."

Cal stares at me for a second, then nods, sheepish. "Thanks, man."

"Don't make it a habit. And buckle up."

He chuckles, and I shut the door. I wait until it pulls away before I let out a slow exhale.

I meant it when I said I'd figure it out.

But I sure as hell didn't plan on needing to.

Pulling my phone out, I open the ride share app, thumbing through to get an Uber. The screen lights up indicating the car's three minutes out.

I drop onto the stone bench outside the entrance, elbows on my knees, empty glass dangling between my fingers.

I think of Sloane in that dress. In her car. In her penthouse.

And me—sitting here, chasing restraint like it's some kind of moral high ground.

Every cell in my body is pulled toward her.

But I don't move.

Because I'm not that guy anymore.

Because I'm trying to do the right thing.

Because wanting her doesn't make me worthy of her.

My Uber pulls up.

I stand, tip the glass into the valet's trash can, and climb in without a word.

We drive toward The Apex in silence, the city blurring past.

When the car stops at the front entrance, I get out and walk into the building I've lived in for a little over a month now, nodding at the night doorman.

In the elevator, the PH button taunts me. But I stab the number seven button like it personally offended me, heading to my apartment.

Alone.

Because for now, restraint still wins.

But I know damn well it won't last through the night.

CHAPTER NINETEEN

Maddox

THE CITY'S still lit when I walk into my apartment.

Not that I notice any of it.

I toss my keys into the tray by the door and scrub a hand over my face, still wired from the gala.

From her.

From *everything*.

Two floors. That's all that separates us now.

Sloane fucking Carrington is two floors above me, probably unzipping that green dress I haven't stopped thinking about since the second she walked into that ballroom.

And I'm down here—pacing my apartment like a lunatic.

I pour myself a drink, only to find the only taste I want is of her.

The image of her—flushed from dancing, lips parted from laughing, hair falling loose around her shoulders—won't let go.

Neither will the memory of her eyes finding mine across the room. Or the feel of her body in my hands, moving with me like it meant something.

It *did* mean something.

I don't care how many lines are between us. Don't care that

she's my boss, or that I'm the last man someone like her should want.

Because I do want her.

I want her in every way I've spent the last six weeks trying not to.

And pretending otherwise isn't noble anymore.

It's *bullshit*.

I stare out the floor-to-ceiling windows of my apartment, chest tight and blood hot.

She's up there. Two floors above me.

Probably still awake. Probably pacing like I am.

Or maybe not. Maybe she's curled into silk sheets with the weight of the night pressing down on her shoulders like it always does.

Maybe she's already dreaming, face soft and vulnerable in a way no one else gets to see.

Maybe she's wishing someone would *come to her*.

My body moves before my mind catches up.

I grab my key card and head for the door.

No more waiting. No more pretending.

I need to see her.

The elevator dings once, low and sterile, as I step into the lobby of The Apex.

Midnight hush blankets the marble floors, the sleek black walls throwing back my reflection in slashes of steel and glass.

The concierge behind the desk looks up, startled, because it's late, and I'm sure I look like a man gone mad.

Because I have.

I've gone mad for my boss.

The only woman who looks and sees me.

And I'm about to break every rule I've set.

"Evening, Mr. Lasker," the concierge says, his voice overly polite as he straightens in his chair.

His name tag says Aaron, and he's maybe twenty-three,

fresh-faced and eager in a way that makes me feel ancient. "Is there anything I can—?"

"I need to go up to the penthouse floor."

I say it flat and direct. Like I'm asking for something simple.

But his expression freezes for a beat too long.

"The penthouse floor is restricted access, sir," he says, shifting slightly in his chair. "I can call Ms. Carrington and—"

"No."

I don't mean for it to come out so sharp, but it does. I scrub a hand over my jaw and try again, this time softer. "Don't buzz her."

Aaron hesitates, hand hovering near the console. "Mr. Lasker, I really shouldn't let anyone up unless the resident—"

"I live here," I cut in, jaw tight. "Seventh floor. You know that. You know who I am. "

"Yes, sir, but the penthouse—"

"I need to speak with her," I say, locking eyes with him. "And I'm asking you to let me up. Just this once."

His gaze flicks toward the elevator. Back to me.

He's young but not stupid. I'm sure he can see it in my eyes. He knows exactly what this is.

Still, he hesitates.

The silence stretches.

And then he exhales, nods once, and taps a key on the panel.

"You've got five minutes, sir."

The elevator doors slide open behind me with a hiss of judgment.

I step in without looking back. But just before the doors close, I lean out.

"One more thing."

Aaron glances up.

"Don't ever let another man go up to her floor without buzzing her first. Got it?"

His eyes widen a fraction. "Yes, sir."

I nod once.

Then the doors slide shut, sealing me inside a box of mirrored walls and reckless intent.

She's just a few floors away.

And I'm done pretending I can keep this clean.

———————————

The soft *ding* of the elevator barely registers.

All I hear is the thud of my pulse and the voice in my head telling me to turn around.

To be smart.

To *stop*.

But I don't.

I cross the penthouse hallway, every step deliberate, heavy, echoing off marble and glass.

She owns the whole floor, and I know which door is the one I need. I've walked past it a hundred times in my head, usually with my fists clenched and my jaw tight.

This time, I lift my hand.

Knock once.

The door opens almost instantly.

And there she is.

My heart nearly stops, and my dick is fighting the constraints of my pants.

At least I still have my tux jacket on.

Hair still pinned in that elegant twist, a few strands slipping loose like she's been pacing.

The dress still clings to her like it was sewn to her skin— dark green and glittering, low in the front, slit high enough to haunt me.

Barefoot.

Just her.

And me, barely breathing.

There's something intimate about her being barefoot and in a dress that glitters.

She's also shorter than I thought without the heels, but that just makes me want to possess her and protect her even more.

"Maddox," she says, like she wasn't sure it would be me, but hoped anyway.

I don't answer.

I step inside, crowding her backward without touching her. She doesn't move to close the door—it swings shut behind me like it knows what's coming.

"I can't do it anymore," I rasp. "I can't keep pretending this tension between us isn't fucking real."

She backs up until her spine hits the wall. "What are you doing here?"

"You know what I'm doing here."

My voice is low. Ruined.

I crowd her space, bracing one hand beside her head. The other slides to her hip, grabbing a fistful of that glittering green fabric like I'm starving for it.

"I should've taken you in that elevator," I whisper against her mouth, "should've stripped you bare and made you scream my name with the whole damn city listening."

Her eyes flare. Her chest rises.

But she doesn't stop me.

Her perfume wraps around me—sweet, expensive, and maddening. She's so close, I can feel the heat radiating off her skin.

Can see the shiver ripple through her when I press harder into her body, every inch of me wound tight and reckless.

"You think I don't remember the way you looked at me?" I growl. "The way you breathed my name when I had you caged in that corner?"

Her fingers curl into my shirt. "We can't—"

"We already are."

I crash my mouth to hers.

Not soft. Not sweet.

Hungry. Raw. All teeth and tongue and the kind of groan that's been living in my chest since the first time she walked into my Boston apartment.

She kisses me back like she means it. Like she's breaking open for me in real time.

I grip her thighs and lift her—dress hiking up, her legs wrapping tight around me.

Her back hits the door with a thud as I grind against her, every hard inch of me pressed between her legs.

"This what you wanted?" I growl into her neck, biting the skin just under her jaw. "Me pinning you just like before? Except this time, I'm not walking away."

She moans, low and desperate. "Maddox—"

I shift my grip and tug the dress up over her hips.

"You wore this to kill me, didn't you?"

"Maddox—"

"Say it," I demand. "Tell me you want this."

"I want it," she breathes, wrecked and honest and so fucking beautiful I could die.

That's all I need.

"You gonna stop me?" I rasp, voice dark and low against her mouth. "Tell me this is reckless? That you're the boss and I should know better?"

She bites my bottom lip, eyes flashing.

"Not a chance."

"Fuck," I groan, grinding into her as I press her harder against the door. "You have no idea what you're doing to me."

"I think I do."

I shift her weight in my arms and slide one hand beneath the slit of her dress, finding nothing but heat and bare skin.

No panties.

Jesus Christ.

"You wore this with nothing underneath?" I rasp, breath catching.

"I told you I wanted this."

"I don't know whether to punish you or call you a good girl," I growl against her neck.

She gasps when I slide my middle finger inside her pussy, pumping it in and out, her wetness soaking my hand.

"Fuck me, you're soaked. That's all for me, isn't it?"

"Yes…it's all for you."

"Well, then I guess that makes you a good girl."

I slide in another finger and her hips move against my hand, her chest heaving against mine.

When I add pressure against her clit with my thumb, my name is like a prayer on her lips.

Control slips out of reach, and I fumble with my pants like a damn teenager.

I press into her, one arm braced against the doorframe, the other gripping her thigh as I angle my hips.

She's already wet, already arching into me.

That's when I realize there's something different—

"Fuck," I ground out, "I don't have a condom."

Her eyes meet mine, those green depths glazed with lust but also something that looks like earnestness.

"I'm on the pill and safe. And I know you just had a physical."

"Yeah, I'm safe too."

And I've never, *ever* had sex without a condom.

I press into her. "Too late to run, sweetheart."

"I'm not running anywhere."

When I finally, *finally* push inside her—fast, deep, *raw*—her cunt clasps around me like a fist.

Her head hits the door, and she moans my name like it's the only one she remembers.

I fuck her like I've been starving for it. Like this is my last night on Earth and I want nothing more than to go out with my cock inside her.

But beyond the animal lust that's driving my hips to meet hers, there's more.

Every sharp breath, every bite of her nails in my shoulders, every hoarse whisper of my name against my ear—it all confirms what I already knew.

This isn't a mistake.

It's the truth I've been denying since the moment we met.

I want to drag it out, so I can savor every second of her falling apart in my arms.

But I can't hold out. I've wanted her so bad for so long.

And when she comes—shuddering, clinging, panting against my neck—I lose whatever restraint I have left.

I spill into her with a groan, forehead pressed to hers.

We stay like that for a moment. Breathing hard. Shaking.

When I finally catch my breath, I carry her to the bedroom, her legs staying wrapped around me. Her hair falls loose, and her eyes don't leave mine.

"I'm not done with you yet, Sloane. Not even close."

"Thank God."

I squeeze her ass when she kisses me, her tongue tangling with mine.

No, I'm not done in the slightest.

But this time, when I take her, it's won't be with the animal, caveman type lust that I had fucking her against the wall.

It'll be about everything we haven't said.

And everything we can't stop feeling.

CHAPTER TWENTY

Sloane

HIS HANDS ARE EVERYWHERE.

Not frantic, not greedy.

Claiming. Certain.

He lays me down like I'm something he's fought for—bled for—and now that he has me, he's not wasting a second.

The dress slips under his palms as I shift back on the bed, satin catching on skin. He watches the motion like it's sacred, like he'll memorize every inch before he lets himself taste it.

"You're unreal," he mutters, voice hoarse. "Laid out for me like this…"

He swipes a hand down the inside of my thigh, his knuckles grazing the slit in my dress. "This was all night. *All fucking night.*"

The fabric pools at my ribs as he works it up slowly, his breath heavy above me. When I lift to help him, he shakes his head.

"Don't. I've got you."

It's like he wants to unwrap me, worship me.

I fall back against the sheets, arms above my head, giving him everything.

He draws the dress over my head with maddening care, inch by inch until I'm left completely bare for his eyes to feast.

His gaze rakes down my body, heat and hunger colliding with something deeper—reverent and raw.

"I've imagined this," he says, low and rough. "Too many goddamn times."

"Maddox…"

"Couldn't sleep. Couldn't think. Not after watching you in that dress, dancing with every man who wanted a piece of you."

His hands slide up my calves, over my knees, along my thighs until they're braced wide on either side of him.

"But you were *mine* the whole time, weren't you?"

I don't answer.

I don't have to.

My body arches, and I gasp as his mouth finds the top of my thigh, then higher. He doesn't rush this time.

Just takes his time, leisurely kissing my skin around everywhere but where I want it the most.

My hands find his hair, and I try to guide him where I want him. Where my body *needs* him to be.

When he drags his tongue up my seam and sucks on my clit, I nearly lose my damn mind.

His mouth works me over with heat and possession until I'm writhing, whispering his name like it's a vow.

And just about when the crest begins to build higher and higher, he pulls away.

I can't help it.

I beg.

"Maddox, come back please."

His smirk just makes the flames licking in my core hotter.

Especially since he's unbuttoning his shirt and I get to see that gorgeous chest again.

"Patience, pretty baby. I got more for you."

I lick my lips like the cat in heat I am while I watch him undress.

My eyes widen slightly when I get a look at his cock. I've felt it inside me so I knew it was big, but I didn't expect it to look as perfect as it felt.

His smirk widens as he strokes himself. "Like what you see, don't you?"

I lift my gaze to his, wanting to be coy but finding that at this moment, I just don't have it in me. "Yeah, I do. And I want more of it."

His eyes darken and he growls, crawling his way up my body.

Yessss... is all I can think when his bare skin touches mine. He's warm and strong and hard in all the right places.

Something shifts in my chest, and while I know this should only be about sex, I can't help but feel that it's more.

I just hope I'm not alone in that feeling.

By the time he presses into me—slow, deep, and anchoring—I'm nearly ready to detonate.

His head drops to the curve of my neck as he moves, his hips meeting mine over and over.

Each thrust is thick with everything we've never said out loud.

This shouldn't happen.

It was always going to.

"I should stop," he growls, driving deeper. "Tell me to stop."

"I won't."

He lifts his head, eyes black with need. "Then tell me you're mine."

"I'm yours. I've been yours since I first saw your picture."

That breaks him.

His rhythm turns desperate, hips snapping harder, one hand tangled in my hair.

He kisses me like we'll burn for it later, but every singe is worth it.

Every thrust drives me higher and higher until I'm once again begging him not to stop.

And when I shatter beneath him, he lets go too, spilling everything into me with a growl I feel in my bones.

Leaning his forehead against mine, he kisses me softly, our breath mingles.

Then he rolls us over and wraps his arms around me like he's holding the only thing tethering him to this world.

The room is quiet except for the soft whisper of the HVAC and the rustle of sheets as I shift. His arm tightens around me.

He's awake.

Has been, maybe. Or maybe the movement stirred him.

I don't open my eyes at first. I just let myself feel it—the warmth of his skin, the steady beat of his heart, the way my body fits into his like it was built to belong there.

"You ever gonna sleep?" I murmur against his chest.

Maddox huffs a breath that might be a laugh. "I can't. Not when I'm this close to you."

I glance up, eyes meeting his. He brushes a piece of hair off my cheek, fingertips lingering.

Laying there, I just watch him for a moment.

His hair's a mess. His mouth is still kiss-bitten. There's a faint pink scratch on his shoulder from my nails.

God help me—I've never seen anything more beautiful in my life.

He stares back at me with that look.

That same look from the elevator, the look in his eyes when he entered my body.

Raw. Real.

"You always like to stare after?" he murmurs.

I smile, lazy. "Only when the view's this good."

He huffs a quiet laugh and closes his eyes, his long lashes brushing the top of his cheekbones.

Damn, I'd kill for lashes like that. It takes a stupid expensive bottle of mascara to make that happen.

Silence stretches between us, but it's not awkward. It's heavy with something…softer.

Safer.

I trail a finger across the line of his ribs. "So," I say, keeping my voice low, "how'd you end up playing hockey?"

He doesn't answer right away.

For a second, I think maybe I've stepped somewhere I shouldn't, but then his voice comes, rough and quiet.

"My mom used to flood the backyard in the winter. We didn't have a lot, but she made sure I had skates. I'd stay out there for hours. I think it was the only time I didn't feel like the walls were closing in."

I go still.

He doesn't elaborate, but I don't need him to. I hear it.

The silence between words.

The kind of childhood that shapes you.

"You were good early?" I ask gently.

He shrugs. "I was fast. Aggressive. Had a mean slapshot." A pause. "It gave me somewhere to put the anger. Somewhere it made sense."

My throat tightens.

I know what it's like to carry a storm inside. To need somewhere to put it.

"Your mom must've been proud."

"She died before I got drafted," he says quietly. "Cancer. Fast and mean. Like everything else in our life."

My heart breaks for him, and it's one more thing that ties us together.

I know what it's like to lose your mother to cancer.

"How old were you?"

"Eighteen. Which was a good thing so I didn't have to live at home anymore."

He doesn't elaborate on what that means, and I get the sense that I shouldn't push.

God. I reach out, covering his hand with mine.

He doesn't pull away.

"Thank you for telling me," I whisper.

He looks over again, eyes searching mine like he's trying to decide if I really see him now.

I do.

And maybe that's why, when he finally speaks, his voice sounds different.

Less guarded. More *him*.

"I've never done that before." His voice is low and rough, yet soft.

His voice alone is a turn on.

I blink. "Told someone about your mom?"

"No." His gaze drops to our tangled legs. "Had sex without a condom."

I freeze.

Not because I'm worried, but because I can *feel* the weight of what he just said.

"You're serious."

He nods once, jaw tight. "Always been careful. Didn't want to screw up someone's life. Or mine."

My chest pulls tight.

"But with you…" His voice lowers. "I didn't even think about it. Not once. Just—knew. Like it was supposed to happen."

The ache that blooms behind my ribs isn't lust. It's something deeper.

A recognition.

A promise.

I lean in and kiss him—slow and reverent.

"Thank you for trusting me."

He rolls on top of me, mouth brushing mine, voice like gravel and heat.

"Next time, you'll thank me with your mouth."

I run my hands in his hair, loving the feel of his body heavy and delicious between my legs, and arch a brow.

"Oh, you want me to thank you with my mouth, huh?"

His grin is slow and dangerous, all dark edges and dimples.

"I'll even say please."

"Maddox Lasker saying please for something?"

His gaze pins me to the bed. "For you? I'll do whatever it takes."

I bite my lip, trying to keep all the emotion flooding my body in check.

It's almost too much to bear.

So I fall back on the physical to keep from losing all of myself this soon.

"Well, since you put it that way…"

Pushing on his shoulder—and yes, the one with the scars that he didn't hide and I didn't say anything about—I roll him over before sliding down his body in one fluid motion.

I drag my fingers across his chest, his abs, the sharp cut of his hips.

Dear God, the V of his hips is sexy as hell.

He watches me the whole way, propped on one elbow now, mouth parted like he's already halfway gone.

Good.

I settle between his legs, one hand braced on his thigh, the other wrapping around him.

He's already hard again. Already thick and hot in my palm.

I lick him once—just the head—slow and teasing.

His groan is immediate, low and broken.

"Fuck, Sloane."

"I said I'd thank you," I whisper, eyes locked on his. "Let me."

And then I do.

I take him into my mouth, deep and wet, slow at first—because I *want* this for him.

Want to worship him the way I just know in my soul he's never been worshipped.

I want to undo him and ruin him like he ruined me.

His hips jerk, and his head falls back against the pillow. He threads a hand into my hair but doesn't push—just holds.

Lets me take control.

Lets me give.

I hum against him, feel him throb against the back of my throat.

His hand tightens and his breath shortens.

And right when he's on the edge, I pull off with a pop and crawl back up his body.

"You're a fucking menace," he growls.

I smile sweetly.

Then straddle his hips, take him in my hand, and sink down on him in one slow, slick slide.

His hands clamp hard around my hips and the delicious burn there makes my pussy clench around him. "Christ."

I roll my hips once just to feel it. The stretch, the ache, the way he fills every inch of me like he was made for me.

His head drops back against the pillow, jaw clenched like he's trying to keep control, but his eyes stay locked on mine.

Like he needs to see me take it.

All of it.

"You always this bossy in bed?" he grits out.

I dig my nails into his chest, grinding down until his breath punches out.

"You don't like it?"

"Didn't say that." His hands slip up, fingers brushing over the curve of my waist. "I fucking love it."

I brace one hand beside his head, the other dragging down the slope of his chest. "Good," I whisper. "Because I'm not done yet."

And then I move. Slide up and down his cock, dragging out the motion to make him crazy like he did me.

I ride him slow, every roll of my hips a taunt.

A promise.

A confession.

This isn't just sex.

I'm claiming him like he claimed me.

I'm surrendering to him, even while I'm in control above him.

His hands roam—hips, ribs, thighs. He cups my breast, strokes his thumb over my nipple, and watches the way I gasp and clench around him.

"Sloane." My name breaks from his throat like a warning.

"Come for me, Maddox," I breathe. "I want to feel you."

His hands tighten. His eyes flare. And when he comes, it's with a guttural sound that cracks something wide open inside me.

My hips pick up speed and I chase down my orgasm until I collapse against his chest, his arms wrapping tight around me as our hearts pound in tandem.

For a long moment, there's only the sound of our breathing and the soft rustle of sheets as he shifts to hold me closer.

I could fall asleep like this.

Wrapped in him.

Wrecked by him.

But he kisses the top of my head, then murmurs, "You're gonna be the death of me."

I smile against his chest.

"Then I guess I'm doing something right."

CHAPTER TWENTY-ONE

Sloane

THE SUN'S STILL LOW—LIGHT not quite reaching the skyline—but the bed next to me is empty.

For one stupid second, my chest squeezes.

I tell myself not to be surprised. Not to expect anything.

But then I catch the scent.

Coffee.

Fresh and rich. With that dark roast bite that can only come from my coffee beans.

I sit up slowly, the sheets falling to my waist. My muscles ache in the best kind of way—like I've been thoroughly, repeatedly ruined.

My hair's a mess, my lips are still swollen, and I'm pretty sure I've got whisker burns on the inside of one thigh.

But I don't care. I love every single swell and burn.

I also love the smell of coffee.

And the sound of movement coming from the kitchen.

What I don't love? The flood of relief through my body.

But that's to think about for another day.

I slip out of bed, tugging on the first robe I find—his tux

jacket still draped across a chair but definitely not enough to cover what needs covering.

The floors are cool under my feet as I make my way toward the kitchen, pulse rising for reasons I don't want to name.

And then I see him.

Barefoot, bare-chested, low-slung black pants riding his hips like a fucking sin. A white dish towel tossed over his shoulder, one hand on the handle of the frying pan, the other reaching for a coffee mug.

My coffee mug.

He moves like he owns the place.

Like the night we had never ended.

Like this isn't a mistake.

And something in me—the part that always braces for abandonment, for regret—eases.

He's got bed hair and stubble and a bruise blooming low on his side—one I didn't put there—but I know the scratch marks across his back are mine.

There's something about seeing him like this, loose and barefoot in my kitchen, that guts me more than any night of sex.

I can see those marks clearly from here, and heat rushes low and deep at the memory.

He turns when he hears me.

Eyes sweeping over my body in that slow, hungry way that makes me forget every reason I should've kept my distance.

"Morning," he says, voice still rough from sleep and sex.

"You made coffee."

"Figured I owed you something after last night." A smirk curves one corner of his mouth. "Or this morning. Or both."

He crosses to hand me a cup, and when our fingers brush, something in my chest catches.

His warmth lingers. So does the memory of his mouth on my skin.

I lean against the doorframe, heart thudding slow and thick. "You cook too?"

His grin deepens, warm and cocky. "You're about to find out."

I step farther into the kitchen, watching him crack eggs like he's done it a hundred times.

"Where did I get eggs and bacon?"

"There's this handy thing called Uber Eats."

"Ah…so, do you always cook after completely ruining someone's life in bed?"

He chuckles, low and unhurried. "Only the ones who beg real pretty."

I arch a brow. "I didn't beg."

"You did." He glances over his shoulder. "Twice."

Heat flares under my skin. "Cocky much?"

He shrugs, scooping eggs into a hot pan. "When I'm right, I'm right."

"You're lucky you're pretty."

"Baby, I'm lucky you let me in."

That stops me. The words hang between us, too raw, too real —and for once, he doesn't backpedal.

He just flips the eggs.

I clear my throat and cross to the counter, stealing a strip of bacon from the plate beside him. "So you make a habit of early morning kitchen takeovers?"

"Only in penthouses I've fantasized about for weeks."

I nearly choke on the bite.

He smirks, sliding the eggs onto two plates with an ease that makes it all feel terrifyingly normal.

"I used to dream about what it'd be like up here. What you were doing. If you ever thought about me the way I couldn't stop thinking about you."

My voice comes out quiet. "I did. All the time. I couldn't stop it."

His jaw flexes, but he nods. "I know."

He hands me a plate, and we sit at the bar, bare knees brushing under the marble counter.

That tiny contact sends a low pulse through me—heat and history and something dangerous.

A flash from last night echoes in my mind—his voice rough in the dark, his hands locked on my hips, telling me to take what I want.

For a few minutes, the only sound is quiet chewing and the low hum of the city below waking up.

But then it starts to crack.

The silence.

The spell.

Because now we're in daylight. And daylight doesn't lie.

The shift would be imperceptible to anyone else, but not to me. I can already feel Maddox's guard returning.

Maddox pushes his plate away, expression unreadable. "You gonna tell the board you slept with your newest contract?"

I flinch. "Don't do that."

"I'm not judging. Just reminding you of the mess we're in."

"I haven't forgotten."

"Good." He leans back on the stool, the muscles in his chest flexing with the motion. "Because you're not the only one who has to answer to people."

That lands.

Heavy.

I want to be pissed off at him for how he's acting, but he's not wrong.

He's not just a player. He's the player I signed under scrutiny.

The gamble everyone's watching.

And I'm the boss who's supposed to stay above board.

But nothing about last night was above board.

"I didn't plan for this," I whisper.

"Neither did I."

The silence stretches again, but now it's tighter.

Brittle.

And I hate it.

His eyes find mine, something sharp behind them.

"What do we do now?"

I don't have an answer. I only know I don't want him to leave.

"I don't know. But I'm not pretending last night didn't happen. I'm not wired like that."

He watches me, unmoving.

I set down my fork and meet his gaze head-on. "It happened. And I don't regret it."

His breath punches out low. "Thank fuck."

Something eases between us.

Not the tension—it's still there, humming like a live wire—but the fear of misstep, of saying the wrong thing.

He stands and rounds the counter, stopping right in front of me. His hand brushes mine, warm and firm and grounding.

"We keep it quiet," he says, voice rough. "We don't let it touch the team."

"And when the season ends?"

"We reassess."

I nod.

"We're careful, Sloane. I mean it."

"I know how to be careful." My voice dips. "I've been careful my whole damn life."

He lifts my chin, eyes burning into mine. "Not with me."

No. Not with him.

And I don't want to be.

We don't say it's us against the world, but it's there—in the space between us, in the slow slide of his fingers down my arm, in the kiss he presses to my temple like a vow he doesn't have to speak.

When I glance down, I see his tie crumpled on the floor beside the island.

I bend to pick it up. "This is mine now."

He smirks, leaning his forehead against mine. "You already took my breath. You might as well take that too."

"Stay," I say softly.

He pulls back slightly. "You sure?"

"I'm positive. Besides, it's Sunday," I murmur. "Let the rest of the world wait one more day."

He runs his knuckles over my cheek. "Yeah," he says. "I could use one more day."

I loop the tie around his neck and pull him to me, where his mouth crashes into mine.

It's more than just a kiss. It's a possession.

And I'm here for it.

He picks me up and I wrap my legs around his waist, feeling the weight of his hardness in my center.

When we get to bed, we rip at each other's clothes, frantic to feel skin on skin again.

And when he finds my entrance wet and ready for him, he slides home, stretching and filling me like it's the first time all over again.

That's where we stay the rest of the day, exploring each other again and again, using our hands, tongues, and bodies to talk.

Reality will come knocking tomorrow.

But today—today, we stay right here.

CHAPTER TWENTY-TWO

Maddox

THE PUCK SLAMS off my pad with a satisfying *thud*, but I don't flinch.

Drop. React. Reset.

I track the next shot out of the corner of my eye, already moving before the rookie's blade makes contact. Low and left.

I smother it with my glove and fire it back to center with a flick of my wrist.

Coach Holt blows the whistle, but I don't stand. Just stay crouched, watching the ice like it owes me something.

"Someone's dialed in today," the assistant coach mutters.

I block out the noise and focus on my breathing. In through the nose. Out slow through the mouth.

The cool sting of the rink air anchors me, but it doesn't quiet the burn still lodged behind my ribs.

She kissed me goodbye this morning like it wasn't a big deal.

Like we hadn't spent two days fucking and talking and pretending the outside world didn't exist.

Like she wasn't the first person I've ever let see *anything* of me—and didn't run.

I tap the post with my blocker and push to my feet.

Keep your head in the game, Lasker.

Everything outside this crease is noise. This is the only place I still know exactly what to do.

The drill resets. Riley skates past with a smirk. "Whatever you did this weekend, do it again."

I plan to do as much as Sloane will let me. And often.

But I don't take the bait.

Don't let them see that I'm doing my damnedest not to think about the way she made coffee in nothing but a robe, or the way she curled into my chest when she got cold, or the way she said *stay* like it was a lifeline.

None of that belongs here.

Here, I'm just the goalie who shows up and doesn't fuck up.

Coach Holt watches from behind the glass, arms crossed. "You keep this up, Lasker, we might actually win something this year."

The boys laugh, but I don't.

I crouch again and tap both posts, centering myself.

Because as much as I want her, as much as I'm already in deeper than I planned—I can't let it show.

Not here.

I push thoughts of her away and watch down the ice as Cal misses his line change.

Even from my post, I catch it immediately.

Riley skates past him, barking his name, but the kid's in his own head.

Slow to react, late to the bench, shoulders tight like he's bracing for a hit that never comes.

Coach Holt doesn't blow the whistle, just lets it ride—probably hoping someone else will light him up instead.

The next rush comes fast. Logan threads a puck through traffic, and Cal fumbles the reception so hard it ricochets off his stick and bounces straight toward me.

Easy glove save.

But I don't feel good about it.

The drill ends and the guys circle center ice, chatting and catching their breath.

Cal hangs back.

I skate over slowly, not close enough to draw attention, but near enough to keep an eye on him.

He leans on his stick like his legs are giving out. Mouth tight. Jaw locked.

And that same look is back—the one I saw the night of the gala when he damn near drove himself home shitfaced.

I didn't say anything then.

Should've.

But I made damn sure he didn't get behind that wheel. Gave him my car and stood in the freezing wind waiting for a blacked-out Uber like I was some twenty-year-old rookie instead of the guy they signed to save this franchise.

Didn't regret it for a second.

Still don't.

Now I see the same cracks forming.

"Reid!" Holt barks. "Get your head on straight or get off my ice."

Cal nods once, sharp and silent, but he doesn't lift his eyes.

Something's wrong.

And I know that look. Hell, I wore that look for most of my first season.

The one that says *I can't ask for help because I don't think I've earned it yet.*

The whistle blows again, and practice resumes.

But while the others are skating drills, I stay back. Watch him fumble a pass, whiff a shot, bite the inside of his cheek so hard I see the muscle twitch from thirty feet away.

Rookie or not, that kid's drowning.

And I've seen too many guys sink because no one ever threw them a rope.

Soon, Coach is blowing the whistle calling practice and giving us an end of practice pep talk before we make our way into the locker room.

I head for the showers and take a stall in the far corner away from the noise of the younger guys.

I'm in my head and need to think. Now that I'm off the ice, all I can think about is Sloane.

When I turn on the water, it's cold.

I let it hit me full blast, no steam, no heat. Just a punishing slap to the spine to scrub the morning off my skin.

But it doesn't work.

Because I still feel her.

The silk of her sheets twisted around my legs.

Her robe hanging open while she stole bacon off my plate.

That sleepy, raspy laugh she gave me like it belonged to no one else.

I brace my palms against the tile and drop my head under the spray, eyes shut.

I can still smell her shampoo on my skin.

Her voice floats back to me—soft and quiet like dawn.

It happened. And I don't regret it.

I shouldn't have stayed the weekend. Should've left the second the sun rose.

But I didn't. I couldn't.

And now I don't want to pretend.

I step out of the shower and grab a towel, rough with bleach and team logos. The locker room's half-empty now. Most of the guys already gone or sprawled on benches, scrolling their phones xor bullshitting like it's just another Monday.

For them, maybe it is.

I tug my hoodie over my head, sit on the bench, and check my phone.

No message.

Not surprised. Not mad. But something in my chest pulls tight anyway.

I flip the phone face-down and scrub a hand over my jaw.

We said we'd keep it quiet.

Said we'd reassess when the season ends.

But the way I feel right now?

The way I felt when she looked at me like I was worth choosing?

That's not something I want to hide.

And that thought—more than anything—scares the ever-living shit out of me.

Because I don't *do* visible. I don't ask to be seen.

But damn if I don't want to be seen by her.

Fuck.

This is why I've avoided catching feelings like the plague. It makes me want things I have no business wanting.

And from people who deserve better than me.

I grab my bag and head out, ready to be home in the solitude of my condo.

Or am I?

The fact that she's in the same building as me right now ignites the need to see her like an obsession.

Instead, I head to the rink. Maybe the sharp, cold air will ground me like it usually does.

Ground me and tell me to go the fuck home.

Do not pass go.

Or Sloane's office.

But when I get to the ice, it isn't empty.

Cal's still out there, skating a loop with his head down, stick dragging like he's running through sludge.

A puck slips off his blade mid-drill and careens toward the boards.

He mutters something under his breath and goes after it.

I hover in the exit tunnel, dressed in my off-ice gear, but with one glove still clutched in my hand.

I should leave, let the kid have his space to wallow.

But I don't.

Wallowing in his misery isn't going to help get his head out of his ass and keep him off waivers.

I watch him stumble through another drill—tight turns, puck control, a cross-body pass that sails too far and hits the boards with a crack.

He exhales hard, shoulders tight, skates back to start it again.

No one's watching. No one left to impress.

Except me.

I start to walk away. Get as far as the top of the stairs before something in me—something I don't usually fucking listen to—pulls me back.

I drop my bag, put on my skates, and step onto the ice. "Reid."

Cal jerks around like I caught him shoplifting.

He skates toward me, sheepish and flushed. "Hey. Uh… didn't think anyone was still here."

I toss him a puck from the nearby bucket. "You're not keeping your top hand high enough. You're losing accuracy in your follow-through."

He nods slowly. "Okay. Got it."

I step into position. "Again. From the dot."

We run the drill.

No praise. No pep talk.

Just sharp angles, quiet ice, and the slap of sticks.

I correct his stance. Force a reset. Make him skate the same route until he gets it clean.

He doesn't whine.

He works.

After the third round, we pause at center ice, sticks resting across our knees.

Cal's breathing hard. Sweat dripping from the ends of his curls. He glances at me, eyes uncertain.

"You don't have to do this, you know," he says. "I've read all the articles. You don't really…do people."

I tap the blade of my stick against his. "Don't get used to it."

He huffs a laugh. "Why help me, then?"

I shift my weight, eyes tracking a faint scar in the glass.

"You remind me of someone," I say quietly. "And I didn't have anyone when I looked like that."

His gaze sharpens.

"Thanks," he says.

"Go another few rounds and then get home for some rest before the road trip starts tomorrow. They're tiring and can be brutal."

"Got it. Thanks again, Lasker."

I nod once and skate off the ice.

He doesn't follow right away.

Good.

He's not done yet.

I should take my own advice. Head home and get ready for a long road trip stint starting in New York and ending in Seattle.

But I haven't even caught a glimpse of her all day except for what I see in my mind's eye.

And I need to see her.

Not because I want to talk about the game.

Not because I've got something to say.

But because after practice, after Cal, after the echo of her laugh in my head while I stripped off my skates—I need to know she's real.

My feet take me in the direction of the elevators and up to the front office floor.

Thankfully, it's quiet; most of the suits cleared out a long time ago.

But her light's still on.

Her assistant isn't at her desk. The door's cracked just enough.

Yeah, I should definitely go home.

Instead, I knock once.

Her voice drifts out, low and tight. "Come in."

She's at her desk in a slim black dress, legs crossed, laptop open. Her hair's up and her heels are off.

There's a coffee cup in her hand and tension in her spine.

She looks like power.

She looks like the woman I had under me hours ago, nails in my back and breath in my mouth.

And she looks tired.

She blinks once when she sees me, like she wasn't expecting this—like maybe she figured I wouldn't follow through on all the things I said to her.

"Hey," she says, setting down the cup.

I shut the door behind me. "Hey."

Her eyes flick over me—damp hair, fresh clothes, the hoodie I yanked on in the locker room. Her mouth softens slightly.

"Practice go okay?"

"Fine."

She quirks a brow. "That it?"

I cross the room, slow steps on the hardwood floor, and stop in front of her desk.

I don't touch her.

I don't kiss her.

I just look.

And she gets it.

Because something shifts in her posture—less boss, more… Sloane.

She closes the laptop and leans back. "Lock the door."

I raise a brow, and my cock suddenly stands at attention.

And I lock the door.

She stands and walks around the desk, then stops in front of me.

Up close, I can see the tired in her eyes. The fight behind it. The crack she's keeping sealed by sheer will.

I slide a hand to her hip, palm resting just enough to anchor her. "I needed to see you."

"You're seeing me."

"Not the version with the armor on."

Her breath hitches. "It's Monday, Maddox."

I lean in, mouth near her ear. "Then give me five minutes to pretend it's not."

CHAPTER TWENTY-THREE

Sloane

I BARELY GET OUT, "MADDOX—" before he's on me.

His mouth finds mine in a hungry kiss, hands in my hair like he needs to feel all of me.

Suddenly I'm not thinking about the meeting or the board or anything but the weight of him pressing me back against my desk.

"This is a terrible idea," I murmur as he tugs the hem of my blouse free from my skirt.

"Then stop me."

I don't.

He lifts me like I weigh nothing, sets me down on the desk, and pushes my knees apart with his hips.

His mouth trails down my throat, his hand sliding under my skirt with that low growling sound I now know means he's losing control.

I grip the edge of the desk, heat curling between my legs, pulse thundering. "Someone could walk by."

"There's no one here."

His voice is a rasp as he kisses along my jaw, his fingers

already finding me beneath my panties. "You've been in my head all damn day. Couldn't think straight on the ice."

"And this is your solution?"

"No," he says, breath hot at my ear. "This is your punishment."

I bite my lip to stifle a moan as he sinks two fingers inside me, curling them just right while his thumb circles exactly where I need him.

The desk shudders beneath me. My head tips back, my breath catching, a needy sound slipping free before I can swallow it down.

"You're soaked for me," he whispers, watching my face like it's his favorite play. "And you're gonna come on my fingers before I ever get my cock out."

I dig my heels into the edge of the desk, everything inside me coiling tighter with every stroke. My hand fists in his shirt, dragging him closer until our mouths crash together again—hot, messy, and desperate.

And then I fall. Hard.

Silently, shaking, my body clenching around his fingers as I cling to him and ride it out.

Before I can even catch my breath, he's unbuckling his belt.

"Thought this wasn't a good idea," I manage, still panting.

He gives me a look that's pure trouble. "It's a fucking terrible idea."

He yanks me to the edge and drives into me in one long, hungry stroke.

I bite his shoulder to keep from crying out.

He sets a brutal rhythm, one hand over my mouth to keep me quiet, the other gripping my thigh as he pounds into me like doing so is the only way he can keep breathing.

My desk creaks. A pen rolls off and clatters to the floor.

All I can do is hold on.

He slams into me once, twice more and groans low in my ear

as he comes, shuddering against me, burying his face in my neck like he wants to live there.

We stay like that for a second—bodies tangled, breath short, hearts wild.

Then he pulls back just enough to press a kiss to my jaw.

"We've got to be more careful," I whisper, still trying to catch my breath.

He nods, brushing a hand down my thigh. "Yeah," he says softly. "We really do."

But neither of us moves for a moment.

When we finally do, there's a silence between us, but it's not uncomfortable.

Just quiet. Settled.

The kind of hush that comes after need is met, and something deeper is left behind.

I fix my skirt while Maddox buttons his pants. He grabs a tissue from the corner of my desk and wipes his hand, then catches my chin gently between his fingers, lifting my face to his.

"You okay?"

"Yeah." My voice is still a little hoarse. "You?"

His mouth quirks. "Better now that I've seen you."

I smile, but the weight of the day settles back on my shoulders.

The moment is over. The world's creeping back in.

I turn toward my desk and start rearranging the mess we made. The pen that rolled off. The folder that nearly fell open.

The ownership binder I had out before he came in.

His voice comes softer now. "How was your day?"

I hesitate.

Tell him.

You should tell him.

But the words don't come. Because once I say them, they're

real. And he already has enough pressure without taking on mine too.

I settle for a shrug as I start packing up my stuff. "Shitty. Meetings. Nothing exciting."

That's a lie. But only by omission.

Because the board meeting was a mess.

I replay it like a silent reel in my mind as I straighten the files.

Dean had that smug look on his face the entire time. He's gunning for a vote of no confidence if the team doesn't hit Q1 performance metrics.

And I already know he's talking to the legacy members behind my back.

"You don't have the experience," one of them said.

"You're gambling with the franchise," another warned.

I sat there in that glass-walled room with every credential I've ever earned stacked in front of me and still had to justify my ownership, my decisions, and Maddox's contract like I was a teenager playing dress-up with Daddy's checkbook.

They don't see me.

They never will.

"Hey." Maddox's voice cuts through the memory.

I blink and turn.

He's watching me, eyes narrowed slightly. "You sure you're okay?"

"Just tired." I force a smile. "It's been a long day."

He doesn't look convinced.

But he nods.

Then his expression softens a little, mouth curving into something close to a smile. "You free tomorrow tonight?"

My brow lifts. "You planning another desk ambush?"

He chuckles. "No sex. Just dinner. My place."

"Dinner?"

"Actual food. Conversation. You get to learn how I became this charming."

I laugh. "What's the catch?"

He shrugs. "No catch. Wednesday is the beginning of a road trip, and I just want to spend some time with you. So, you show up. We eat. We talk. That's it."

That shouldn't make my heart skip, but it does.

Because this is Maddox trying. This is him letting me in without letting me fix him first.

"I'd like that," I say quietly.

His grin turns slow and sure, then just like that, it fades a little. "I'll walk you to your car."

My smile falters. "You don't have to—"

"I want to."

I hesitate, glancing at the window. "There are cameras."

"I know." He opens the door but doesn't touch me. "I'll keep my hands to myself."

He holds the door for me, letting me go first. I school my face and even out my expression.

Because I feel like floating.

But I can't.

Not here.

We head down the hall side by side, the space between us charged in a way no one would guess.

And still, I want to reach for him.

His hand brushes close to mine once, and even though he doesn't touch me, I swear I feel it anyway—like static on skin, like the warning before a storm.

Neither of us speaks.

The elevator ride is short and silent, filled with fluorescent light and unsaid things.

When the doors open to the executive lot, he steps out first, scanning the perimeter like it's instinct. Like he always has to stay alert.

Like being seen with me would put a target on both our backs.

I lead the way across the pavement toward my car, heels echoing in the quiet.

The breeze catches my hair and flutters it against my cheek, and I feel him watching me as I tuck it behind my ear.

"Here," I say as we reach my car. I click the key fob. The lights blink. The locks chirp.

He doesn't reach for me. Doesn't lean in.

But his eyes burn into mine like he wants to.

"Wait for me here, and I'll follow you," he says, low.

"Okay."

There's a pause.

A long one.

Like we're both waiting for something neither of us can do.

The silence pulls tight around us, weighted with the kiss we don't dare have and the touch we can't risk.

I grip my purse tighter.

"I'll see you at The Apex," he says finally.

I nod. "Okay."

Another beat. His jaw tics.

"I'm looking forward to tomorrow tonight," he adds, softer now.

My chest clenches.

"Me too," I whisper.

He steps back then. Just one step. Just enough to let me go.

I open the car door and get in, hands trembling more than I'd like.

When I glance up, he's walking toward his car, but looking over his shoulder at me.

The drive home only takes ten minutes.

He follows me the whole way, headlights two cars behind like a shadow I invited.

We don't text. We don't call.

But when I park in the garage at The Apex, he's right there, pulling into his usual spot like this is normal.

Like we've done it a hundred times before.

I grab my bag and head to the elevator, pulse thudding with every step.

He doesn't rush to catch up. Just falls into step beside me like we've been walking together forever.

The elevator dings, and we step inside.

I swipe my card and press PH.

He presses seven.

A charged silence wraps around. Like there's a string pulled tight between us, vibrating with every breath I take.

We stand apart from each other, me on one side, him on the other. It's like we know if we're too close, we'll do something to get us caught.

He doesn't say anything, and I'm too aware of the fact that we're alone in a box with mirrors and secrets and nowhere to put either.

The elevator glides past the second floor, and stops at the third.

The doors slide open and Jace Rourke is on the other side.

Holy shit.

He clocks both of us immediately. His eyes flick from me to Maddox and back again.

"Evening," he says.

I manage a tight smile. "Hey, Jace."

Maddox gives him a nod. "Cap."

He steps in, earbuds out, towel slung around his neck, water bottle in hand. Judging by his shirtless chest, gym shorts and running shoes, he's headed to the fifth floor fitness center.

Pressing the fifth floor button, he just leans back against the mirrored wall, one brow raised like he's taking mental notes.

No one says anything else.

The tension shifts—less electric now, more watchful. I can

feel Maddox's posture shift, can feel Jace observing both of us like he already suspects.

The elevator stops at five.

"Have a good night," Jace says as he steps out.

The doors close.

It's just us again.

I exhale slowly, staring straight ahead. "Well, that wasn't awkward at all."

Maddox's voice is low and rough. "You handled it."

"I know, but…"

"You didn't panic either."

"No," I murmur, glancing sideways. "I'm saving that for later."

He gives the smallest smile, just a flicker.

When the doors open at his floor, he doesn't move to leave. Not yet.

His eyes find mine. "I'll see you tomorrow?"

"Looking forward to it."

He nods once, then steps into the hallway. The doors close behind him, sealing off whatever that just was.

I blow out a breathe and as I ride up to the Penthouse floor, I wonder how the hell I'm supposed to survive a date with Maddox Lasker without falling deeper.

CHAPTER TWENTY-FOUR

Maddox

I'VE FACED slap shots from guys built like brick houses and stared down sold-out crowds at the Garden, but none of that gets under my skin like waiting on her.

The steak's already on its way from Charred—medium-rare, black pepper crust, side of grilled asparagus.

I even added the damn truffle mac.

Now the place smells like sandalwood-scented candles the girl at the store swore Sloane would love, and I've rearranged the living room twice like it's gonna impress her.

I'm not even trying to get laid tonight, and somehow that makes it worse.

Because this time it's not about sex.

It's about her walking through that door and deciding to stay.

I check the time again.

She's not late. I'm just impatient.

I'm not used to this version of me—the one that gives a damn if the playlist sounds like background noise or if the lighting's too bright.

I glance at the mirrored backsplash in the kitchen and catch my reflection. The sleeves of my black henley are shoved up my forearms and my jaw's a little too tight.

I look like I'm trying not to care.

"Trying" being the operative word because I care way too damn much.

My phone buzzes on the counter.

Sloane: Be down in a few.

I exhale slowly, setting the phone face-down.

She's really coming.

Even after the board meeting she wouldn't tell me about yesterday, even after all the ways this could blow up in our faces, she's still walking into my place.

And not for sex. Just for dinner.

Which feels more dangerous.

I take one last lap through the condo, straighten a throw pillow I didn't know I had and not sure I like, and stop just as I hear her at the door.

Three knocks. Confident. Measured.

Hers.

When I open the door, my brain short-circuits.

She's in jeans that hug her legs like a second skin and a green sweater that brings out her eyes and clings in all the right places. Her hair is loose, her makeup soft, and her smile hesitant.

And fuck me, I think I fall a little harder right there.

"Hey," she says, holding up a bottle of red. "I brought wine."

"All I care about is that you're here," I say, stepping back to let her in.

A pretty pink blush stains her cheeks as she walks past me, and everything about her—the citrus and spice of her perfume, the swish of her hair, the way her eyes sweep the room like she's memorizing it—makes my pulse tick up.

I shut the door and lean against it for a second, watching her move.

"Didn't peg you for a candle guy," she says, arching a brow at the flickering votive on the counter.

"Didn't peg you for a woman who'd willingly step into a goalie's condo."

Her lips twitch. "Touché."

She walks further into my place, giving it a once-over. "Place looks good."

"I cleaned," I say.

She turns, amused. "For me?"

"No," I deadpan. "For the wine."

Her laugh spills out—light and unguarded—and it does something to me.

A reminder of that morning in her kitchen, barefoot and radiant in the aftermath of everything we didn't say.

I clear my throat. "Dinner's on the way. From Charred. Hope that's okay."

"More than okay. That mac and cheese is borderline erotic."

"Good thing I ordered it."

She flashes a smile and tucks a loose strand of hair behind her ear. "You nervous?"

I don't answer right away.

Because yeah, I fucking am.

This isn't sex. This is worse. This is her in my space with no game plan. No walls between us.

Just…here.

"Maybe," I admit. "You?"

She nods. "A little."

There's a beat of silence. Not awkward. Just full.

Then she lifts the wine bottle. "You got a corkscrew?"

"Drawer by the sink."

She moves into the kitchen like she belongs there, and I

follow. Watching her struggle with the cork for a second before I step in behind her.

"Let me."

Her fingers graze mine as she hands it over, and I feel the contact in my chest.

When I get the cork free, she holds out two glasses from the cabinet without needing direction.

I pour. She hands one back.

"Toast?" she asks, tilting her glass toward mine.

I pause.

"To doing this differently," I say.

Our glasses clink.

And for a second, her eyes soften in a way I'm not ready for.

But I don't look away.

Because she's here.

And I want to do this right.

She steps away with her wine, her eyes trailing over the far wall near the hallway. A moment later she stops.

"Is that a comic book?"

I follow her line of sight. The signed copy of *ChronoBlade #1* is mounted in a black shadow box. The ink still looks fresh under the glare of the recessed lighting.

"My cousin Griffin used to love these," she says, leaning in. "We'd buy issues from the gas station near his house and read them in the treehouse until it got dark. He was obsessed with time travel and twin storylines."

My brow lifts. "Solid taste."

"It's signed. Did you know the artist?"

My throat works around the sip of wine I just took. "Not exactly."

She glances over her shoulder. "That sounds like a story."

I shrug, but my voice roughens. "Not really. I recently bought it at auction, actually. Connor, the kid I met at the hospital visit, draws comic books and reminded me how much I loved drawing. So when I saw it come up for auction, I bought it."

Her face softens. "You draw?"

"Used to. A lot. Mostly on the road. It helped."

"Do you still have anything?"

I shake my head. "Doesn't matter."

"That's not an answer."

"It's not for anyone else to see."

"Maddox. Please."

I grit my jaw. She says my name like it's a key, like she already knows it'll unlock something I've kept locked up tight for years.

"I'm not trying to analyze you," she says gently. "I'm just… curious."

Her voice is soft but direct. And I'm shit at saying no to her.

I sigh, set down my glass, and walk to the hall closet. Pulling a small black portfolio from the top shelf, I hand it to her without opening it.

She takes it over to the table and sits down. Taking her time, she opens the zipper slow, like the contents deserve reverence.

Inside there's a few inked panels, mostly from memory. A goalie with a cracked mask. A girl with green eyes and a sharp tongue. A city that looks suspiciously like Boston and burns in the background.

She flips through carefully, not speaking at first. Just taking it in.

Finally: "Maddox…these are incredible."

I shake my head, uncomfortable. "Just something to kill time."

"No," she says, firm now. "This is storytelling. This is pain and heart and character. You ever think of doing more with it?"

"No."

Her eyes lift to mine. "You should."

I don't know what to say to that.

But when the knock comes at the door, I swear I've never been more grateful for a damn steak in my life.

"Food's here," I say, setting my wine down and moving to grab it.

Sloane zips the portfolio back up and sets it aside before following me, hovering just behind as I take the bag from the delivery guy, tip already handled.

The scent of seared steak, garlic, and truffle hits the air, and she groans.

"God, is that the filet?"

"With the black pepper crust," I say, holding the bag up like a trophy.

She grins and gestures toward the kitchen. "Let's eat before I commit a felony."

We set up at the island, plates stacked, silverware already laid out. I hand her the takeout box with her name scribbled across the top in red sharpie.

Charred always labels with care, which is the kind of detail I didn't care about before.

Now I do.

Because she notices that kind of thing.

"I love this place," she says, opening the lid and sighing in appreciation at the perfectly cooked filet and roasted asparagus. "Have you had a chance to experience it yet?"

"Not yet. But I've been looking for a replacement steakhouse since I left Boston."

"Is this a test run?"

I give her a look. "If they fuck up the mac and cheese, I'm filing a formal grievance."

Sloane chuckles and takes a sip of wine. "I'm skipped lunch, so I'm starving."

"Then dig in."

There's a comfortable silence between us and being the fuck up I am sometimes, I'm about to break it.

But now feels like the time to tell her about Boston.

The whole truth.

Not what the Freeze's spin doctors came up with.

I set my fork down and swallow hard before speaking. "You said once that I was a risk."

She looks up, fork paused halfway to her mouth.

"You were right," I add. "But not for the reason you think."

She sets her fork down. "Tell me."

I lean back on the stool and run a hand over my jaw. It's hard to start.

Harder to find words that don't come out like excuses.

"There was this rookie. Young. First year pro. Barely spoke up in the locker room, but he was fast. Smart and different."

Sloane watches me, her expression still. Open, but not pushing.

I continue. "He was gay. He hadn't officially come out, but a couple of guys overheard him talking to his partner on the phone in the locker room one day. He thought he was alone."

I take a sip of wine before continuing. "Unfortunately, one of those guys didn't keep his fucking mouth shut, and it got around. Most of us didn't care. But one guy…."

I have to stop. My blood still boils to this day about the entire situation.

Not just because it was wrong, but also because it brought back way too many thoughts that hit too close to home.

"One guy—a veteran no less—decided to make it his personal mission to break him."

Her brow furrows. "Physically?"

"Not at first. It started small. Verbal shit. Pranks. Cutting the kid's laces. Turning his gear inside out."

My hands clench into fists before I can think about it. "Then it escalated. Slashing him in practice. Elbowing him during drills. Just enough to look like bad luck if you weren't paying attention."

"Were the coaches really not paying attention?"

"Oh, they saw. But this guy was one of theirs. Legacy player. Face of the team for years. They weren't going to call it what it was."

She's quiet for a second, but I can tell her gears are turning. "What did you do?"

I exhale slowly. "At first? I told the rookie to stay away from him. Keep his head down. Just play."

She nods once, like she understands why that might've been my first instinct.

But she's still watching me closely.

"But it didn't stop," I say. "And one day I lost it. Practice had ended, and I saw him push the kid into the boards from behind. Unprovoked. Just mean. I snapped."

I can still feel the sharp echo of my skates cutting across the ice. The way my fists found that asshole's collar and slammed him into the glass.

"It turned into a full-blown fight. I didn't just throw a punch—I beat his ass. Told the team exactly what he'd been doing and dared anyone to defend it."

Sloane's face shifts. Not shock. Something closer to admiration flickering under control.

"They suspended me. Called it 'conduct unbecoming.'" My voice turns flat. "The official line was that I'd attacked a teammate and violated team code. They never investigated the reason. Never made a statement about the rookie. Just buried it. Quiet. Clean."

"And then they didn't pick up your option."

I shake my head. "Nope.

"What happened to the kid?"

I shake my head with a bitter chuckle. "They were going to keep him on. Even with all the bullying. But he asked for a trade and evidently got it. It was kept quiet too."

"And the vet?"

"Still on the team. Still getting praise."

She blinks. "Jesus. It's Joshua Leonard, isn't it?"

I take a bite of steak and nod, not trusting myself to speak.

"Ugh." She flops back in her chair. "I've always hated that guy. He's the only player in the league that my father and I agreed was the most overrated player to set foot on ice. Of course, Dean wanted him on the team last year for our inaugural year."

Dean's a fucking asshole, but I don't say that aloud.

I tilt my head. "I have to admit, a lot of things I've heard about your father haven't been positive, but that's nice to hear. My father would've sided with the prick."

She raises a brow. "Seriously?"

"Oh yeah." I pause a moment, deciding how much I want to reveal to her.

Because once I do, she may leave and never come back.

I take a chance anyway because I need her to understand.

"My father was just like Josh. A bully who loved to pick on the weak, kicking them while they're down."

When she doesn't say anything, I keep going. "On one hand, I have to thank the bastard. If I hadn't wanted to stay out of the house so much when he drank, I wouldn't be the player I am today."

I blow out a breath. "On the other hand, he also gave me his temper, and I have to fight it every day. Because when I don't— like during the fight with Josh—it costs me."

Sloane lays a hand over mine. "Hey, we all get some of our parents worst traits. But listen to me…"

She stops talking, waiting for me to look at her.

And when I do, I know I'm in way over my head with this woman. "Yeah?"

"I'm not running, Maddox."

"I'm beginning to see that."

We hold the stare for a few beats longer.

Sloane Carrington isn't like any other woman I've ever known. She's wise beyond her twenty-eight years, and that scares the shit out of me.

With her, I forget the years between us, and she makes me... *want*.

Everything. With her.

Finally, she pulls her hand away, picking up her wine glass. "Have you talked to the kid since then?"

I'm glad one of us can fucking speak. I'm having trouble finding my voice. Where the hell did that come from?

I clear my throat before I can speak. "No. Last I heard, he's overseas and playing well." I turn my head and look out the wall of windows in the living room. "You know one of the worst parts of the deal?"

"What's that?"

I look back at her, meeting her gaze. "I didn't defend the kid for a thank you. But after the incident, he refused to speak to me. Like I'd been the one to bully him."

She pursues her lips. "Do you know why?"

"Nope. And I didn't ask." I push my plate away, most of my appetite vanishing. "I thought it was better off that way, especially given the fact I'd been suspended."

We're quiet a moment before my eyes meet hers, my hands loose on the edge of the counter. "So, yeah. When people say I'm hard to work with, they're not wrong. I just don't back down when it matters. And for me, that situation mattered."

Sloane shakes her head, her voice soft but fierce. "You did the right thing. You protected someone when no one else would."

"That's not what the media said."

"You really care what they say?"

I pause. "Not until it started costing me teams. Then, yeah. It got to me."

There's a flicker of something in her eyes, but it's gone so quickly, I think I imagined it.

She gets up and crosses around the island to stand in front of me. I expect her to touch me, but she doesn't. She just looks me dead in the eye.

"Thank you for telling me." She glances toward the portfolio again before looking back at me. "And thank you for sharing your drawings with me."

I swallow, throat tight. "You still think I'm a risk?"

She lifts a shoulder. "Sure. But now I think I'm the one who should be protecting you."

A laugh huffs out of me.

She doesn't say anything at first. Just slides her fingers over mine—light, soft, no pressure to speak.

I don't deserve her comfort, but I take it anyway.

When I finally look up, she's watching me. Not with pity. Just knowing.

"You always carry that much weight around?" she asks.

"Only on good days."

She chuckles quietly and sits back down.

"So I told you a story. Time to tell me one."

She nods once. "Fair. What do you want to know?"

"That day you wrapped my shoulder, you said you skated competitively. Tell me about it."

She draws in a breath, tucks her long legs up beneath her.

"I started figure skating competitively when I was seven years old."

"You started young."

Her gaze drops to her almost empty plate. "My mother died the year before, and my father said I needed something to do. So he hired the best coach around and got me out on the ice."

When she stops to drain her wine glass, I want to reach out. I know what it's like to lose your mom as a kid, though I can't imagine being just a small child.

Before I can say anything, she continues.

"So I did as my father wanted and threw myself into skating.

By the time I hit sixteen, I was ranked top five in the southeast. Nationals. Junior Olympic qualifiers. It was my whole life."

I blink. "Seriously?"

She nods. "Dead serious. Had the routines memorized, the costumes stitched, the whole damn schedule taped to my mirror."

"So why'd you stop?" I ask, already knowing I won't like the answer.

She doesn't meet my eyes this time. "When I failed to make the Olympic team the second time, my father fired my coach and said I needed to do something I wasn't a failure at. And since I was his only child—his legacy as he always loved to remind me —that meant I went into business with him. So that was that."

My jaw tightens, and I can't help but think I'm glad I'll never have to meet the man. "And you just...quit?"

"Didn't have a choice. I buried it. Went to school, learned the business, and became who he wanted me to be."

I let the silence stretch between us, let the weight of that settle. Because I know what it's like to be shaped by someone else's hands. To carry a version of yourself around that doesn't feel like yours.

And hate every minute of it.

"You still skate?" I ask quietly.

"Sometimes." She smiles, but there's something wistful underneath. "When no one's around. Late nights at the practice rink."

Fuck.

That image hits hard—her out there under the dim lights, alone on the ice, chasing ghosts and memories.

"You ever let anyone watch?"

She shakes her head. "Never."

I don't know why that gets to me the way it does, but it does. Like she's offering me a piece of herself no one else gets.

I clear my throat. "How' bout a race?"

Her eyebrows shoot up. "You're kidding."

I shrug. "Let's see if you still got it, Carrington."

She laughs—bright and unexpected—and it punches through the quiet like sunlight.

"If you lose," I add, "you're watching *Slap Shot* with me. No complaints."

"And if you lose?" she fires back.

"I won't."

She narrows her eyes. "Cocky much?"

"Only when I'm right."

She stands and starts to clean up, but I stop her. "Leave it for now. I want to see you skate."

Her eyes are lit up, a fiery green competitive gleam in them. "Meet me at the rink. And prepare to eat ice."

When she looks like that, I'd rather eat her, but I'm the one who made the no sex rule tonight.

What the fuck was I thinking?

So, instead, I follow her out, grinning like a fucking idiot the whole way.

CHAPTER TWENTY-FIVE

Maddox

WE RIDE down in separate elevators.

After running into Jace the other day, we mutually decided it was best not to risk anymore run-ins with Vipers players or staff.

Going separately, we won't get splashed across a tabloid site, social media, or handed to the board on a silver platter.

But it doesn't stop the way my chest tightens when I watch her disappear into the other car.

Doesn't stop the way I glance at the security camera and think about ripping it down.

By the time she pulls up at the rink, I'm waiting in the parking lot.

She tosses me a grin as she approaches, keys in hand. "You ready to lose?"

I lean against the hood of my SUV, arms crossed, and let my eyes drag over her. "You sure you want to skate in those jeans? You might need something more aerodynamic to catch up when I lap you."

She snorts. "You're cocky for someone who's about to get his ego handed to him."

"I'm a goalie," I shoot back. "We're built for humiliation."

She laughs, and it's the kind that gets under my skin—light, unguarded, and real. I haven't heard her laugh like that outside a closed room.

Not around anyone but me.

She steps up to the side door and punches in a code on the keypad. The lock clicks.

The place is technically closed. But she's the owner, so "technically" doesn't apply to her.

She's the boss. This is her ice, her world.

Her name on every piece of paper I signed.

But here she is, holding the door open like this is just for us.

I follow her inside, the sharp scent of chilled air and rubber hitting me all at once. The rink is dark, echoing, and empty.

But it doesn't feel lonely.

It feels like something's about to happen.

"I've got skates in my office. Want to meet in the locker rooms or center ice?"

"Wherever you plan to undress me, princess."

She rolls her eyes with a smile. "Behave, Prince Charming. I'll be right back."

"I'll be at center ice when you get back."

I head for the locker room to get my skates, taking my time to lace up.

But I get lost in my head thinking about us because by the time I come back out, she's at center ice.

The lights are low, just the main track lighting over the ice on. No music, no noise, just the quiet hum of the refrigeration system.

And there she is, spinning slow, arms tucked close, her movement so effortless it takes my brain a second to catch up and realize she changed into leggings and a fitted hoodie.

I didn't think Sloane Carrington even owned clothes like that.

But it's not her clothes that have me staring. It's her movements.

It isn't just skill. It's muscle memory, grace, and precision. The kind of thing that doesn't come from casual practice.

It's in her bones.

She sees me, and for the first time since I've known her, she looks like someone else.

Not the owner, not the boss. Just a woman doing something she once loved.

And fuck if that doesn't level me more than anything she said tonight.

If I'm going to lose this bet, I'll at least make her work for it.

And if I'm lucky?

She'll let me stay long enough to watch her fly.

She glides my way, cheeks flushed, hair pulled back in a low braid, and something about the way she looks—comfortable, grounded, and light on her feet—makes my throat tighten.

It's the most arresting thing I've ever seen.

She looks *home* here.

"Ready to get your ass handed to you, Lasker?" she asks, stopping inches from me with a controlled spray of ice.

I arch a brow. "You mean, are you sure you can handle the humiliation?"

She just smirks. "I was landing triple lutzes when you were still learning how to tie your skates."

"Big words for someone who's about to eat my snow."

She snorts. "Please. I'm a figure skater. I don't fall. I descend."

I bark out a laugh and skate backward, giving her space. "Fine. You set the terms."

"Three laps. Full length of the rink. First one back to the blue line wins."

"And what's on the line?"

"If I win," she says, tapping her blade against the ice, "you buy me dinner again. And this time, *I* pick the movie."

"And if I win?"

"You won't."

I lift a brow. "That confident?"

"That terrified?" she tosses back.

Christ. She's having fun and it's fucking gorgeous.

We take our marks at the blue line, and she does a little bounce on her skates like it's nothing. Just a casual weeknight duel with the guy she's been riding all weekend.

"On your count," I say.

"Three…two…one—go!"

She takes off like a shot.

For a second, I keep pace easily. I'm bigger, more powerful. My strides cover ground, and I know how to cut corners like I'm guarding the net from hell itself.

But by the second turn, I start to notice something.

She's *cleaner* than me.

Every push is efficient. Her blade edges bite perfectly into the ice. She doesn't muscle her way through—she *flows*. There's no wasted movement. No effort burned on anything that doesn't matter.

By the start of lap two, she's ahead. By the end of it, she's so far in front I'm questioning my entire damn athletic career.

Lap three is just damage control.

She crosses the blue line with both arms in the air and a triumphant, breathless laugh that echoes off the walls.

I coast in behind her, panting, stunned, and grinning like an idiot.

"What—" I gesture wildly. "What the *hell* was that?"

"Told you," she says, turning toward me with flushed cheeks and bright eyes. "You're all power. No finesse."

"Did you lace your skates with rocket fuel?"

"Steroids, actually. I keep them in my bra."

I bark a laugh and double over, hands on my knees. "Jesus Christ."

She skates over and nudges me with her shoulder. "Want a tip, hotshot?"

I stand and nod, still catching my breath. "Lay it on me."

She moves closer, motioning to my skates. "Your stride's solid, but you're pushing from your heels too much. You've got to engage the toe pick—push through the ball of your foot and roll your weight across the blade. It gives you better acceleration."

I blink. "That's real advice."

"You expected me to gloat and skate away?"

"I expected a lot of things. None of which included getting humbled on home ice."

She shrugs. "You're teachable."

"Try me."

That's all it takes.

She positions herself a few feet away, demonstrating a clean push-off, then turns and has me copy her. I do, wobbly at first. She corrects my angle, adjusts my stance, then nods when I finally get it right.

"Better," she says. "Now again. With more pressure through your inside edge."

I take off and feel the difference. More speed. Cleaner glide.

When I stop, she claps.

"Gold star?" I ask, grinning.

"Yes, and lucky you, I won't make you watch a rom-com next movie night."

"Even better."

I skate back toward her and catch the way she's watching me —quietly pleased, a little surprised, and maybe just a bit proud.

"You really miss it, don't you?" I ask.

She blinks. "What?"

"The ice. Skating."

Her smile softens. "Every day."

I want to say something more. Something about how she looked like poetry out there, how I've never seen anyone own a space so effortlessly. But I don't. Not yet.

Instead, I just watch her for a minute. The way she stands so still in the middle of the rink, like the rest of the world doesn't exist here. Like it never did.

And damn if I don't fall just a little harder for her in that moment.

We're both quiet for a while.

She leans against the boards, cheeks flushed and hair coming loose from her braid, looking out at the wide-open rink like it's holding something I can't see.

"You okay?" I ask.

Sloane nods slowly, then glances my way. "I haven't skated like that in a long time."

"You looked like you never stopped."

A wry smile curves her lips. "I used to have a routine. For competitions. I could still probably skate it in my sleep."

I tilt my head. "Show me."

She laughs, startled. "It's kind of silly without music."

"Don't care. I want to see."

She hesitates. Not because she doesn't want to—because part of her *does*, and that scares her. I can see it in the way her fingers curl over the boards like she's grounding herself.

But after a second, she pushes off.

And just like that, she transforms.

Her body shifts into muscle memory, graceful and sure. No hesitation. No performance for me. Just her cutting elegant curves into the ice with speed and control that make my chest go tight.

She moves through turns, crossovers, and jumps—not big ones, but clean and intentional. Arms out, posture perfect. She

flows with a quiet rhythm only she can hear, and it's…
breathtaking.

Power and softness. Precision and heart.

It's not a show. It's a part of her.

And watching it—watching *her*—wrecks me in a way I don't
know how to explain.

She finishes at center ice with a final spin that slows into
stillness, her hands at her sides, chest rising with effort. She
doesn't look at me right away. Just breathes, letting the ghost of
music fade into silence.

I take a step onto the ice. Then another.

By the time I reach her, my throat's tight.

"You still skate like it matters," I say quietly.

Sloane lifts her eyes to mine, unsure. A little raw. "It did. For
a long time."

I reach out, brushing her hair back behind her ear, then slide
my hand around the back of her neck.

"You were incredible."

Her breath hitches and the air between us thickens, not with
tension—but with something reverent.

Deep. Unspoken.

I pull her to me, and her hands clasp my shirt when our
mouths meet.

We're slow this time, as though any other way would break
the moment we're having.

I kiss her like she's precious—because God knows she is—
and like I may never get this moment again.

She moans under me, her lips parting beneath mine, and I
take the opportunity to claim her softly, slowly.

It's the most erotic kiss I've ever had in my life.

When we pull away, our breaths come out in small puffs of
clouds around us, and I keep my hand against her cheek, feeling
the ice-cold flush in her skin and the heat rising beneath it.

Letting her know she's seen.

And that I won't forget what she just gave me.

Not ever.

The silence stretches between us as we step off the ice. Her fingers brush mine as we walk, but she doesn't grab my hand. Doesn't need to.

As we change out of our skates, the tension's already there—woven through every movement we make.

It pulses under my skin, right behind my ribs, hotter than it should be for a night skate.

"Ready to head out?" I ask.

Because while I said no sex and I'm trying hard to keep to that, I want to hold her in my bed, skin on skin.

Just to know she's real and for now, all mine.

She smiles softly, but shakes her head. "Not yet. I want to show you something."

"Oh yeah? What's that?" My voice is rough and low and the look she's giving me makes my heart pound.

But she doesn't answer.

Instead, she walks toward the far wall of the rink—one I hadn't paid much attention to before. Her heels echo faintly now that she's back in boots. There's a narrow black panel mounted beside a sleek steel door.

I watch her key in a code and press her thumb to a scanner. The red light turns green. A small screen flashes: **CAMERAS DISABLED – PRIVATE ACCESS GRANTED.**

She turns over her shoulder, eyes locking with mine.

"Follow me," she says.

The door opens, and cold air rolls out from a narrow private corridor. Concrete walls. Low lights. Silence.

I follow her.

Every footstep echoes like a countdown.

She doesn't speak. Just walks ahead with purpose, her spine straight, her chin high. Like this isn't the first time she's done this.

But it is the first time it's meant something.

At the end of the tunnel is a dark wood door with a finger-print reader and brass lettering I almost miss:

OWNER'S SUITE – AUTHORIZED PERSONNEL ONLY

She presses her thumb. The lock clicks.

And when she opens the door, I stop breathing.

Because there's no turning back after this.

Not after the way she skated. Not after what I felt watching her. Not after the look in her eyes right now.

"You sure?" I ask, voice hoarse.

She lifts her chin, eyes steady. "I wouldn't have brought you here if I wasn't."

And that's it.

That's the end of me.

CHAPTER TWENTY-SIX

Sloane

"You sure?" he asks, voice hoarse.

My stomach dips in anticipation. I lift my chin, gaze steady on him. "I wouldn't have brought you here if I wasn't."

My legs are still shaky, and my lungs are raw from the race on the ice.

Every inch of my skin is hypersensitive—awakened by adrenaline and sharpened by the fact that Maddox Lasker is looking at me like I'm the only thing on earth he hasn't conquered yet.

And he wants to.

His knuckles graze my side, the gentlest brush, but it lands like lightning. "Sloane…"

"I don't want careful," I whisper. "Not tonight."

I want to surrender to him here in my private sanctuary. The room I never let anyone see.

Not board members, not press, not even Tessa.

This is my secret, my last safe place.

And now Maddox Lasker fills the doorway, hair wild from our race, eyes blown wide with want and something darker.

Something desperate.

He steps in. Kicks the door closed with his heel. The lock slides into place, soft but final.

Then silence. A breath held between us.

Until he moves.

His hands find my hips, warm and sure, and he backs me into the room like a force of nature.

Every step erases another line I swore I'd never cross.

When his mouth crashes onto mine, it's not a kiss—it's a declaration.

He's savage as he consumes me, possessive and real.

He guides me until my ass hits the table, his body crowding mine, and I gasp when his tongue sweeps across mine exactly how I like it.

"You have no idea," he mutters into my mouth, voice shredded, "what you do to me."

But I do. Because he's doing the same thing to me.

Unraveling every stitch I've sewn into my armor.

Making me feel everything I've worked years to avoid.

His hands are everywhere—spanning my ribs, dragging down my hips, fisting the hem of my hoodie.

I tug it over my head and he growls, rough and low.

"Fuck." His gaze eats me alive. "Take the leggings off. Slowly."

My lips part. I hesitate just long enough for heat to spark in his eyes.

Then I obey.

I sway my hips as the leggings slide down my thighs until they pool at my feet, and I kick them away.

His stare lands on my pussy, and he growls. "Fuck me, Sloane. All night with no underwear? You really are trying to kill me."

I'm so turned on all I can do is exhale, every inch of exposed skin feeling like a promise he's about to collect on.

He lifts me onto the table in one fluid motion, and I wrap my legs around his waist, arms clinging tight to his shoulders.

The sound he makes as he unbuttons his pants—half groan, half growl—burns through me like fire.

"Mine," he rasps, grinding against me. "Say it."

The word is a flame in my chest. "Yours."

That single syllable destroys what little composure we have left.

He thrusts into me in one rough, hungry stroke.

My cry rips out of me, echoing off the suite walls.

"Jesus, Sloane." His forehead drops to mine, breath ragged. "So fucking tight. You were made for this. For me."

I clutch at him like a lifeline. "Don't stop."

"I have no plans to ever stop."

His thrusts are brutal. Deliberate.

Every inch of him drives into me like he's trying to brand me from the inside out.

His mouth is everywhere—my jaw, my neck, my collarbone. His words fall hot and filthy in my ear, every one of them a sin I want to commit again and again.

"You like being fucked in your private little tower, don't you princess?"

"Yes," I gasp. "Yes."

"Bet you've never let anyone up here. Never let anyone see you like this. But me?" His teeth graze my throat. "I get everything."

"Yes, yes. Only you. Only ever you."

He's seeing the version of me I hide from the world. The one who wants to be held, claimed.

Wanted without conditions.

My orgasm crashes into me like a tidal wave. My legs tremble, my hands clawing down his back as I ride it out.

He grabs my wrists and pins them over my head with one

hand, the other gripping my thigh as he keeps thrusting, harder now, more erratic.

The table creaks beneath us, but I don't care. I want more. I want all of him—this heat, this power, this desperate claiming.

Without warning, he pulls out. I cry out at the loss, but he spins me fast and rough, bending me over the back of the couch before I can breathe.

"Hands flat," he growls, voice a snarl at my ear. "Back arched. Ass up. You wanna be mine? Then show me."

My palms brace on the couch cushion, heart slamming in my chest. I feel his hand whisper down the curve of my spine, fingers splaying across my hips like he owns them.

And he does.

"You think I haven't dreamed about taking you like this?" he rasps. "Watching you fall apart for me. Seeing what you look like bent over the throne you rule from."

He thrusts into me again—deeper this time, angle brutal, possession written in every stroke.

"Fuck," I gasp, head dropping forward. "Maddox…God you feel so good."

"Say it again." His palm smacks my ass, a sharp bite that makes me whimper and my second orgasm climb higher. "Say who you belong to."

"You," I choke out. "I'm all yours."

"That's right." His hand fists in my hair, tugging just enough to make me feel it. "My smart-mouth boss. My ice queen. My fucking addiction."

The rhythm builds. Maddox pounds into me, breath ragged, skin slapping against skin, filthy praise pouring from his lips like a litany.

"So wet for me. So fucking tight. I could stay buried in you all night and still want more."

I'm already there—right at the edge, heat coiled tight in my belly. His hand slips between my thighs, fingers finding that spot, rubbing fast and relentless.

"You gonna come again for me, Sloane? Gonna soak my cock while I ruin you?"

I break.

The orgasm tears through me like fire, shaking every inch of my body. My moan rips out of me, half sob, half plea.

Maddox thrusts twice more, then spills into me with a hoarse shout, hips grinding deep like he never wants to leave.

For a moment, there's nothing but the sound of our ragged breathing.

We collapse onto the couch in a tangle of limbs, hearts pounding, skin damp. His arm bands tight around my waist and anchors me against the broad wall of his chest.

For the first time in years, I feel…safe. Not alone.

His breath slows against my hair. I let my eyes drift shut, lulled by the steady thud of his heart.

But I can't let myself fall too far.

I never could.

So I speak.

"I have a question for you. Something I've been wondering."

His smile is faint but there. "Okay, shoot."

"At the hospital visit, why were you hesitant at first?" I ask softly. "With the kids. You looked like you wanted to run."

His body stiffens just enough to notice.

"Because I haven't had any role models in my life on how to act with kids," he says, voice quiet but steady. "I mean, I had my mom for a while, but how to act like a man but gentle with little ones? I have no idea."

Emotion swells in my throat.

"I didn't want to walk in there and have one of them see me like I saw my dad when I was seven. I know I got my temper from him, but thankfully I didn't get his addiction. But still, I just don't know how to be. All I know is that I didn't want to be that."

"But you weren't," I whisper. "You weren't that guy."

"No," he says. "Because of you."

He presses a kiss to my temple.

And that's when it happens.

The shift I've been fighting finally takes hold.

I realize I'm in love with him.

Not just attracted. Not just infatuated.

In love.

It hits with full force, cracking open the hollow space inside my chest where nothing has lived for years. I feel it in every part of me—the weight of it, the terror of it, the inevitability.

And I know.

It can't work.

We've let ourselves blur the lines. We've been reckless with our hearts and our reputations.

And now I'm lying here in the wreckage, listening to the steady rhythm of his heart while mine breaks quietly inside my ribs.

He shifts beside me, completely unaware. Still holding me like I'm something precious.

I let my eyes close again, committing the moment to memory.

Because I know what comes next.

The world outside will come for us.

And I'll be the one who opens the door.

We weren't careful. Not with each other. Not with the world outside these walls.

And if the world saw us tonight… there will be no taking this back.

CHAPTER TWENTY-SEVEN

Maddox

THE HOTEL CEILING has thirty-six tiny holes in the acoustic tile directly above my bed.

I've counted them twice.

Once after we landed, once after the game.

It's past midnight now, and the room's too quiet. Too clean. Too cold in a way that has nothing to do with the thermostat.

The blackout curtains don't block enough city noise. The bed's too soft. The air smells like lemon disinfectant and recycled air, not bergamot and leather and something sharp like a warning.

Not like her.

I scrub a hand down my face and shift on the mattress, shoulder twinging from the hit I took in the second period.

Doesn't matter.

The ache I feel isn't in the muscle.

It's under the skin.

Between being on the road and sneaking around, I haven't heard her voice or touched her skin since I kissed her goodbye seventy-two hours ago.

But I can still taste her in my mouth, feel the imprint of her thighs around my waist, the drag of her nails down my back when I pushed into her like I was starving.

And I was.

I still am.

Fuck, I thought that night in the suite would burn it out of me. Instead, it lit something I can't put out.

I roll onto my side and grab my phone off the nightstand. No new texts. No missed calls. No headlines—yet.

But that doesn't mean anything.

And we weren't careful.

Center ice. Her in my arms. Mouths locked, like we were alone in the world.

And then her hand pulling mine into the tunnel. Her voice in the dark. That kiss that stripped me bare.

We were reckless. Bold. Feral.

And I'd do it all over again.

But now, lying here alone, surrounded by things that aren't hers, I can't stop thinking about the cost.

If someone saw us.

If someone talked.

If this whole thing explodes.

What happens to her then?

I thumb over her name in my phone. Just her first name. No last name. No emojis. No photo. Just *Sloane*.

I don't text.

I don't call.

Instead, I toss the phone back on the nightstand and stare up at the ceiling again.

Thirty-six holes. Perfectly spaced. Probably machine-punched.

She'd hate them.

I turn my head to the right. My duffel bag sits in the chair, half-zipped. On top of the pile is the gray hoodie I shoved in last-minute before we left.

The one she wore once.

I drag it toward me like a fucking lunatic and bury my face in the cotton. It still smells faintly like her shampoo.

Like lavender and ambition and late-night sin.

I let myself hold it there, just for a minute.

Just long enough to remember what it felt like to be wanted by someone who knows what it costs.

Ice time on the road always feels like borrowed space. Neutral walls, neutral lines, no logo under your blades. Nothing to ground you.

You have to make your own edge.

Which works fine for me.

I've been edge and nothing else for years.

I hit the ice first, do my usual warmup drills, and let my body take over while my head tries to level out.

It doesn't. The glide's off. The rhythm's wrong. My balance is fine, but something inside feels...misaligned.

Sloane's voice is still in my head. Her nails still on my back. The taste of her still in my goddamn mouth.

"You always skate like a psychopath, or just today?"

Finn. Loud as hell, gliding up beside me like he owns the rink.

"Don't you have some chaos to go cause elsewhere?" I mutter.

He grins. "I am the chaos."

I cut away from him, chasing speed. If I can't get her out of my head, maybe I can at least burn her out of my muscles.

After drills, we head to the weight room. The usual noise— jokes, shit talking, music that's too loud.

I towel off, neck still damp, and grab a bottle of water. That's when I feel it.

The rookie shadow.

Cal's not obvious about it. He's not clingy. Doesn't ask questions. He just…watches. Studies.

I catch him mid-set, lifting clean, form tight, eyes flicking to me between reps.

I take a swig of water and nod at his stance. "You keep your knees locked like that, you're gonna blow' em by midseason."

He pauses. Adjusts. "Thanks."

He doesn't say more. Doesn't puff up or over-apologize like some wide-eyed rookie looking for approval.

It's not the first time he's hovered nearby, either. He's quiet. Steady. Like he's trying to download everything just by standing close enough.

Later, in the locker room, the vets are laying into him. Nothing brutal. Just the usual quips.

"You still bringing your mom's casserole to team dinners?" Finn throws out.

Riley smirks. "Bet he's got his name stitched in his jockstrap."

"Better stitched than scratched," Cal fires back, voice deadpan.

That earns a few laughs. Finn claps him on the back.

The kid doesn't flinch. Doesn't laugh too hard either. He just takes it. Rides it out.

I like that.

There's something there.

"Don't let' em smell blood," I tell him as I drop to the bench next to him, unwrapping tape from my wrist. "If they do, they'll start circling and they won't stop."

He nods slowly, chewing on that. "So what—you just take the hits and pretend you like it?"

I shrug. "You skate through it. You hit back later. On the ice."

He's quiet a second, then says, "Guess that means I've gotta skate hard enough they choke on it."

It's not cocky. Not clean, either. But it's got teeth.

I glance sideways at him. Cal's watching me again, but not like he wants to be me. Like he wants to *understand* me.

And that unsettles me more than I care to admit.

The hotel lounge is too damn bright. Overhead lights buzzing, TV blaring some late-night highlight reel. Half the team's spread out on couches and barstools, nursing recovery shakes or picking at overpriced snacks from the counter.

I've got my back to the wall, legs stretched out, hoodie pulled over my head like I'm off-limits. Doesn't stop them.

Riley drops onto the armrest beside me, shaking a granola bar in my face. "You gonna stare at your phone all night or finally admit you're in your feelings?"

I don't look up. "Fuck off."

Finn pipes up from the couch, sprawled across it like a golden retriever in a frat house. "Pretty sure he's writing poetry in his Notes app. Real deep stuff."

He clutches his chest dramatically. *"Her eyes were like skates on fresh ice…her touch, a penalty I'd take twice."*

Laughter rolls across the room.

I stay silent. Let them have it.

Because the worst part? They're not entirely wrong.

My phone's in my hand. Again.

Sloane hasn't texted.

And I sure as hell haven't either.

Which is smart. Professional. Clean.

But it fucking sucks.

Across the room, Cal's sitting at the high-top table, protein bar in one hand, water in the other. He's not laughing with the others. Not chiming in.

He's watching me again.

Not with judgment. Not with curiosity either. Just…focus. Like he's learning the game off the ice too.

I let my head fall back against the wall, eyes closed, jaw tight.

Kid doesn't know what he's seeing.

But he's seeing it.

I should head up to my room, but for once in my career, I'd rather be around my teammates, even if it means they make me crazy.

I'd rather be with them than be alone. And I don't quite know what to do with that.

After a while, the room thins out.

Beau's phone buzzes, and when he sees the name, his whole face softens. "Hey, my baby girl," he says under his breath, already standing.

He throws a casual wave over his shoulder as he heads for the hallway, smile still tugging at his mouth.

Thankfully Riley and Finn—arguing over some player's stats —decide to hit the weight room again, the silence in their wake like a rumble.

Logan and Eli peel off next, quiet and efficient, mid-conversation about zone entries and defensive breakdowns.

Jace lingers a little longer, throwing me a sharp look like he wants to say something, then thinks better of it and leaves without a word.

That just leaves Cal.

He finishes the last bite of his protein bar, crumples the wrapper, and drops it into the trash. Then he walks over—not close, but just enough that I can't ignore it.

"You good?" he asks.

It's not nosy. Just simple. Direct. Like he actually gives a shit.

I nod. "Fine."

Cal doesn't move. Doesn't push. Just watches me for a second longer, then says, "You've been different lately. Quieter."

I arch a brow. "That your subtle way of saying I'm off my game?"

"No." He shakes his head. "You've been sharp in net. Just… different. Like something's shifted."

I lean back against the couch, eyeing him. "You ever think maybe the shift's just settling in?"

He shrugs. "Maybe. Or maybe it's something else."

There's a pause, just long enough to make me feel like he's trying to read me.

"You don't talk much," I say. "Most rookies won't shut up."

He smiles faintly. "I talk when it matters."

That actually earns a quiet laugh from me. "Smart."

Cal nods again, then glances toward the hallway. "Night, Lasker."

"Hey."

He turns back.

"Don't let them break you," I say. "The noise, the pressure, the bullshit. You keep skating your game, and you'll last."

He holds my gaze. "I know. Thanks."

And just like that, he's gone.

I sit there a while longer. Long after the last joke fades, the last screen clicks off, and the lounge settles into silence.

By the time I make it back to my room, my legs are heavy, and my shoulder's already starting to stiffen.

I grab an ice pack from the mini freezer, a fresh towel and drop it on the ache, before crashing back against the mattress like the night's been waiting to cave in around me.

After a while, the ice pack's gone warm against my shoulder, sweat beading where it's soaked through the towel. I should get up and swap it.

Move. Shower. Sleep. Something.

But I don't.

I lie there in the dark, one arm draped across my chest, staring at the faint green glow of the clock on the nightstand.

1:47 a.m.

I scroll through my phone. Again.

No messages.

No headlines.

No pictures.

But I feel it.

That night is still under my skin.

The look in her eyes when I touched her like she was mine. The way she let me in—truly in—not just to her body, but her space.

That suite. That hidden part of her world no one else gets to see.

She let me see it.

And fuck if it didn't undo me.

I swipe to her contact. Just her name, still sitting there.

She's probably asleep.

Or working. Or locked behind whatever steel-plated walls she's built back up since I left.

She's not mine. Not really.

But it felt like she was.

And that's the problem.

I drop the phone on my chest and close my eyes.

And then, without warning, Cal's face flashes in my head.

That quiet way he watches. That steady presence. The way he didn't laugh when the others did.

He's twenty-four. Barely out of college. He has no idea what he's walking into every night. But he's already learning. Watching me like I'm someone worth mirroring.

And that—

That might scare me more than anything.

Because I'm not built to be followed.

I'm built to survive.

But now I've got a rookie watching my every move, and a woman I can't stop wanting—even if wanting her might burn the whole damn thing down.

I drag the towel off my shoulder and turn onto my side, staring at nothing.

I don't know how to be what either of them needs.

But I know this much:

I'll move heaven and earth not to let either of them down.

CHAPTER TWENTY-EIGHT

Sloane

My HEEL TAPS once beneath the boardroom table, a soft click only I can hear.

The screen at the end of the room shows a clean spread of stats and projections. Attendance is up. Social engagement is up. Even merchandise sales have ticked higher since the season opener.

And still—

Still, I can feel the way they're looking at me.

Dean, of course, is seated at the other end of the table, elbows on the arms of his chair, fingers steepled like he's running this meeting instead of me.

The other board members hover in degrees of silence and deference, some flipping through the printed decks in front of them, others pretending to follow the numbers on the screen.

But Dean doesn't pretend. Dean waits.

"I'd like to shift into community engagement next," I say, letting my voice slice clean through the room. "The numbers are in from the October activation series, and response has been stronger than projected. Midtown skate clinics were at full capacity. We're seeing strong social traction on both Instagram and TikTok. Sponsors are happy."

I tap the remote. The screen changes again, now a clean mockup of the new campaign.

"For December, we'll roll out the Vipers Holiday Drive. We're partnering with Hope & Home Atlanta to collect toys for underserved kids across North Georgia. Players will be present at the pickup event. We'll be hosting it here—on home ice, post-practice, open to the public. PR will hit next week. Charitable sponsorships are already in review."

A couple nods around the table. A few murmurs of approval.

Dean, of course, stays silent. Until he doesn't.

"And the players are all confirmed?" he asks casually, eyes not on the deck but on me. "No pushback on appearances?"

"No," I say. "Attendance is required, barring injury or medical restriction."

"And Lasker?"

The question drops like a stone in the middle of the table.

I don't blink. "He'll be there."

Dean lifts one eyebrow. "How's he doing?"

It's a simple question. Measured. Professional.

But the pause that hangs after it isn't.

"He's contributing," I answer smoothly. "He's top five in save percentage across the conference. Locker room reports are neutral to positive. He's stayed out of the penalty spotlight."

I hear myself say it—clinical, practiced, bulletproof—but my pulse still kicks once, hard.

Because I know what Dean's doing.

He's not asking about stats.

He's poking the bruise. Watching for the flinch.

"He's an expensive gamble," Dean says mildly, flipping to the next page of the printout. "We'll want to make sure the optics hold, especially with press invitations going out for the toy drive. Cameras will be everywhere. Social interns tend to wander."

"I'm aware," I say evenly. "We're monitoring optics closely."

Dean smiles. Thin.

Another board member clears her throat. "Sloane, while we're on the subject of performance…"

Here it is. The pivot.

"We'd like to reiterate what was outlined in the ownership continuity clause."

I nod once. "Of course."

Dean picks it up like they rehearsed it. "The board expects a postseason berth this year—and next. No exceptions."

I anchor my hand against the table and force my body to stay still.

"We've seen improvement," another member adds quickly, trying to soften the blow. "But given the size of the expansion investment and the shift in ownership, we need back-to-back playoff appearances to justify long-term retention."

Retention.

Like I'm a player. A gamble.

"Let me be clear," Dean says, voice smoother now. "We all want you to succeed, Sloane. But this is still a business. And results matter."

There it is.

Not a warning.

A line in the ice.

I incline my head. "Understood."

The rest of the meeting rolls forward—updates from legal, some financial notes from the interim CFO, Tessa piping in with a few calendar reminders.

But I barely register any of it.

Because I can still feel Dean's words clinging to my skin.

Lasker.

Optics.

Playoffs.

Gamble.

I sit straighter. Tighter. My posture textbook perfect. My face unreadable.

I give them nothing.

Not my nerves. Not my memories.

Not the press of Maddox's mouth against mine in the darkened suite three nights ago.

I'm Sloane Carrington.

I own this team.

I built this empire from the ashes of a man who never wanted me to hold the torch.

And I will not burn for wanting something that was never in the rulebook to begin with.

I should be asleep.

Instead, I'm curled on the couch, bourbon in hand, hair unpinned, a knit throw blanket slouched around my bare legs. The only light in the room comes from the city outside—soft amber wash from the streetlights below, and the occasional blink of a plane overhead.

The board packet sits unopened on the coffee table. My laptop's in sleep mode. My second glass of bourbon is almost gone.

And Maddox's name is still sitting at the top of my screen.

I haven't called him in three days.

We agreed—without saying it—that space was safer. That silence meant strength.

And yet...

My thumb hovers over his name.

I shouldn't.

But I do.

The call connects before I can second-guess it.

He answers after the first ring, voice low, rough with sleep. "Hey."

That one word kicks something loose in my chest.

"Hey," I whisper back, eyes falling shut as I sink deeper into the couch.

There's a beat of silence. Then a slow inhale on his end, like he already knows where this is going.

"You callin' me this late for a reason?" he asks, voice dipping.

"I needed to hear you," I say. Truth, laid bare.

He groans, soft and guttural. "Fuck, Sloane. You can't say shit like that when I'm a thousand miles away."

My breath catches.

"What are you wearing?" he asks.

I glance down. "A robe."

"That's not an answer."

I swallow. "Nothing under it."

"Jesus." His voice fractures, and I feel it—like heat through the phone. "You touching yourself yet?"

"No."

"Do it."

I shift under the blanket, nerves fraying. "Maddox—"

"Do it," he growls again, command tight. "You called me. Let me take care of you."

My hand slides beneath the robe, fingers brushing bare skin, the sound of his voice already lighting me up.

"That's it," he breathes. "Nice and slow. I want you thinking about my mouth on you. About the way I'd drag my tongue down your body, make you beg before I let you come."

A sound slips out of me, soft and desperate.

He groans again, but it's different now—raw, strained. "Fuck, I'm hard just thinking about you."

There's a rustle on his end. The unmistakable shift of sheets. A breathless curse.

"Maddox?"

"I'm stroking my cock, baby," he says, low and filthy. "Thinking about how sweet you tasted. How fucking tight your cunt is around me."

I squeeze my thighs together, breath trembling. "Tell me."

"I'd have you under me again, spread out, shaking. My mouth on your pussy, my fingers deep inside you. I'd keep you there—right on the edge—until you scream."

My fingers move faster, hips lifting.

"You close?" I whisper.

"Yeah," he grits out. "Touch yourself harder, Sloane. Let me hear you fall apart."

"Maddox—"

"God, I want you under me," he pants. "Want to fuck you so deep you forget every damn boardroom and stat sheet. I want you messy. Mine."

The orgasm takes me like a riptide, sudden and hard. My breath catches on a moan, head thrown back, thighs trembling as his voice drives me over.

He lets out a sharp gasp—low, broken, desperate.

"Jesus…Fuck," he groans. "You should've seen how fast I came, princess. You wreck me."

Silence stretches as we both catch our breath. The only sound is the soft hum of the city around me and the ragged cadence of our breathing.

Then his voice comes again, quieter this time. Unsteady.

"You ever think about what this could've been if we weren't who we are?"

The question scrapes across my chest like broken glass.

"I try not to," I whisper.

"Yeah," he says. "Me too."

But he doesn't stop. Like something in him is cracking wide open in the dark.

"You don't leave my head, Sloane. Even when I want you to.

You're just…there. Embedded. Like you rewired something in me and now I don't know how to turn it off."

My fingers press to my lips, holding in everything I want to say.

I close my eyes, throat thick.

"I don't know what the fuck I'm doing," he admits. "I don't know how to do this right. But I know I don't want to be just a mistake you regret."

The silence after that is crushing.

So I give him the only thing I can. The one sure and true thing I know when it comes to Maddox.

"You've never been a mistake."

It's not everything he needs. Not even close.

But it's all I have tonight.

"You've still got another day on the road," I say finally.

"Yeah."

"And then a long home stretch before Thanksgiving. And then the toy drive party."

"You want to talk about work now? After what I just said to you?"

I flinch at the bitter disdain in his voice.

Sitting up a little straighter, I adjust the blanket over my legs. My heart pounds, but not for the same reasons it did a minute ago.

"I should go."

"Sloane—"

"Maddox, I can't do this right now."

"Do what exactly?"

"Have this conversation. About us. Look, I shouldn't have called."

His silence is louder than a scream. I can practically feel him putting those walls back up through the phone.

"Good night, Sloane."

I close my eyes against tears that threaten to spill over. He doesn't call me princess and as much as I hated it at first, I've come to treasure it now.

But I can't tell him that now. It won't look genuine. So I respond the only way I can.

"Good night, Maddox."

My phone screen goes dark, and I toss it on the floor.

The silence feels heavier now. My body's still humming from the orgasm, but the end of that conversation left my chest too tight to breathe easy.

This was supposed to be about control. About owning the risk.

But I feel more exposed than ever.

I stare out the window for a long time, my bourbon empty, my phone dark.

This thing between us isn't just dangerous. It's unsustainable.

The woman who never loses is about to lose it all.

CHAPTER TWENTY-NINE

Maddox

PRACTICE ENDS with a clatter of sticks and a whoop loud enough to rattle my skull.

I yank off my helmet and roll my shoulder, the deep ache in the joint pulsing like a bastard.

Ice isn't helping much lately, not when I've been logging thirty-plus saves a night and pretending I'm not one bad hit away from being on the injured list.

Still, we're winning more than losing, and that means everyone's cocky, loud.

Buzzing on the high of back-to-back road victories and the promise of heading home tomorrow with a near perfect October record.

But right now?

If the Vipers were a kindergarten classroom, I'd be the substitute with a concussion and no lesson plan.

Riley's halfway out of his pads, giving Cal shit about some rookie mistake he didn't actually make. Cal takes it like a champ, even fires back with a dry one-liner that gets a laugh. Kid's learning—on the ice and off.

Eli and Logan are off to the side, heads close, talking

low. Game strategy or family stuff, hard to say with those two. Eli's got that look again, the one he wears when he's thinking too hard. Logan's the only one who can pull him out of it.

Beau's gone with one of the coaches to look at some film before tonight's game. Something about needing his eagle eye for the opposing team's plays.

And Jace?

Jace leans on his stick near the boards, watching the chaos like a war-weary general. No helmet, just that permanent calm he wears like armor.

He doesn't say much, but he doesn't have to. One look from him and half the guys pipe down without knowing why.

I nod at him as I pass. He nods back. Nothing said.

Just one of those days where the ice doesn't feel like work.

Riley flings his helmet into the net and yells, "Who's got two assists, one flawless faceoff, and a Tinder date lined up for tonight after the game?"

"Yo mama?" Finn fires back.

"She's a lovely woman," Riley deadpans. "You should be so lucky."

Finn flips him off and then immediately takes a puck to the skate from Cal, who winces and speeds over, hands up in surrender.

"Shit, sorry, man! I was aiming for the boards, I swear—"

Finn glares. "You calling me a board now?"

Cal's face flushes. "No! I just, uh. Momentum."

He glances over at me like I might offer a lifeline. I don't.

But I don't let him flounder either.

"Next time, aim with your stick. Not your hopes and dreams."

Cal grins sheepishly, cheeks still pink. "Yes, sir."

I roll my eyes. "Don't call me sir. Makes me feel like I should be collecting retirement benefits."

I stretch one last time, pop my neck, and skate toward the bench to unclip my pads.

Cal skates up beside me, helmet pushed back, cheeks still red from the Finn mishap. He looks like he's trying to summon courage.

"Hey," he says, voice a little higher than usual. "Can I ask you something?"

I side-eye him while unclipping my chest pad. "You just did."

He gives a tight laugh. "Right. Okay, well…real question."

I nod once, waiting.

"How do you, uh—how do you stay so calm out there? Like, when guys start screwing around. Doesn't it mess with your focus?"

I pull my glove off and flex my fingers, shoulder twinging.

"It used to," I admit. "Now I just expect it. Anticipate the noise. Tune it out."

He nods like he's memorizing every syllable. "That's hard."

"Yeah. So's keeping your stick on the ice. Try that next time instead of punting pucks into people."

His mouth opens. Closes. Then he laughs. "Got it."

I sling my gloves over my shoulder and start for the tunnel.

He calls after me. "Hey—seriously, though. Thanks."

I don't turn around. Just lift a hand in acknowledgment as I walk off.

Let him earn the rest of it.

I had just enough time to shower and change before returning to the rink for a community outreach event. And when I get there, the rink's gone full circus.

Kids are on the ice, sponsors mill around, and local press snap shots for the paper.

Most of the team's kept it together. Signed jerseys, posed for photos, did the good citizen act. Now we're standing at the mouth of the tunnel waiting to see where else we're needed.

But not Finn.

He's going the extra mile by having the Zamboni drive him around the rink. Standing on the back of the machine, he's holding court, waving like a homecoming king on a parade float and tossing candy to the kids he got from God knows where.

He's still in half gear—jersey untucked, shorts hanging too low, mouth moving too fast

Then it happens.

He turns to wave at someone, and his waistband snags on a metal piece on the back of the Zamboni. There's a rip and then all hell breaks loose.

His ass is out on full display for all eyeballs in the rink to see.

Worse, he's about to have a dick slip with his boxers caught low, jock strap barely hanging on, and enough thigh to ruin someone's childhood.

Thankfully, he's fast enough to keep from showing the family jewels.

But the damage is done.

A collective gasp echoes from the boards. One of the kids shrieks with laughter.

Phones are already out.

I close my eyes. "You've got to be fucking kidding me."

Riley nearly chokes on his water. "Tell me that just happened."

"Oh, it happened," Logan mutters, rubbing his temple like he's aging in real time.

Jace walks up beside me, gaze flat. "That gonna hit socials before or after PR calls in sick?"

We watch as Finn scrambles to yank his shorts up, laughing like it's the best joke of the year.

"I swear to God," I mutter, "he's proud of it."

Cal, trying not to laugh, leans in. "Is this… normal?"

"No," I say flatly. "This is Finn."

A photographer cackles. One of the interns turns green.

And just like that, we're trending.

All I can think is that Sloane is going to lose her shit when this lands on her desk.

And wonder whether or not I should give her a heads-up.

Last night she said she couldn't do this right now, whatever the fuck that means. So I've let her be.

But would calling her about Finn be a professional courtesy or a boyfriend thing to do?

Shit, I don't know what to do.

Before I can decide, the event coordinators shut it all down real quick after the incident and we head back to the locker room.

And it's nothing but fucking chaos when we get there.

Finn's off somewhere basking in his accidental OnlyFans debut. Riley's running post-game commentary like he's on a damn podcast. Cal's trying not to laugh but failing. Logan and Eli have dipped already.

Across the room, Jace leans against the brick wall, calm and unreadable.

He doesn't speak until the noise thins out, until the air starts to settle.

"Think she'll suspend him?"

I glance up. "For the accidental nudity or the pride in the aftermath?"

His mouth tics at the corner. "You know it's not the video that'll piss her off."

I raise a brow. "What, then?"

"That it happened on the road." He pauses. "When you're not there."

That flickers something in my chest. I cover it with a shrug. "I'm not the captain."

"Doesn't matter. You're the anchor."

I snort. "Pretty sure I'm just the goalie."

He doesn't blink. "You're the reason the ship doesn't capsize. She knows that. Everyone knows that."

There's something too careful in his tone. Something behind it.

I narrow my eyes. "What are you really saying?"

"Look, I don't care what's going on with you and Carrington. Not my business."

The silence crackles between us.

"I've seen a lot of shit in this league. Seen guys throw careers away because they forgot which part of the world was watching."

"Nothing's happening," I say, voice even.

But I say it a little too quickly.

He gives me a look. Not judgmental, just steady. Unshakable.

"I'm not gonna say a word," he says quietly. "But if there is something? Be smart. You've worked too hard to build this comeback. Don't hand it over for free."

That lands like a body check I didn't see coming.

I want to argue. To tell him he's wrong. That it's not what he thinks.

But the worst part is—he's not wrong. Not really.

Jace pushes off the wall. "Just be careful, Lasker," he mutters. "Some lines don't come with second chances."

Then he walks away.

And I'm left staring at the empty bench across from mine, my mind spinning with every possibility I thought I had under control.

CHAPTER THIRTY

Sloane

THE FIRST THING I notice is the silence.

Not the usual kind—the focused, caffeinated hum of a professional sports franchise spinning up for another day. This is the other kind.

The dangerous kind.

The kind that smells like smoke before the fire even touches your skin.

Tessa's already standing at my office door when I round the corner.

Still in her coat. Bag slung over one shoulder. Hair pulled back in a severe bun, like she didn't even pause at her desk.

She holds a tablet in both hands like it's radioactive.

Not a word. Just lifts it and taps the screen.

The video starts playing before I can ask.

And then I see it.

Finn.

Waving from the back of a fucking Zamboni like he's in the damn Macy's Parade. Jersey untucked. Shorts hanging low.

He turns to throw candy—and his waistband catches.

Rips.

And just like that, the entire arena gets a clear full-screen shot of Finn McCade's ass.

Boxers sliding. Jock strap clinging for dear life. One bounce away from a dick slip and a lawsuit.

My jaw doesn't clench.

My expression doesn't change.

Not even a blink.

I reach out, take the tablet from Tessa, and tap to pause the video.

Once is enough.

I hand it back.

"Get rid of that."

Her voice is low. "It's already viral. X, TikTok, IG, Reddit. Buzzfeed's got a meme up that says *'Finn-tervention Needed.'*"

I nod once.

I don't ask who was supposed to be watching him. I don't ask why no one stopped it. I don't ask why my phone wasn't ringing off the hook two hours ago.

I say the only thing that matters.

"Get PR, comms, legal, Dean, and security."

Tessa's already two steps ahead. "They're on your calendar. War room will be ready in twenty minutes."

I finally exhale. "You really do love me."

She hands over the coffee. Black. Extra strong.

I take a sip, then check my phone out of habit.

Nothing.

No text. No warning.

Just silence.

The kind that isn't neutral—it's intentional.

And that? That burns more than the video ever could.

I stare down at the screen, thumb hovering like maybe if I tap it again, something will change.

That the name I want to see will light up.

That the man who touched my body like a prayer and kissed me like a fucking war would bother to say something.

But no.

He stayed quiet.

He let me wake up to this—with cameras and chaos and headlines on fire—and didn't even send a warning shot.

Not even a single damn word.

But what did I expect? The last time we talked two days ago, he made me come, made himself vulnerable, and then I told him I couldn't do this right now.

What the fuck did I even mean by that?

I tuck the phone away like it doesn't matter.

Like it's not a fresh crack in a foundation I already knew better than to build.

Then I straighten my spine, square my shoulders, and take another sip of the coffee that won't fix any of this.

Time for damage control.

Dean strides into the room like he's auditioning for a roast special. He's holding a tablet and grinning like the damn Joker.

"Do we fine him for public indecency," he says dryly, "or send a thank-you note to Buzzfeed for the free marketing?"

I don't look up. Just keep reading the internal comms thread on my phone. The messages are coming in too fast to track. Sponsors, media, community partners.

Everyone wants to know what the hell just happened at a youth skate on the road.

Join the damn club.

Tessa's already booted up the smart board. PR, Legal, and Comms are seated, watching me like they expect me to detonate.

I don't.

Instead, I tap the screen and pull up the trending clips.

Finn, waving like a parade clown. The snag, the rip, the horrifying near slip. The viral caption underneath: "#Zamboner".

My jaw tics. I say nothing.

PR clears her throat. "We suggest a soft-touch response. Keep it light. Make it a 'boys-will-be-boys' moment without saying those words. Position Finn as the lovable goof. Public tends to be forgiving when we give them permission to laugh."

Dean leans back in his chair like it's a beach lounger. "God bless the idiot brand."

Legal jumps in. "We can't hit him too hard or it raises questions about uniform policy and equipment liability. The incident happened at a team-sanctioned event with minors present, but technically there was no exposure. The boxers stayed on."

"For the most part," Dean mutters.

I raise a hand. The room goes still.

"Here's what we're doing," I say. "We draft a three-line statement. Emphasize it was an unfortunate wardrobe malfunction during a community event. Add that we're reviewing internal protocol to ensure it doesn't happen again. Full stop."

PR nods, already typing.

"Internally," I continue, "he's on a leash. No media, no side interviews, no solo events. He's glued to Logan or Eli for the next month. Every sponsor appearance, every youth partnership, every fucking breakfast fundraiser—we own his calendar."

Tessa slides something across the table. A sticky note in her handwriting.

> FAN FOOTAGE. MADDOX IN THE BACKGROUND.
> LOOKS FURIOUS.

I don't react. Not visibly. I fold the note in half and place it under my phone.

Dean notices. Of course he does.

"What?" he says, eyes narrowing. "Lasker didn't step in?"

I look up. Slowly. "He's not the hall monitor, Dean."

"He's the veteran. The anchor. He could've pulled Finn off the damn Zamboni."

My smile is ice. "Maybe he didn't want to create a bigger scene."

Maybe I told him I wasn't ready.

Maybe I pushed him away and let the silence grow between us until it turned into this.

Dean keeps going. "If he's going to be a leader on this team, he needs to act like it. Especially on the road."

"Enough." My voice cuts clean.

The room falls quiet.

Tessa clicks her pen but doesn't say a word.

PR slides the draft statement toward me. I skim it, make two edits, and nod.

"This goes out in ten. We pivot immediately to the toy drive announcement and flood socials with partnership content. Give them something else to trend with."

Comms nods. "Already queued. Photos, press copy, captions."

Legal pushes back from the table. "I'll loop back on any risk factors."

As they pack up, Dean hangs back a beat too long.

"You good?" he asks.

I don't answer right away.

Because I am good. I'm great. I'm ice and fire and calculated precision.

Except for the part of me that's unraveling quietly under my skin. The part that regrets not calling him back.

That wonders if he would've warned me if I'd let him in.

Instead, I give Dean the look that ends meetings.

"I'm always good."

He smirks. "That's what scares me."

When they all clear out, I'm left with nothing but the silence and the folded sticky note under my phone.

Maddox saw it happen.

He didn't call. Didn't text. Didn't do a damn thing.

And the worst part?

I can't even blame him.

Heading back to my office, I'm exhausted and it's barely nine in the morning.

A coffee IV would be the most appropriate thing for me at this point.

"PR campaigns are spinning up across socials," Tessa announces as I approach.

"Thank God one thing is going right today."

"So far."

"Keep that positive spirit for me, Tessa."

I step into my office and close the door behind me, the soft snick of the latch far too loud.

The silence hits like a slap.

I drop my phone on the desk and sink into the chair I haven't had five minutes to sit in all morning.

My inbox is overflowing, my calendar looks like a battlefield, and the toy drive campaign launch is in three hours.

But I don't open my email.

I pick up my phone instead.

No missed calls.

No texts.

Not even a meme.

The space between us used to buzz with static. With heat. With the things we didn't say out loud but still knew.

Now it's just air. Cold and quiet.

I tap the screen again like that might change something.

Still nothing.

The last time we spoke, I asked for space. Maybe not in so many words.

But I pulled back just the same, giving him some flimsy ass excuse.

I shut the door because I didn't know how to walk through it without breaking.

And that's on me.

But part of me—some small, traitorous, aching part—still thought he'd reach back anyway.

A single message. One line.

Even just *"You okay?"*

I open the viral clip. Not the one from the news outlets, but the raw fan footage from a parent's Instagram story.

Finn waves, spins, flashes half the crowd, then almost flashes the rest.

The angle shifts, panning to the crowd behind the glass.

And there he is.

Maddox.

Frozen in the background, jaw tight, hands curled at his sides like he's holding back the urge to punch something.

I pause the frame.

His eyes don't track the camera. They track Finn. The incident. The fallout.

He saw it all.

And he didn't call.

I stare at his face, searching for something—regret, frustration, maybe even guilt.

But the still image doesn't give me any of that. Just the sharp angles of a man who keeps everything locked behind his ribs.

I should've reached out.

Should've told him I was scared.

That I wasn't shutting him out—I was just trying to breathe without needing him so much.

But I didn't.

And now?

Maybe he's giving me what I asked for.

Clean lines.
No blurred boundaries. No blurred hearts.
I exhale through my nose and press play again.
"You wanted clean lines," I whisper.
The video plays.
Finn's laugh echoes.
I don't laugh with it.
My hand shakes as I press rewind.
And watch it again.

Later that afternoon, the team's returned from off the road and Finn McCade slouches into my office like he's here for a damn massage.

Still in joggers, hoodie unzipped halfway, hair damp from a post-workout rinse he probably didn't even shampoo.

The grin on his handsome face is automatic, wide and smug, like this is just another day and not a PR crisis with his ass at the center of it—literally.

"Hey, boss lady." He winks, flopping into the chair across from my desk without asking. "Didn't expect to be summoned so soon. You trying to keep me from going viral twice?"

I don't smile.

Don't respond.

I just slide a single printed frame across the desk. It's from the paused video. The one where his shorts are halfway to hell and Maddox is blurred in the background, mid-flinch.

Finn blinks down at it. His mouth twitches.

"Okay, first—objectively hilarious. Second—those shorts were team-issued. Technically, this was a wardrobe malfunction. Shouldn't I get hazard pay or something?"

I lace my fingers together on the desk. My voice stays level.

Calm.

Controlled.

Clipped with a serrated edge.

"You mooned a child in front of six sponsors, three local reporters, and the mayor's wife. From the home team's city."

Finn winces. "She laughed. She definitely laughed."

"She also called Dean to ask if your next stunt will involve streaking the holiday parade."

He doesn't answer.

I lean forward a fraction and let my tone cool a few more degrees.

"This isn't just a locker room prank gone rogue, Finn. This is a viral headline. It's a meme. It's a potential liability. And it's a warning shot for every exec on the legacy board waiting for me to screw up."

His posture shifts slightly. Not cocky now. Just quiet.

I continue.

"You want to be the class clown? Great. Own it. But you're also a professional hockey player with a seven-figure contract, a marketing clause, and a dozen kids out there who look at you like you're something to become. If you can't be that without treating every event like a circus act, I'll stop inviting you."

His mouth opens. Closes. He looks like he wants to argue.

But I give him nothing to push against.

No heat.

No emotion.

Just cold, brutal truth.

"You embarrassed this organization. You embarrassed yourself. And whether you realize it or not, you embarrassed your teammates—who now have to field questions about your ass instead of their game."

Finn swallows hard. The grin's long gone.

"I'm not suspending you. But I *am* pulling you from the next community event. You'll still attend, but you'll be on logistics duty. No media, no spotlight. Just grunt work."

His brows lift. "I'm getting benched from *handing out toys*?"

"Correct."

"You do know I'm the favorite Viper, right?"

I don't blink. "Not today."

The silence stretches. Then he nods once, jaw tight.

"Got it."

He stands slowly, less swagger this time, and turns for the door. But just before he opens it, he pauses.

"It really was an accident."

"I'm sure it was, only it doesn't look like it on video. It looks like showboating."

"I was just going with the flow. Thought I'd be funny."

I meet his eyes, finally letting something flicker behind mine.

"It's only funny until someone else pays for it."

He leaves without another word.

I wait a full thirty seconds before I let my shoulders drop.

Then I pull my phone out again.

Still no message.

Just clean lines.

And a whole lot of space I don't know what to do with.

CHAPTER THIRTY-ONE

Maddox

THE LOCKER ROOM hums with the usual pre-game chaos—sticks clatter, tape rips, someone's blasting a remix of a Taylor Swift song Riley insists is for "vibes only."

It should ground me.

This room.

This rhythm.

It's what I know.

But my focus keeps slipping.

I run tape along my stick in slow, precise rotations. The stretch-pull-snap is mechanical, something to do with my hands while the rest of me spirals.

It's been a day.

A full day.

No call.

No message.

Not even a damn emoji.

Sloane's silence is louder than any headline.

And maybe that's fair.

Maybe I should've called her. Just said, *Heads-up—Finn's dick made the rounds on TikTok.*

I don't know what the rules are between us anymore.

But I know I broke something.

I roll my shoulder, just enough to feel the ache spike down my back. It's tight. Overused. Pissed off.

I haven't told Holt. Haven't told our trainer. Hell, I haven't told *myself*, not really.

Because admitting it means slowing down.

And I can't afford slow. Not when the only thing keeping me sane is moving fast enough to outrun everything I feel.

"Cal, you're lacing up like a twelve-year-old girl at summer camp."

Cal throws Riley a look. "You learned that from me yesterday."

Riley grins. "Yeah, and I'm workshopping it."

Cal shrugs and goes back to lacing up. He's quieter than usual. Focused.

Not nervous. Just…still.

Like he's trying not to show something.

Jace leans against his stall, taping his own stick with slow, even passes. He hasn't said a word, but his eyes cut toward me. Observing.

He doesn't ask what's wrong. Doesn't need to.

The guy sees everything.

And that's the problem. I can't afford anyone *seeing* me right now.

I duck my head and finish my tape wrap. The last turn snaps tight at the blade. The sound echoes sharp through the room.

Then the door swings open.

Coach Holt walks in—clean navy suit, no tie, expression like we're already down by two.

And he's not alone.

Sloane steps in behind him, heels quiet on the concrete, coat open over a soft black sweater. Next to her is a woman I don't recognize—shorter, polished, holding a tablet like it's a weapon.

My whole body locks.

I wasn't ready to see her tonight.

And yet…here she is.

Sloane Carrington, in the flesh.

And just like that, the air in the room shifts.

I sit straighter. My pulse spikes. The noise around us dulls to static.

She doesn't look at me. Not even once.

But she doesn't have to.

I *feel* her—like electricity against my skin, like the shadow of a memory that won't leave quietly.

I take in everything in one hungry sweep.

Hair pinned back, sleek and simple. Diamond studs in her ears. Red lip. That soft black sweater pulled tight across her breasts.

My hands ache to have those tits in my hands again.

But under all of that, there's tension she's barely holding together.

She's doesn't show it, but I can see she's rattled.

It's in the set of her jaw, the flick of her eyes. In the tight grip on the cuff of her sleeve that only I would notice because I notice everything about her.

She's pissed. Controlled, calculated—but angry.

At Finn.

Maybe at herself.

At me.

And I probably deserve that.

Still, a selfish part of me wants her to look at me.

Just once.

I want her to give me something I can hold on to.

A flicker of softness. Of heat. Of *us*.

But she stays cool. Regal. Unshakable.

And I hate how much I still want her anyway.

Coach Holt steps forward, clearing his throat, and the spell snaps.

"All right, gentlemen. Eyes up."

Coach Holt steps back with a nod. "Carrington's got a few words before we hit the ice."

Sloane moves forward. Not rushed. Not timid. Just *certain*. Like she's done this a hundred times.

Like there isn't a room full of men and steel and sweat watching her every move.

I swallow hard.

She stops at the front of the room, coat open, hands loose at her sides.

"First off," she says, voice calm and clear, "thank you. I know this season hasn't been easy."

No one dares move. Even Riley shuts up. Her voice is silk over steel. Cool, polished, but carrying weight.

"You've shown up. You've played hard. You've put wins on the board. And I see it. I appreciate it."

She lets that hang for a beat. Then shifts.

"But I won't lie to you."

My chest tightens.

"This team is being watched. Not just by fans. Not just by the media. But by people with influence. People who think I don't belong here."

There's a rustle—chairs adjusting, gear creaking.

She breathes once. Then lays it down.

"If we don't make playoffs this year *and* next—if we don't start building a Cup-worthy reputation now—those people will use it as justification to pull this franchise out from under me."

The silence is total.

My jaw locks. I didn't know that part. She never told me.

Another truth she kept in that glass-and-gold vault of hers.

And I hate how much it fucking hurts.

Especially when I laid my cards out to her.

She nods toward the center of the room, eyes sweeping the

space. "That means every penalty matters. Every fight. Every headline. It's all ammunition—for or against."

Her gaze cuts sharper now. "So stay clean. Stay sharp. Keep playing like the whole damn league is watching—because they are."

That twist in my gut pulls tighter. Because she's not just talking to *them*. She's talking to *me* as well.

And I still don't know if I failed her by doing too little, or by walking away when I should've held on.

She exhales slowly, tone softening just a notch. "Now, on to something a little more festive."

She gestures beside her. "This is Noelle Jennings. She's the lead event planner for our holiday toy drive and charity gala in December. She's here to make magic happen."

Noelle steps forward, smiling like a damn holiday commercial in heels. "Hi, everyone! Don't worry—I won't keep you long. Just know I'll be coordinating your charity outreach for the next several weeks."

Riley makes a joke under his breath about ugly sweaters and elf hats. Jace elbows him.

But I barely hear her. Because across the room, Cal's gone dead quiet. And his eyes? Locked on Noelle like someone just knocked the wind out of him.

Interesting.

Sloane glances at Noelle, then back to the team. "Whatever she needs, you give it to her. No excuses. No ghosting. Or you answer to me."

The corner of Riley's mouth twitches. But he doesn't test her.

She turns slightly, like she's about to walk out—then stops.

Her eyes find mine.

Just for a second.

Everything freezes.

We don't speak. We don't move.

But it hits me like open ice contact.

I see the ache in her chest, the storm behind that smooth exterior. And I wonder if she sees it in me too. The regret. The restraint. The goddamn need.

I want to say something. *Anything.*

But the moment ends.

She turns away.

"Wait."

The voice comes from Finn.

He stands slowly, helmet in hand, grin nowhere in sight. "Before we go out there…"

The locker room stills again.

He clears his throat. "I want to say something. To all of you."

A beat. Then another.

"I know I embarrassed the team this week. I know it wasn't just a joke or some harmless stunt. It mattered. And it wasn't okay."

Riley shifts, but stays quiet. Jace watches him like a hawk.

Finn rubs the back of his neck. "I'm not great at…boundaries. Or thinking ahead. But I want you to know I get it. And I'm gonna be better. For the team. For the front office. For her."

His eyes flick to Sloane, quick and respectful.

"And if I mess up again?" he adds, mouth tight. "I'll own it. No excuses."

Nobody claps. But nobody mocks him, either.

I nod once.

Jace follows. Even Riley doesn't mouth off.

Sloane's still near the door, frozen in place.

But her posture loosens. Just slightly.

"Thank you, Finn."

Then she leaves—coat whispering behind her like smoke—and the war begins.

They drop the puck, and everything else disappears.

I don't think about the video. The silence. The way her voice cracked beneath all that polish when she said she couldn't do whatever this is.

I just watch the ice.

Nashville comes hard. Fast break out of the zone, their right wing testing me early with a wrist shot glove side. I snag it without flinching. Toss it to the ref like it didn't cost me anything.

Even though it did.

Even though my shoulder's on fire already, that deep, dull burn that wraps around the joint and bites with every extension.

But I'm still standing. Still in it.

They cycle through fast. Pucks flying, bodies crashing, chirps echoing off the glass.

I let it wash over me. Let it scrape something raw and focused inside me.

The Vipers are holding, but Nashville smells blood. They push harder.

Riley gets caught deep. Eli's slow on the backcheck. My crease clogs up, and I lose sight of the puck for half a second.

That's all it takes.

Top corner. Blocker side.

I don't even turn around. Just skate to the net, tap the post, and reset.

1–0, Nashville.

Eli bangs his stick on the boards, frustrated. Riley throws a gloved hand in the air. Holt's shouting line changes from the bench.

I breathe.

One. Two. Three.

Next shift, Eli barrels in toward the net, tip-in off a beauty of a feed from Cal. It's dirty. Scrappy. A garbage goal if there ever was one.

But it counts.

1–1.

The bench erupts. Cal's face lights up, flushed and focused as Riley grabs his cage and yells something about "finally earning that damn locker."

They're pulling together.

Finn's next on the ice. Eyes sharp. He's all elbows and attitude, but he draws a penalty the clean way—drew his man out of position, and when the guy hooked him, Finn just grinned and kept skating.

No chaos. Just grit.

I nod to myself behind the mask.

Redemption in real time.

Power play doesn't convert, but the tone shifts. We're controlling the puck now. Slowing Nashville's rush.

Jace throws a monster hip check at the blue line that nearly rattles the boards loose.

Second period winds down, and we're still knotted.

Until Riley catches a blindside hit.

It's late. Dirty. Shoulder to jaw. He goes down hard, helmet skidding across the ice.

My heart spikes.

I slam my stick against the post. "Are you fucking kidding me?!"

The ref doesn't move. Doesn't blow the damn whistle.

I lunge out of the crease—just two feet—rage boiling behind my eyes.

But Jace skates in front of me, calm and commanding. He mutters something I don't catch, but I fall back.

Barely.

Riley gets up under his own power, wobbly but waving it off.

He's fine. Or pretending he is.

I look up.

Owner's suite. Top right corner above the glass.

And she's there.

Sloane.

Backlit by the arena glow. Hands folded at her waist. Jaw tight. Eyes locked on the ice.

Locked on *me*.

My pulse hammers in my throat.

I don't blink. Don't look away.

I skate back to my net and crouch. Feel every muscle in my body scream as I reset.

Whatever pain's in my shoulder, whatever noise's in my head, it doesn't matter.

She's watching.

And I need this win like oxygen.

So I give them the rest of the game.

I block three breakaways. Kill a four-on-three. Snap a glove save on a point-blank wrister that should've tied it late in the third.

We hold.

Eli gets the empty-netter in the final thirty seconds.

Final score: 3–1. Vipers.

The crowd explodes.

The horn still echoes through the rafters when Riley launches his stick in the air and whoops like we just won the Cup.

We didn't.

We won a divisional game on a Thursday night in November.

But right now, to them? It's everything.

I stay in the crease, crouched, mask on, chest heaving.

My shoulder's gone numb. The good kind of numb—the kind that means you gave everything and still came out clean.

Finn gets a hard clap on the shoulder from Logan. Jace even grunts out a "nice work" as he passes him on the way to the handshake line.

Cal looks dazed—like he still can't believe he belongs here

—but when Jace lifts a hand, Cal meets it with a quiet, stunned high-five.

The crowd is still on their feet.

And then the announcer's voice booms over the system.

"Tonight's First Star of the Game... Number thirty-three, your Vipers goalie, Maddox Lasker!"

I glance up once—top right, Owner's Suite.

She's already gone.

Applause swells. I raise one glove, give the barest nod, and skate toward the bench. My teammates bang their sticks in rhythm on the boards.

I should feel something.

Pride. Relief. Satisfaction.

Instead, my shoulder throbs. My lungs burn. And all I can think about is the empty space behind the glass where she used to be.

The locker room is chaos.

Steam rising. Music thumping. Beers cracked open and half-spilled on the floor.

Riley's dancing shirtless in front of his stall. Finn's trying to convince Jace to wear his lucky boxers next game. Eli's arm is slung around Cal's neck like they've been teammates for a decade.

Laughter bounces off the tile walls.

I sit in silence.

Still in my gear, pads unstrapped but not removed. Tape hanging loose from one glove. Helmet at my feet.

My shoulder's a firestorm, but it's the hollow in my chest that hurts more.

She saw the game.

She saw *me*.

And still—nothing.

Not a nod. Not a text. Not a signal from behind the glass.

I gave her everything I had tonight. Shut it all down. Led this team like I'm supposed to.

But it didn't fix a damn thing.

The scoreboard says we won.

But all I feel is the ache.

The space where something used to live.

You can win the night and still lose the person who made it matter.

CHAPTER THIRTY-TWO

Maddox

THE BUZZ of last night's win hasn't even worn off when my phone lights up with Peter's name. I almost let it go to voicemail.

I'm halfway to the gym, windows down, music up, trying to get out of my head. But the second buzz hits and something in my gut turns.

I thumb the call. "Yeah?"

He doesn't waste time. "It's out."

My whole body goes still. Had Jace said something after all?

"What's out?"

"The Boston thing," he says, voice tight. "Someone leaked it."

The air in the car goes razor sharp.

"No names yet, but it's bad. A blind item on some sports gossip site hit this afternoon, and now X is tearing it apart. They're calling it Locker Room Loyaltygate." A pause. "The way it's worded? Someone knew details. Enough to point fingers."

I grip the steering wheel like I might tear it off the column.

"You're not mentioned—yet. But if it spreads, it's only a

matter of time. The rookie's name isn't in it either, but the time-line and team details line up too fucking clean to be a guess."

"Who?" I rasp, throat tight. "Who the hell would say anything?"

Peter sighs. "I've already gone down the list. Boston's front office hasn't budged. Rookie's been quiet. Josh could ruin his career if he said anything."

"Only if Boston wants him to be ruined. He's the golden boy."

"What's his incentive?"

I don't have an answer for that. And that only leaves one variable.

Sloane.

The silence that follows eats a hole through my chest.

"Sloane knows," I say flatly. "Not just what happened. The details. What it meant."

"How the hell does she know?"

"I told her."

Peter sighs long and hard. "Please tell me I did not just hear that." He pauses. "Why and when did you tell her this?"

I suppose telling him I decided after I'd been between her thighs is not a good idea.

"It's been a few weeks, and I figured she needed to know."

"Hold on a minute. Are you and Carrington…?"

"No, Peter."

But once again, I say it too quickly. And Peter's not stupid.

He doesn't respond right away, and he doesn't press, but I can hear the gears turning. "Look, I'm not saying it was her. But this didn't come from nowhere. And she's got enemies on that board who'd love to leak something toxic."

My jaw flexes until it aches. "If she told anyone—"

"If she did, she just put a target on your back and her own."

I hang up without saying goodbye.

My blood's buzzing like it did the night of the fight. The

weight in my chest, that sharp push of betrayal—God, it feels the same.

Like a scar cracking open from the inside.

I try to breathe. Try to tell myself this isn't what it looks like.

But every time I give someone the benefit of the doubt, I end up burned.

And this time?

I fucking told her everything.

By the time I pull into the Venom District garage, I've run through every version of this that doesn't end with her name on the tip of someone's tongue.

None of them hold.

Security clocks me at the private elevator, but no one stops me. They know my face now. Or maybe I just look pissed enough to make way.

The upstairs lights are low except for the corridor leading to her office. I hear muffled voices from a conference room—PR, maybe Legal—trying to get ahead of the wildfire.

But her door's closed. No assistant. No cameras. Just silence and the click of my boots across the tile.

I knock once, sharp.

No answer.

I open the door anyway.

Sloane stands near her window, back straight, arms crossed over her chest like armor.

The room smells like printer toner and espresso. Her desk is a war zone—printouts, marked-up press releases, two phones side-by-side. One of them buzzes, unanswered. A hardcopy of the blind item lies open on her keyboard, my name circled in red ink.

She doesn't flinch when I enter. Doesn't even turn.

"You leaked it?" My voice comes out lower than I mean it to. Rougher.

Still, she doesn't move. "Don't come in here barking accusations."

"Too late for that." I shut the door behind me, the click like a gun firing off.

She turns then—slow and measured. Her mouth is painted sharp, her expression unreadable. But her eyes give her away. There's something cracked behind the frost.

"I didn't leak a goddamn thing," she says.

I stare at her. Waiting. Daring her to blink first.

She doesn't.

She exhales through her nose, sharp. "I've spent the last twelve hours putting out fires you don't even know about. Three calls with Legal. Two with PR. Our lead sponsor wants a meeting tomorrow. The board is circling like vultures."

She throws a file folder onto the desk, the contents spilling out—internal memos, clipped news articles, half a dozen flagged emails.

"You think I had time today to casually sabotage both our careers?" she says tightly. "You think I wanted to put myself in the crosshairs of my own board for fun?"

"Then how did it get out?" I step closer, heat pounding under my skin. "You're the only one outside Boston who knew the whole story."

"I didn't tell anyone." Her voice breaks, just slightly, at the edge. "You think I'd do that? After what you told me? After what it cost you to say it?"

I stare at her, lips parting, but the memory hits too fast: her curled into me on that hotel bed, fingers resting over the scar on my chest like it meant something.

Like I meant something.

"I don't know what to think," I bite out. "Because I haven't heard from you in two days. Not after the video. Not after the fallout. Not after I opened my fucking chest and handed you the pieces."

Her chin lifts. "And what, you wanted me to say thank you? That I'm fixed now? That I know how to be yours?"

"That's not what I—"

"You want to talk betrayal?" she cuts in, eyes gleaming now. "You didn't text. You didn't call. You didn't warn me that Finn was about to set the team on fire from the inside. And now you're standing in my office acting like I'm the one who lit the match."

The silence between us stretches, raw and ugly.

I want to yell. I want to pull her into my arms. I want to smash every wall between us. But all I can do is breathe hard through my nose and clench my fists.

"I told you I needed space," she says quietly. "That's not the same thing as saying I didn't need you."

The second she says it—"That's not the same thing as saying I didn't need you"—it slams through me like a puck to the chest.

And still, I can't let go of the anger curling around my ribs.

"You don't get to play semantics with me, Sloane," I grind out. "You said you needed space and then went radio silent. What the hell was I supposed to think?"

She steps back, folding her arms tighter, like she's physically holding herself together. "That maybe I was scared. That maybe this—us—isn't something I've ever been allowed to want before."

Her voice cracks again, but she doesn't look away.

And I can't look away from her.

The weight of what's happening—the leak, the fallout, her silence, my silence—sits heavy between us.

But under it, something more fragile flickers.

Something like pain. Regret. Maybe even longing.

But the damage is done. We're both standing in the wreckage now.

"You think I wanted to be the one who leaked it?" she says softly. "You think I wanted this?"

I shake my head. Not because I believe it. But because I don't want to believe she could ever betray me like that.

She crosses to her desk and rests her palms flat on it like she's bracing for impact. "Dean already thinks I'm compromised because of you. The board's looking for a reason to clip my wings. So no, Maddox. I didn't leak your past to the press. Because I'm not stupid enough to hand them the knife they're dying to use on me."

I watch her, heart pounding, throat dry.

And suddenly the anger in me buckles, cracking open something colder.

"I came here thinking you'd deny it," I say. "Thinking maybe I could still believe you."

"You still can."

But the silence afterward feels like a void.

I step toward the door. My hand closes around the handle.

I don't leave.

"You can hate me all you want," I say quietly. "But if you didn't leak it, you'd better find out who did. Fast."

I look over my shoulder one last time. She's staring down at her desk, shoulders rigid, like she's trying not to shake.

"Because if the league runs with this the way Boston did," I add, "they won't just take me down this time. They'll come for you, too."

A knock slams against the door before I can open it.

I jerk it open, jaw still tight and chest heaving—

And Dean's standing there.

Wide-eyed.

Listening.

And with a smirk that can only mean trouble.

I DON'T MOVE.

Not when I feel Maddox's stare burning between my shoulder blades.

Not when the silence grows so thick I can taste it.

He's still by the door, not leaving.

I can feel the weight of him in the room like a storm front pressing in.

My fingers tighten around the edge of my desk, my heart a snarled mess of anger and something softer I can't name.

If I turn around, I'll break. If I say too much, I'll say something I can't take back.

"You got what you came for," I say, voice cool as glass. "Now go."

The words scrape my throat raw. But I don't let it show.

Behind me, nothing but silence. A heartbeat passes before his boots shift once on the tile.

The handle clicks.

But when I finally turn, it's not Maddox leaving.

It's Dean walking in.

Son of a bitch. How long has he been standing on the other side of the door?

His brows lift, one slow rise of smug satisfaction as he takes in the scene. Me at my desk and Maddox inches from the door.

The storm in the air we didn't quite clean up.

"Well," Dean says, stepping inside and letting the door swing shut behind him. "Don't let me interrupt the lovers' quarrel."

Neither Maddox or I move.

For once, we're aligned.

Dean folds his arms. "I was coming to let you know the board's called an emergency session. Later tonight. Boston's blown up bigger than expected."

My stomach drops.

Dean glances between us. "But I guess there's two crises to address now, huh?"

The silence snaps like a bone. Maddox straightens, stepping forward just enough to send heat up my spine.

"There's nothing the board needs to discuss about this," I say.

Dean doesn't blink. "You sure about that? Because the optics aren't great. And considering the story leaking out of Boston, it's a hell of a coincidence."

I open my mouth to speak, but Maddox beats me to it.

"She didn't leak it."

Dean gives him a slow, mocking nod. "Maybe not. But now the *timing* is a story. This scandal was bad enough. Now the owner of the Vipers is sleeping with the player at the center of it? That's two fires, not one."

I close my eyes.

Just for a second. Just long enough to find my footing again.

When I open them, my voice is iron.

"This is my team. If the board has questions, I'll answer them. But I won't be interrogated in my own office over a relationship that has nothing to do with the Boston leak."

Dean's smile is paper-thin. "Then be ready to defend both. Because the vote tonight? It's not going to be about Boston anymore. It's going to be about whether you're still the right person to lead."

He lets that sink in, then turns and leaves without another word.

The door clicks shut.

And for a long, breathless second, I just stand there. Hands braced on the desk. Jaw clenched so tight my teeth ache.

Maddox doesn't say anything.

He doesn't have to.

The boardroom is colder than usual.

Unforgiving.

Dean is already seated when I walk in.

Because of course he is.

His smirk barely hides behind his professionalism. He nods to the board members filing in, most of whom I've known for years when I was cutting my teeth on quarterly projections while my father ruled this table with a cigar in one hand and a warning in the other.

Now they look at me like I'm a scandalous burden.

"Maddox Lasker will join us shortly," Dean says, all casual like he didn't just listen to my private life get torn apart through a door I never heard open. "Shall we begin?"

I don't sit. Not yet.

"We're here to discuss two things," I say, voice even, crisp. "The leak concerning the Boston incident, and any concerns regarding my relationship with Mr. Lasker."

There's a flicker of surprise across a few faces.

Good. Better they hear it from me than let Dean drip it out like poison.

A moment later the door opens quietly, and Maddox walks in.

He's dressed in a black pullover and slacks, hair still damp from the shower.

I hate the punch to my gut seeing him dressed like he belongs in a boardroom.

He looks damn good. But also different. Almost like I don't know him.

Maybe I don't.

Because he doesn't look at me, doesn't speak. Just takes the open seat like he's been called into a post-game review, not into the room full of folks who might cut his legs out from under him.

One of the board members clears his throat. "Mr. Lasker. It's been brought to our attention that you and Ms. Carrington were —are—engaged in a personal relationship. Is that true?"

Maddox doesn't blink. "Yes."

Dean's mouth twitches like he wants to cheer.

"And is that relationship ongoing?"

A pause. Long enough to make my pulse thud.

Then Maddox says, "No. It's over."

It hits me like a slap. I don't flinch. I don't move. But every muscle inside me goes rigid.

He won't even look at me when he says it.

The questions shift to me. Expected. Practiced.

"Did you leak the Boston information, Ms. Carrington?"

"No." My tone is sharp steel. "The matter was closed legally. I was briefed internally on the incident at the time of acquisition. Only two other members of that legal team had access to the records. None are employed by this organization."

"Were you aware of the optics of bringing Mr. Lasker onto the team?"

"Yes. Which is why I ensured all internal protocols were followed. His performance speaks for itself."

Dean leans forward. "Performance doesn't negate perception. Or distraction."

"If perception's enough to override talent," I say coldly, "we should fire half the roster."

He doesn't respond. But the dig lands.

Another board member—one of the older ones, with silver hair and a thick Southern accent—leans in. "Ms. Carrington, are you emotionally compromised in your role?"

"No."

His brow lifts. "Are you sure?"

"Yes."

No hesitation. Even if it's a lie.

They turn back to Maddox. "Mr. Lasker. Do you believe Ms. Carrington leaked the story?"

His jaw works. Slowly, finally, his gaze lifts to mine.

For a moment, there's something there. Not softness. But clarity.

"No," he says. "She didn't."

Dean doesn't like that answer. "Regardless, the optics are messy. Fans and sponsors are asking questions. There's concern about judgment, leadership, and locker room fallout."

"I've done my job," Maddox replies coolly. "You asked me to play like a franchise anchor. I did. That's the job."

The silence stretches. Measured. Calculating.

Then the board chair clears his throat. "We'll adjourn for two hours. During that time, we'll call in Coach Holt to review any impact this may have had on locker room culture and team focus. At the end of the recess, we will vote."

Dean doesn't hide his glee now. "Very good."

They rise. One by one. No handshakes. Just silence.

Maddox stands too. Starts for the door.

I don't stop him. I want to. God, I want to.

But I can't. Not now and judging by the way this meeting went, not ever.

We're over before we began.

And just like everything else with this team, it feels like what I had to say or what I feel means less than nothing.

So fuck all of them.

Let them vote. Let them rip this legacy out from under me. But I will not fall apart while they're watching.

And I will not beg a man to stay who's already decided to leave.

———

Two hours on the dot later, the board files into the conference room.

Their faces betray nothing. It's stoicism at its finest.

But the air has shifted. It's heavier, like a sentence has already been written and we're all just pretending this part matters.

Dean's tie is loose around his neck now, his sleeves pushed up, a worn-out performance of casual authority.

Maddox sits two seats down from me. Stone-faced. Arms crossed. Eyes unreadable.

I wish my body would behave and not be on high alert knowing he's around.

"We've reconvened after reviewing the materials submitted by both parties," Chairman Weatherby says, his voice even. "Including the written statement from Coach Holt and internal player reports from preseason through current standings."

He adjusts his glasses. Doesn't smile.

"There are two matters on the table. Let's begin with Ms. Carrington's ownership review."

My spine straightens, but I don't move.

I don't flinch.

I already know what they're going to do.

"You'll retain ownership of the Atlanta Vipers."

A brief murmur rolls through the room.

"However," he continues, "effective immediately, your voting share will be reduced by fifteen percent until the conclusion of the season. During that time, all roster decisions must be approved by the board, and you are to refrain from direct player contract negotiations or signings."

Dean leans back in his chair, satisfied.

Like he didn't just gut my power in front of everyone.

Like I didn't fight tooth and nail to get here.

"We'll revisit your full reinstatement in the off-season, pending performance and compliance."

I nod once. No emotion. No blink.

If I show how badly that burns, I'll unravel.

And if I unravel, I lose everything.

The chairman clears his throat.

"Now, regarding Mr. Lasker."

Maddox doesn't shift. Doesn't breathe.

"There's no evidence of a policy breach on your part outside of a personal relationship that has now, per your statement, ended."

That word lodges in my chest.

Ended.

He said it. Out loud.

"Given your importance to team performance and current league standing," Weatherby continues, "you will remain on the roster through the remainder of the season."

Maddox's jaw clenches.

"However, your contract will not be renewed. This decision is final."

Dean jots something down like it's just another box checked.

"And any off-ice promotion or franchise branding involving your image will cease immediately."

Another cut. One I didn't see coming.

I swallow hard, but it doesn't go down.

"Is that clear?"

Maddox gives a single stiff nod.

He doesn't look at me.

Not when the votes are recorded.

Not when the board begins to adjourn.

Not even when the words *relationship is over* hang between us like barbed wire.

By the time I stand, my hands are trembling.

I curl them into fists and pretend it's from anger.

But it's not.

It's grief.

And no one here will ever know the difference.

They let me keep the team.

They just made sure I couldn't keep the one man who played like he believed in me.

CHAPTER THIRTY-FOUR

Maddox

THE GAME'S ON, but I couldn't tell you who's playing.

It flickers in front of me, colors blurring across the screen like it's underwater. The sound's off. Has been for over an hour.

The bourbon in my hand has gone warm. I haven't taken a sip in a while.

The ice pack on my shoulder slid off a long time ago, dripping cold puddles onto the wood floor I haven't bothered to clean up.

My phone buzzed at least ten times earlier. Peter for sure. Probably the league. Probably more press.

I haven't looked.

My eyes are fixed on the corner of the room where the Owner's Suite keycard sits. Right where she left it.

I don't even know when she dropped it. I just saw it there when I walked in, and it's been staring at me ever since.

It's not just the symbol of what we were. It's the last safe place she ever let herself have.

The thing is, I don't regret what I said to her in that room or on the phone that night.

I meant every word.

And I really don't want to regret the words I said in front of the board tonight either.

I stood in front of the board and gave them what they needed to hear.

That it was over.

That she didn't break any rules. That the relationship was personal and private and terminated.

I did it to protect her. To keep her ownership safe. To keep her future intact.

But now I can't get the image out of my head—her, standing across from me, not flinching, not blinking, not breathing. Just… silent.

She didn't try to stop me. Didn't ask me why. Didn't show a single crack.

And that, more than anything, makes me want to punch a wall until something gives.

Because I *know* what I saw in her eyes that night in the suite. I *know* what I felt. It wasn't one-sided. It wasn't fake.

And maybe that's the worst part.

Because I didn't just break it off.

I broke her trust.

And I can't take that back.

I lean forward and rest my elbows on my knees, knuckles white around the sweating glass.

The ice has melted. The bourbon sits untouched.

And for the first time since Boston, I can't tell if I did the right thing or just repeated the same fucking mistake all over again.

A sharp knock breaks the silence.

I don't move.

Another knock. Heavier this time.

"Lasker," Jace calls. "I know you're in there."

I scrub a hand down my face, leave the bourbon where it is, and drag myself to the door.

When I open it, Jace doesn't wait for an invitation. He walks right past me like he owns the place, eyeing the mess with the kind of calm that makes me feel even more unhinged.

His gaze lands on the bourbon glass. Then the keycard.

Then me.

"You look like shit," he says, sitting on the edge of the couch and folding his arms over his knees. "Start talking."

I kick the door closed behind me. "Not in the mood."

"Tough."

I don't answer.

Instead, I go to the kitchen, grab a second glass, pour another shot of bourbon, and set it on the coffee table in front of him.

He doesn't touch it.

"So, it was true," he says, after a long beat. "You and Carrington."

My jaw tightens. "It's over."

"That's not what I asked."

I don't want to say it. Don't want to crack it open.

But Jace just sits there, waiting, like he's done this before. Like he's seen this movie, knows how it ends, and still thinks I've got one last plot twist left in me.

I sink into the chair across from him and stare at the drink in my hand. "Started around media day. No, I take that back. For me, it started the first time I met her. When she marched into my apartment in Boston and gave me an ultimatum."

"What was the ultimatum?"

I lean back in the chair. "Forty-eight hours to sign or go out as a washed-up has been."

One side of his mouth quirks up. "Sounds like Carrington."

I blow out a breath that's half sigh, half laugh. "Yep, that's her. But we fought like hell against it. We just couldn't stay away from each other. Didn't mean for it to happen."

Jace lifts a brow. "But it did."

"Yeah." I take a sip and let the fire burn its way down. "She made me feel something I haven't in years. Like I mattered. Like I wasn't just the guy people whisper about when they think I can't hear."

Jace doesn't say anything. He lets me talk.

"We kept it quiet. Thought we could control it. But the board found out. And then the Boston story leaked. Timing was too clean. I thought…I thought maybe she'd told someone."

He winces, just slightly. "You accused her?"

"I didn't say the words." I glance at the keycard again. "But I didn't stop her from believing I did initially."

Jace leans back, jaw ticking. "Tell me what happened in Boston. I've heard the rumors. I want the truth."

I don't want to relive it. But if I don't say it now, I never will.

"There was this rookie," I start, voice low. "Kid was smart, fast, played with his heart on his sleeve. The kind you bet your money on early."

Jace nods once.

"He also happened to be gay," I continue. "Didn't tell the press, but some of the vets figured it out. One in particular—Joshua Leonard—made it his personal mission to break him."

Jace's face darkens. "Jesus."

"I caught Leonard cornering him in the weight room one night. Slurs. Threats. Shit that doesn't belong in a locker room, or anywhere else." My grip tightens around the glass. "I lost it. Pinned him to the wall. Told him if he came near the kid again, I'd break his jaw."

"And that's what got you benched?"

"That, and not keeping quiet when they told me to." I lift my gaze to Jace's. "The team swept it under the rug. PR nightmare, they said. Bad for the brand. They told the rookie to request a trade. They told me to shut up and sit down."

"And you didn't."

"No. I took the heat. Took the suspension. Didn't say a word publicly, because the rookie didn't want his story out. But I still got labeled as the problem." My throat tightens. "Then Carrington gave me a chance. Puts me back on the ice. I let her in—and the past followed me anyway."

Jace blows out a slow breath. "So when it leaked, you assumed it was her."

"I wanted to believe she wouldn't. But part of me…" I trail off. "I've been betrayed before. When you're used to it, you start looking for it."

Silence stretches. Jace finally picks up the bourbon and takes a measured sip.

"You're still an idiot," he says quietly. "But I get it now."

I nod once, jaw tight.

"She didn't leak it," he adds. "You know that, right?"

"I do now. But I already broke her trust. Not only with not believing her but then I essentially broke up with her in front of the board. Told them we were over."

"So you're an idiot and an asshole."

"Thanks for the kick while I'm down."

He shrugs, sipping his drink again. "You're the one who did it."

"Yeah, I did. I hurt her and burned down the only good thing I've had in years."

Jace studies me for a long moment. "You want to fix it?"

I shrug. "Doesn't matter what I want."

"Bullshit." He sits forward. "You stood up when it counted in Boston. You're gonna do the same here. Start by deciding what the hell you want, and stop hiding from it."

I rake a hand through my hair. "Even if I wanted to fix it, I don't know how."

"Then figure it out." Jace stands, finishes his drink, and sets it down with a quiet clink. "But here's the truth, Maddox—if you don't fight for her, you're not just walking away from Carrington. You're walking away from yourself."

He turns toward the door.

"Oh, and one more thing." He pauses with his hand on the knob. "When you're ready to stop letting other people write your ending, write your own."

Then he's gone.

And I'm still sitting in the wreckage, glass in my hand, heart in my throat.

Jace has a point. Several actually.

If I stood up for someone else in Boston without having a safety net, why shouldn't I give myself the same opportunity here.

Because everyone lets you down.

Except they don't.

Sloane didn't. Jace didn't. Coach didn't. Cal didn't. They've all taken a chance on me.

And I'm about to pull a classic Lasker and fuck it all up. And for what?

I'm tired of being alone. Fighting all of this all by myself. Putting my head down and focusing on the game while the game of my life passes me right by.

Yeah, the cap is right.

It's time I start writing the ending to my own story.

CHAPTER THIRTY-FIVE

Sloane

I SHOULD BE GETTING ready for the game. Press walk-throughs, media roundups, pre-ceremony meetings with sponsors.

Instead, I sit in the dark in my office.

Just me, my laptop, and the power-hungry glow of the screen as I open the file I promised myself I'd never touch again.

PLAYER ACQUISITION DOSSIER – M. LASKER

My chest tightens.

It takes a full minute to double-click. Not because I'm indecisive. But because it feels like slicing open a wound just to check if it still bleeds.

Spoiler alert: it does.

The first slide flickers into view.

A headshot of Maddox in his Boston jersey, jaw tight, eyes flat.

He looks like he hasn't slept in a decade. I remember staring at that photo for hours, analyzing every detail.

Trying to figure out if I could trust a man like him to represent everything I was fighting for.

HIGH RISK, HIGH REWARD.

That's the title of the second slide.

God, I was so clinical. So strategic. So in control.

"Potential captain material if emotionally stabilized."

"History of altercations, but team-first loyalty."

"Fanbase response: Polarizing."

I scroll through it slowly, one slide at a time, the corner of my mouth twitching in something that might be a laugh if it didn't feel like a knife scraping against bone.

Everything here was meant to guard me.

To keep this exactly what it was supposed to be: business.

But somewhere between puck drops and center ice kisses, I lost the plot.

And now I'm sitting here like some heartbroken idiot, rewriting a presentation no one will ever see.

My fingers hover over the keyboard. I start a new slide and type:

REALITY CHECK

- Manipulative
- Untrustworthy
- A threat to legacy
- Unprofessional
- Liability

Each bullet feels like a punch. Not to him. He's none of those things.

But every single one of those is me.

I try to blink away the sting in my eyes, but my vision blurs anyway. I swallow the lump in my throat and reach for my water bottle, like that's going to fix anything.

Why is it people ask if you want water when you're hurting or panicking?

Is hydration stronger than heartbreak or anxiety?

The cursor flashes in the corner of the slide like it's waiting for one more truth.

— Irreparable.

I type it slowly. Each letter a confession.

The silence around me is heavy, suffocating. The kind of silence that makes you feel the emptiness in your own skin.

I should be downstairs, shaking hands and making smiles.

I should be plotting something for Dean's removal. Prepping press statements. Watching warmups from the catwalk with a face made of steel.

Instead, I'm here. Alone. Making PowerPoint poison out of the only thing I ever let myself want.

My phone buzzes on the desk.

I don't check it.

I just press my fingers to my eyes and will myself not to fall apart.

Not yet.

Not until I know there's nothing left to salvage.

I don't know why I'm doing this.

Maybe because it's the only place I can bleed where no one will see. Maybe because the slideshow hurts less than walking into a rink filled with whispers and cameras and Maddox's face on every damn poster.

Or maybe because if I control the narrative—at least in here—then I can pretend for five minutes that I still have power.

I click back to the beginning of the presentation.

The first slide loads again, that haunting headshot staring back at me.

I drag the image into the trash bin.

The empty gray box where his photo used to be feels like a hollowed-out organ.

Good.

Let it match the rest of me.

My nails tap against the keys—agitated and erratic. I scroll down to the slide that used to say *"Long-Term Viability."* I retitle it:

Unrecoverable Losses

The words blur.

I blink hard and tighten my grip on the mouse, like squeezing plastic can ground me.

He didn't even flinch.

He said it in front of the entire boardroom like it didn't cost him a piece of his soul.

"It's over."

Not *I'm sorry.*

Not *I had to.*

Not even *This is killing me, too.*

Just final. Brutal. Irrevocable.

The sharp, clean kind of truth you don't walk back from.

My throat thickens, raw and burning. I press the heel of my hand against my chest, like I can push the pain back into place.

Keep it from cracking through the seams of my composure.

But it's already leaking. Into my breath. Into my bones. Into the space where his voice used to echo.

"I want all of you, Sloane."

He said that once.

Now I sit in the wreckage of what it meant.

I hover over another slide.

Projected Impact.

It used to be about fan engagement and defensive rankings.

Now, all I can think is how many pieces of myself I handed over to a man who never promised to keep them safe but I assumed he would.

A knock sounds faintly against the door.

I don't move.

Let whoever it is knock until their hand falls off.

Let the whole world bang down my door. I've already lost the only thing that mattered.

My hand shakes on the mouse as I drag another slide into the trash. Then another. Until all that's left is a blank deck and my reflection in the screen, eyes red, lips trembling, mascara smudged at the corners like a confession I forgot to swallow.

My phone buzzes again. Another notification. Maybe a news alert. Maybe the board. Maybe Maddox.

I don't look.

If it's him, I'll break.

If it's not, I'll break anyway.

The soft knock comes again, more insistent this time.

I don't answer.

But the door creaks open anyway, and Tessa steps inside like she's walking into a room where something already died.

She takes one look at me and shuts the door quietly behind her.

I swipe at my face, but it's pointless. The damage is obvious.

She doesn't say anything right away. Just walks over, sets her phone facedown on the table, and lowers herself slowly into the chair across from me.

I brace for her to say something comforting. Or worse— something kind.

But she surprises me.

"I have something you need to hear."

Her voice is tighter than usual. Strained. Not bossy or brisk or clinical like normal. Tessa only sounds like this when something is about to detonate.

I frown. "What is it?"

She flips the phone over and taps a message. A voice recording starts to play, already queued up.

Two voices.

Dean's.

And someone else I don't recognize at first—until I do.

Joshua Leonard.

The Boston Freeze Golden Boy asshole veteran who went after the rookie Maddox saved.

The one player Dean always wanted on the team, but even my father refused to try to acquire him.

The one with no love lost between him and Maddox.

"…told you it would work," Josh says, smug and low. "You leak the story, he spirals. Carrington's credibility tanks. They're both out by playoffs, guaranteed."

Dean's reply is colder. "It's not just about getting rid of them. It's about restoring order. Maddox was never going to fall in line. And Sloane…she's dangerous when she thinks she's untouchable."

The room tilts.

I stare at the phone like it might bite me.

"They planned this," I whisper. "They—Jesus, they *planned* this."

Tessa pauses the recording and ger voice goes sharp. "There's more. Including how Dean's been feeding rumors to a media contact for months. It's all on here. Time stamps. Identifiers. Enough to bury him."

I blink, barely absorbing the words. "Where did you get it?"

"Total fluke. He has his assistant record their meetings to dictate later. She left her phone in his office by accident and never shut off the recording. When she heard it, she came to me for advice."

I shake my head. "This doesn't make sense. Why would he—?"

But the question dies before I finish it.

Because I know why.

Power.

Control.

Legacy.

The same reason men like him always pull the strings.

And the same reason I'm sitting here now—half undone, fully exposed and with nothing left to hold onto but a broken heart and a handful of truth too late to change anything.

Tessa watches me carefully, as if she's expecting me to explode. To rage. To scream and demand retribution.

But none of that comes.

I fold forward instead, elbows on my knees, face in my hands. My body shakes, a sob strangling in my throat like barbed wire.

It isn't Dean's betrayal that guts me.

It's Maddox's voice in my head, breaking all over again.

It's over.

I choke on a breath. "I told him we'd ruin each other."

Tessa kneels in front of me and grips my wrists with steady hands. "Then *un-ruin* it, Sloane. Fight for him. Hell, fight for *you.*"

But all I can do is cry.

I don't know how to fight for someone who already walked away.

CHAPTER THIRTY-SIX

Maddox

THE CROWD'S already a live wire when I step out of the tunnel, but the second my skates slice across the crease, it explodes.

A low rumble that builds into a roar, echoing off the rafters, rattling straight through my ribs and the steel under my pads.

Feels like electricity.

Feels like home.

The Pit's packed—standing room only, banners snapping from the upper deck, the kind of night you can smell in your bones.

It's a divisional game with playoff points on the line.

And my old team? They're all here for blood.

I flex my left shoulder once, testing the wrap under my chest protector. It's tight, holding everything in place, but the muscle still sings with that old pain.

A reminder. A warning. A pulse I can't ignore.

Across the red line, I spot him.

Joshua Leonard.

Same smirk. Same slow, smug circle through warm-ups, coasting in front of the crease like he owns it. Like he owns me.

My jaw tightens behind the mask. I press the blade edge into the blue paint, focusing on my rhythm: shuffle, slide, set. Stay loose. Stay ready.

Jace glides by, tapping the butt of his stick against my pad. "You good?"

"Yeah." I nod once, eyes locked on the Freeze bench. "I'm good."

"Keep your head."

Then he skates off like he's read enough between the lines.

They announce starting lineups. My name gets the loudest cheer, booming and relentless. Feels like gasoline poured on the fire building in my chest.

I drop into my crease, knees bent, stick out front, glove loose. Joshua's lined up on the wing for the first draw, but his eyes never leave me. Even from forty feet away I can feel the hiss of his breath through the cage.

The puck drops.

Riley wins it clean, and the play moves up ice. I rock back into the crease, tracking lanes, eyes scanning traffic.

The Freeze are pushing early—dump-and-chase, bodies flying at our D.

They want to test me. Given that they know about my shoulder injury, they're testing the shoulder as well.

First shot comes low glove. Easy snag. I hold it a beat before the whistle, just long enough to let the crowd cheer.

Flicking it to the ref, I reset.

Second shift, they stack Leonard at the top of the crease, his ass practically on my pads. I shove my blocker into his ribs, clearing space.

He just laughs under his breath. The fucker is trying to bait me.

Not tonight.

Play cycles to the other end. My defense clears. For a while it's just saves and slides, the normal chaos of hockey.

Riley heckles their goalie from the bench. Cal's back checking like his life depends on it.

We're holding.

But Leonard's circling. Always circling.

I drop into the butterfly for a shot from the point, smother it, and kick the rebound to the corner.

He jabs at my glove after the whistle, a little poke. Just enough to make the crowd boo.

"Easy there," the ref warns.

Leonard just smirks before leaning closer.

"Didn't think you'd show your face, Lasker. Figured the whore got to you first."

I bare my teeth as the words hit like a slash to the gut. Not only because of what he said, but because he said it here.

In my house.

Fucker. I should have beat his ass harder last time.

I grip my stick tighter, pulse pounding against my gloves. Don't look at him. Don't flinch. Jace's voice in my head: Keep your head.

The next few minutes blur. Shots. Blocks. Stick taps.

My shoulder twinges with every push off the post, but I grit through it.

If I leave this game, he wins. And I'm done letting guys like him take things from me.

Midway through the first, it happens.

Puck's up ice, no whistle. Leonard loops behind my net like he's on a casual skate. Nobody close. No cameras focused. Then he barrels in—elbow high, full weight—straight into my bad shoulder.

Pain explodes like a flare.

White-hot and ripping through muscle and bone. I slam into the post, mask rattling, vision splintering.

The whistle doesn't come fast enough.

"Motherfucker!"

It's Jace—his gloves already off, barreling toward Leonard. Eli's right behind him. Riley vaults the bench.

Chaos erupts.

I curl over, gripping the post, gasping through clenched teeth. Everything spins. My arm's numb from the impact, but the burn is deep—old scar tissue tearing, maybe more.

The ref's yelling. The benches are roaring. Gloves litter the ice like a war zone.

And in the center of it all—Leonard, grinning.

He wanted this. Wanted me out.

The trainers get to me fast. I wave them off, jaw locked. "I'm staying in."

"Lasker—"

"I said I'm fine."

Because if I leave, he wins.

I plant my skates back in the crease. Bend. Stretch. Pain flashes but holds. Fine enough.

I glance up toward the owner's suite, just once. She's nothing but a shadow behind glass from this far down, but I look anyway.

Part of me hopes she's watching. The other part hopes she's not, because this isn't clean hockey anymore.

Second period starts. Slow crawl of bone and blood. Every movement in net sends a warning shot through my shoulder, nerves singing sharp enough to cut. But I don't leave.

I won't.

Leonard skates past again mid-play, but this time he gets clipped. Not by me.

By Jace.

Hard. Legal. Surgical. The kind of hit that's less about the puck and more about sending a message.

You don't touch one of ours.

The crowd eats it up.

And it doesn't stop there.

Eli starts skating tighter circles around Leonard, body checking just a little too close.

Riley throws more heat behind every slap shot like he's trying to punch holes through their goalie.

Even quiet Cal gets in Leonard's face after the whistle.

We're not playing pretty anymore.

We're playing Vipers hockey.

My kind of game.

They're doing it for me.

I see it in their eyes when they look at the crease. I hear it in the barked line changes. I feel it in the way every rebound is cleared with violent precision.

This is what a real team looks like.

It takes until the final minutes of the second period, but the payoff comes. Beau slams the puck in from the top of the crease after a cross from Logan.

The crowd loses its mind.

We go ahead. 3–2.

My pulse hammers harder than the scoreboard buzzer. Leonard scowls, jaw tight, and for the first time all night…he looks nervous.

Good.

Win or lose, he's not walking off this ice with his ego intact.

I drop into position as the puck resets. Pain coils in my shoulder like a vice, but I bare my teeth behind the mask.

He can try to break me.

But I've already played hurt.

I've already lost the girl.

And I'm still standing.

The third period feels like war.

Bodies fly. Tempers boil, causing gloves to nearly drop more than once.

Leonard continues to circle me like a vulture, but I block out his smirk. The jeers. The subtle nudges.

I've dealt with worse.

I've survived worse.

My shoulder's on fire, but I lock in. Square to the puck. Vision tight. Every instinct honed.

And then it happens.

Breakaway. Leonard again. Barreling down the ice like a battering ram. He doesn't even try to deke. Doesn't try to finesse. He's aiming for the kill.

I meet him head-on.

Push out to the top of the crease.

Drop low, pads sealed, glove high.

He rips it glove side. I snare it clean, smother it to my chest, roll back into the butterfly and freeze the puck.

Whistle blows.

The arena erupts.

I stay down for a beat too long. Not because I'm hurt—but because the crowd is roaring my name.

MADDOX. MADDOX. MADDOX.

It crashes down like thunder.

I rise. Slowly. Controlled. Glare at Leonard through my mask. He glares back. Doesn't say a word. Just skates away.

I look up again, breathing hard behind the cage. I don't know if she's still there. Don't know if she saw me stop him. But I hope she did.

Because tonight, that save? That was for me. But it was also for her.

And for the first time since this season started… I feel it.

Like I belong to this team.

I turn to the bench. Jace is banging his stick on the boards. Eli's shouting. Riley throws both arms in the air like we just won a Cup. Even Cal's grinning, tapping his stick against the ice like a drumbeat.

The horn blows minutes later. Final score: 3–2, Vipers.
I don't throw my gloves. I don't celebrate like the rookies.
I skate off slow, taking it all in—like it might be the last time.
Because win or not, I know what's coming.
And if I'm going down…
I'll go down as a Viper.

CHAPTER THIRTY-SEVEN

Sloane

THE BOARDROOM SMELLS like old money and fresh blood.

Every chair is filled. Phones silenced. Suits pressed to perfection.

No one speaks above a whisper, but the tension could fracture bone.

I sit at the head of the table, hands folded in front of me, expression carved from stone.

My heart is a thunderclap in my chest.

They know.

Tessa sent the recording to the board's general counsel last night. By midnight, the chair called an emergency meeting. No time for strategy. No space for spin. Just damage control with teeth.

The glass door hisses open.

Dean walks in like he owns the room. Shoulders square, jaw tight, expression unreadable.

He doesn't even glance at me as he takes his seat, like we're on the same team.

God, he's smug.

Chairman Weatherby clears his throat. "Thank you all for

coming on short notice. We have a serious matter to address regarding a violation of trust at the executive level."

He nods to the compliance officer, who clicks a button on her laptop.

My heart's pounding in my ears knowing what's coming next. I flex my fingers around the handle of my chair, the fury I felt the night I heard it coming back to me.

The audio plays.

Dean's voice crackles over the speaker system. "It's already in motion, Joshua. The moment it hits, they'll both be radioactive. Carrington loses her leverage, and Maddox takes the hit. Exactly what we wanted."

Murmurs ripple through the room.

"Unbelievable."

"Jesus Christ, what next?"

Dean's still, feigning composure.

The recording continues, Joshua Leonard's voice next. Arrogant. Cruel. "So we both get what we want. The vet spot opens back up, and your boss gets dragged down by her sins. Perfect, huh?"

The file ends in silence.

Weatherby leans forward, his voice calm but deadly. "Mr. Ward, do you deny that is your voice on the recording?"

Dean's jaw flexes. "It's been taken out of context."

"I think the context is clear," I say, voice smooth as a scalpel. "You conspired with a player from another team to destabilize both our franchise and the reputation of one of our top athletes. You leaked confidential information to the press, and you did it without notifying counsel or the board."

His eyes finally meet mine. "You knew about Boston. You should've told them first."

"I did. And I handled it according to legal and internal compliance. What I didn't do," I say, voice rising, "was weaponize it for personal gain."

He scoffs, low and bitter. "You're acting like you didn't sleep with him."

More murmurs spread around the room.

I don't flinch, but the jab hits. "My private life has nothing to do with this situation, Dean. You're on trial for violating your fiduciary duty and exposing this organization to legal risk. So answer the board—or don't. Either way, you're done here."

He looks at Weatherby. "So that's it? I don't get to explain?"

"Mr. Ward," the chairman says evenly, "we're not here to discuss your personal grievances. We're here because you acted with gross misconduct and undermined the ethical integrity of this organization. This board operates on trust. And you shattered it."

Dean glances around the room, but no one meets his eye.

He's alone. And he knows it.

"So, that's how it's going to be, huh? You're going to let this woman take down the team? You *need* me."

Weatherby straightens his glasses, ignoring Dean's outburst. "The bylaws are clear. Mr. Ward's behavior constitutes gross misconduct. As chair, I motion for immediate termination of his employment. All in favor?"

Every hand but Dean's goes up.

My stomach doesn't lurch. My hands don't shake. I am ice. Precision. Discipline.

But inside? I am fury restrained by protocol.

Weatherby nods. "Effective immediately, Mr. Ward, your badge is deactivated. Security will escort you out."

Dean stands, fists clenched, and for a moment I see the real man beneath the polish.

Petty. Entitled. Mean.

"I hope he was worth it," he spits. "Because this team? It's not making the playoffs without him. And then you're going to lose everything, Carrington."

I meet his glare head-on. "This franchise has survived worse than your ego. I promise you, we will survive this."

Continuing to hold Dean's hateful glare, I address the large man standing at the door. "Please see that Mr. Ward leaves his computer and phone on his desk on his way out."

Security steps in. He doesn't fight it. Just throws me one last look before disappearing out the door.

The board turns to me like wolves circling the next course.

But I don't flinch.

I lift my chin, fold my hands, and brace for whatever comes next.

Let them come for me. I've already lost the only thing that mattered.

I'm back in the same seat a few hours later.

Different meeting, same battlefield. Only this time, I'm on the same side as the Vipers board as we face two Boston executives and their lawyer.

There's also a league lawyer and a couple of assistants trying to look useful while pretending not to eavesdrop.

Dean's chair is empty.

On purpose.

"Let the record reflect that Dean Ward has been relieved of his duties effective immediately," Chairman Weatherby says, voice like gravel.

Boston's legal rep—a trim man with wire-rimmed glasses and a permanent scowl—doesn't even nod. "We appreciate the prompt action. That said, the leak still occurred. And the resulting fallout has damaged the reputation of not only Mr. Leonard, but the Boston Freeze organization."

Joshua's name lands like a weight on the table. I glance to an empty seat next to the executives. The seat Joshua should be occupying.

Typical. Cowards never show up when it's time to face consequences.

"Our concern," the second Boston exec adds, "is less about the contents of the leak and more about how it originated. If internal Vipers personnel were actively conspiring with a player from our roster to—"

"That individual has been terminated," I cut in, voice sharp. "Dean Ward acted alone and against direct policy. I've already made that clear."

"Be that as it may," Boston's lawyer says, "Mr. Leonard's involvement still raises questions."

I lean forward, palms flat on the table. "Then perhaps you should ask yourselves why Mr. Leonard is still skating on your top line instead of being suspended pending review. Because what's not going to happen here is Boston trying to pin its internal rot on my franchise."

The man's mouth tightens. "With respect, Ms. Carrington—"

"No," I interrupt, cool and exact. "With respect, you're here pointing fingers while your player openly conspired to take out a member of my roster and destabilize my leadership. You want transparency? Try accountability first."

Murmurs ripple around the table.

Miriam—one of the older holdouts from my father's era—gives me a rare approving glance.

"You want assurances? Start with your own house. My franchise took action. Yours rewarded the leak with first-line minutes."

Boston's lawyer nervously clears his throat. "The league would prefer to avoid public litigation against the Vipers. However, we're asking for assurances that internal leaks won't happen again. Your franchise isn't in a position to withstand another scandal."

That part's aimed at me.

I nod once. "Understood. We've already tightened our internal security protocols. Perhaps the Freeze should do the same. You'll receive our written agreement by end of day. Assuming all parties are satisfied, I believe we can call this closed."

Boston's execs gather their notes and leave without another word.

When the door shuts behind them, the silence is thick.

Chairman Weatherby rubs a hand down his jaw. "You handled that well, Ms. Carrington. Your father would be proud."

The mention of my father is like a sucker punch to the gut.

It's the first time anyone in his circle has given me any credit.

It feels like a victory. Or, at least, it should.

But it tastes like ash.

Because it doesn't matter.

I still have my team, but it doesn't mean anything without Maddox.

CHAPTER THIRTY-EIGHT

Maddox

THE WEIGHT SETTLES into my chest before I even knock.

Coach Holt's office is still dark, blinds drawn, door cracked open like it's waiting for me.

The rink's quiet now, just the hum of machinery and the distant echo of sticks hitting rubber.

Practice wrapped half an hour ago, but I stayed behind. Pacing. Thinking. Trying like hell to talk myself out of this.

Didn't work.

I nudge the door open with a knuckle.

Coach is behind his desk, scribbling something in a notepad. Doesn't look up. Just flips a page and keeps writing like he already knows why I'm here.

"Got a minute?" I ask.

He finishes his line. Sets the pen down. "Close the door."

The click behind me sounds final. Like the start of something I can't undo.

I sink into the chair across from him, palms sweaty, heart pounding like I'm about to take a slap shot to the chest.

Coach doesn't say anything, just watches me with that quiet, unreadable stare that always makes you feel like you're about to get benched.

I run a hand through my hair. "I'm retiring at the end of the season."

No flinch. No blink. Just a slow nod.

"I wanted you to hear it from me first," I add. "Before the press gets wind or the rumors start."

His voice is low. "You sure about that?"

No. Not even a little.

But I nod anyway. "Yeah."

I can't say her name. Not here. Not now. But she's in every inch of this decision. In the ache under my ribs. In the silence I wake up to now that she's gone.

Coach leans back and folds his arms. "You've got a few good years left, Lasker."

"I know."

"You're finally playing with a team that respects you."

"Yeah."

He studies me. "This about Carrington?"

I let the breath go slow. "This is about me not wanting to lose the only thing that ever made walking away from the game make sense."

He exhales through his nose. "You know what this'll mean for your contract. For trades. For playoffs."

"Doesn't matter. Not anymore."

There's a beat of silence, heavy and still. Then, quietly, Coach nods again.

"All right," he says. No speech. No lecture. Just that. Simple and solid. "You tell Jace?"

"Not yet."

"Start there." He reaches for his notepad again and flips to a fresh page. "Then finish this season strong. Go out swinging."

I rise from the chair, but the weight doesn't leave. It just shifts. Sinks lower, deeper.

Something permanent in the way it settles in my bones.

At the door, I pause. "Thanks, Coach."

He doesn't look up. "Make it worth it, Lasker."

I step into the hallway alone. The buzz of the arena lights overhead, the echo of skates and voices long gone.

I don't know what happens next. Don't know if she'll ever forgive me. Don't even know if I can fix what I broke.

But I do know this…

I'm not running again.

If I've got one shot left to prove she matters more than the game, I'll take it.

Even if it means giving it all up.

The door to the locker room hisses shut behind me.

For a second, nobody looks up.

Riley's sprawled on the bench, taping his stick. Finn's half-dressed, skates still on, a towel around his neck. Cal's in the corner, headphones around his neck, fidgeting with a puck like it holds the answers to the universe.

The second I step in, though, something shifts.

Eyes cut to me.

Not suspicion. Not judgment.

Something else.

Something heavier.

Jace leans against the far wall, arms folded, expression unreadable. He's the only one who already knows. We talked after practice—just the two of us, up in the film room, where the lights are always dim and the silence hits harder than it should.

I told him everything.

Didn't sugarcoat it.

Didn't run.

"I'm out after this season," I say now, to the whole room. My voice is low, but it hits like a puck to the boards. "No contract extensions. No trades. I'm done."

The silence sharpens. Not one guy speaks.

I brace for it—questions, jokes, maybe even disappointment.

Instead, Riley's the first to nod.

"Fucking knew it," he mutters. He shoves the tape roll into his gear bag and adds, "You got that 'I've been emotionally wrecked by a woman' glow."

Finn laughs under his breath. "It's the dead eyes. Real subtle, bro."

Jace doesn't say anything, but his gaze flicks between them. A silent cue.

And like that, the energy shifts again.

Cal crosses the room and nudges me with his shoulder. "You good, Lasker?"

"No," I admit. "But I will be."

They don't push.

They just let it hang there. This truth between us.

That I'm leaving.

That it's not because I want to.

That it's because I found something worth walking away for.

Riley leans back, cracking his knuckles. "You better go out with a bang, old man. Take some bastards down with you."

"Yeah," Finn adds, smirking. "Especially that dick from Boston."

Cal perks up. "Joshua Leonard?"

"Fucking hate that guy."

I glance at Jace, who finally speaks.

"You've got a couple games left to show them what kind of man you are." His voice is steady, low. "Make it count."

I nod once. "Yeah. I will."

And I mean it.

Not just the games. Not just the hits or the wins or the final roar of the crowd.

I've got one shot left to earn the kind of ending I never thought I'd get.

And it starts right here.

In this locker room.

With the team I didn't think would ever feel like mine.

I drag my bag onto the bench and start unzipping it. "One more thing," I say, voice casual.

They all glance over.

I pull out my sketchpad. The one I haven't touched since before everything went to hell.

I flip it open to a page halfway through, one I started in secret weeks ago and never finished. A Vipers logo, hand-drawn. But not the standard one.

This one's got teeth. Edge. Fire behind the eyes. The kind of logo you bleed for.

I hold it up.

"Thinking about leaving this behind," I say. "Something for the next generation."

Finn whistles low. "Damn."

Even Riley looks impressed. "You drew that?"

"Yeah."

Jace nods once. "Hang it in The Hiss Room when it's done."

There's no fanfare. No group huddle or pat on the back. Just a room full of guys nodding like I've already made my mark.

Like I belong.

Maybe for the first time in my life.

Later, when I get home, I don't turn the lights on.

Just drop my bag by the door and head straight for the kitchen, grabbing a Gatorade from the fridge I haven't stocked properly in weeks.

The cold stings my palm. My shoulder's still aching from the hit I took from Leonard. But none of it touches the fire under my skin.

I should be bone-deep tired.

Instead, I'm wired. Alive.

She's still in there—behind my ribs, under my skin. No matter how many times I've told myself it's over, the truth doesn't change.

I want her.

Still.

Always.

And I'm not going out quiet.

I cross the room and grab my sketchpad from the coffee table. It's already open to the Vipers logo I showed the guys. But I flip past it—page after page of half-finished panels, character outlines, old shit that never felt like anything.

Until now.

Until her.

I grab a pencil and start sketching.

Not a game plan.

Not a playbook.

This one's for her.

She called me out the first time she saw my work. Told me not to hide behind it. Not to flinch.

So I won't.

The lines come slower tonight. Not because I don't know what I want to say, but because I want it to be perfect.

The panel starts to take shape. A woman—powerful, head held high, expression unreadable—standing at center ice in heels. Her back's to the viewer. She's facing the boards. The stands.

The spotlight's on her.

Alone.

Except she's not. Not really.

There's a speech bubble forming above the ice behind her. Unspoken. Waiting.

I pause, pencil hovering.

The words will come later.

For now, it's enough that I know what it's supposed to be.

I don't want a press conference.

I don't want to grovel behind closed doors.

If I'm going down, I'm doing it our way.

Loud.

Public.

With cameras and chaos and the team behind me.

I lean back on the couch, sketchpad resting against my thigh, heart thudding like it did the first time she kissed me.

She gave me something I didn't know I needed.

And I let her go.

But not without a fight.

My phone buzzes next to me—probably Jace, checking in again. I don't answer.

Instead, I close the sketchpad and drag in a breath that tastes like salt and ink and maybe, finally, hope.

If I'm going down, I'm doing it with my whole heart on the ice.

<hr>

CHAPTER THIRTY-NINE

Sloane

THE PIT IS ALIVE TONIGHT.

Buzzing, hissing. Unapologetically loud.

There's music pulsing through the air, fans in flashing neon, signs that glitter under the arena lights—one that even says *MARRY ME MADDOX* in all caps, scrawled in black Sharpie on a hot pink poster board.

I should laugh. Roll my eyes. Something.

But I just keep walking, heels sharp against the tile as I move through the tunnel toward the owner's suite like I don't feel like I'm shattering with every step.

Fan Appreciation Night is supposed to be a celebration. The culmination of months of grind and grit.

It's the kind of night where you smile until your cheeks hurt, where the crowd screams loud enough to shake the rafters, and every handshake comes with a compliment about how far the team's come.

And we have.

We made it through chaos. Through scandal. Through fire.

And somehow, I still feel like I lost everything.

The suite doors open ahead of me. A few of the sponsors are

already inside, sipping top-shelf whiskey and watching the pre-game warmups on the triple screens.

A congratulatory basket from one of our luxury brand part-ners sits on the table—leather, silk, something sleek and black with my name embossed in gold.

Dean's absence doesn't even feel satisfying. It just feels...quiet.

"Sloane, you made it," one of the board members says as I enter, smiling too hard. "Big night."

I nod, lips tight. "It is."

I make the rounds like I'm not hollowed out. Shake hands. Smile when I have to. Pretend like I'm not scanning the ice every few seconds for a glimpse of him.

And then I see him.

Maddox.

Helmet on, visor low, jersey stretched tight across his shoul-ders as he circles the far side of the rink like a predator locked in.

Every part of him looks like he was built for this moment—sharp, strong, dangerous. The crowd chants his name before the puck's even dropped.

And I stand there, arms folded, pretending I'm just another executive watching her player prepare.

Not the woman who kissed him in the dark.

Not the woman who fell in love with him too late.

Someone laughs behind me. "Think he'll announce it tonight?"

"Retirement? Hell, I've been hearing that rumor all week."

My stomach sinks.

He hasn't told anyone. Not officially. But Coach Holt informed me of Maddox's intentions.

I stare down at the ice, pulse throbbing behind my ribs. Maddox skates to the bench, jaw set, and my throat tightens.

I don't know what tonight is going to bring.

But I know one thing for sure.

I'm not ready for goodbye.

———

The game moves like a blur, but I don't miss a single second.

Every time Maddox hits the ice, my spine goes rigid.

I feel every blow he takes like it lands on my own skin. The sound of a body slamming into the boards. The whistle slicing through the noise.

His name rising from the stands like it belongs to them.

Because it does.

They love him. Even after everything.

The scandal. The fallout. The tension that's followed him like smoke.

He's still theirs.

And he plays like it.

Aggressive. Controlled. Beautifully brutal. Like a man with nothing left to lose and everything still worth fighting for.

The board members beside me cheer when he slides into a split save and smothers the rebound before the winger can pounce, their laughter cutting through the suite like static.

"Still got it," someone murmurs.

Still got it.

He's never lost it.

Even when the press tried to rip him apart. When the whispers painted him as washed-up and too volatile to bet on.

When they dragged up Boston again like it was a fresh wound and not a scar he carried every damn day.

He's never lost it.

And I can't breathe watching him.

The third period ticks down, and we're only up by one, 2–1. Overtime potentially looms, the tension so thick I can taste it.

Boston wins a face-off in our zone. They pull their top line out—including Leonard, of course. I press a hand to the glass in front of me, leaning forward without meaning to.

He's locked in. Maddox. Every muscle wired, eyes tracking like he's reading the future.

The puck snaps across the slot—

A one-timer.

A rocket.

Straight at him.

And he robs it.

Full extension, glove to the heavens, snatching the shot out of the air like it's personal.

The Pit explodes. The buzzer sounds.

I shoot to my feet, clapping before I even realize what I'm doing, and it takes every ounce of willpower to stop myself from screaming his name like the rest of them.

On the ice, Maddox doesn't even celebrate.

He just straightens from the crease, skates toward the glass, and looks up at the owner's box.

Right at me.

The noise dulls. The pounding of my heart is louder than the crowd now.

He holds my gaze like it's the only thing tethering him to the moment.

Like he knows what comes next.

Like he's already made peace with it.

And I haven't.

"Hell of a save," one of the sponsors says behind me, clapping. "Man's got ice in his veins."

No.

He bleeds.

I'm the only one who saw it.

I sit back down slowly, hands folded in my lap like that will keep them from shaking.

The PA announcer's voice echoes across the arena, booming over the noise.

"With a game-saving stop in the final seconds, tonight's First Star…number thirty-three—Maddox Lasker!"

The cheers erupt again, louder this time. Deafening. Wild.

I barely hear it.

All I can do is watch him skate to center ice as the lights drop and the spotlight finds him.

Alone in the glow.

Stick raised.

A king with no crown.

He nods once.

And something in my gut twists.

He's planning something.

I don't know what. But I feel it in the way the tension shifts. The way the players give him space.

The way Holt stands back with his arms folded, watching like he already knows what's coming.

Maddox is about to do something dangerous.

And I'm terrified I won't survive it.

But the crowd doesn't settle after the save.

They swell.

Voices chant his name over and over, and Maddox doesn't move. He stands at center ice, helmet off now, stick at his side, steam curling off his skin like smoke in the cold.

A storm building.

The spotlight stays locked on him even after the scoreboard rolls into postgame highlights.

The crew doesn't drop the lights. The music doesn't kick on. No one calls the players off the ice.

Something's happening.

And the Pit knows it.

Maddox skates to the nearest ref and mutters something.

There's a brief exchange—sharp nods, clipped words—and then the announcer's mic crackles again, fuzzed with feedback.

"Ladies and gentlemen…" The PA voice drops low, curious. "If you'd give your attention to center ice, Maddox Lasker has something to say."

The noise in the arena crests, then quiets like a wave pulling back.

My heart stops. My lungs lock.

No.

He wouldn't announce his retirement like this.

Not here.

Not like this.

Except he is.

A staff member in a Vipers jacket skates out and hands him something—a black foam core board. From up here, I can't make out the image on it, but he holds it in both hands like it matters.

Like it *means* something.

When he turns to the crowd, the jumbotron catches his face.

His hair is damp with sweat, his jaw scraped from a hit, but his eyes—

God.

They find mine and don't let go.

"I don't like talking," he says into the mic, voice gritty, low, everything in him shaking with restraint. "Never been good at it. And I definitely don't like attention."

A ripple of soft laughter rolls through the stands.

"But there's someone in this building tonight I owe more than a private apology. Someone I hurt… because I thought I was protecting her. Because I was trying to undo the wreckage I'd caused, even if it meant pretending I didn't love her."

A gasp breaks from my throat. Tessa's hand clamps down on my arm.

He keeps going.

"I said some things in that boardroom I didn't mean. I did it so she'd be safe. So no one could take what she built. I thought I was being noble. But I was being a coward."

His voice cracks there, just a little.

"I told her she wasn't a distraction. That she was the reason I still wanted to be better. And then I walked away anyway."

He pauses. Lifts the board.

The jumbotron switches to an image—his drawing.

It's a comic panel. Two figures, unmistakably him and me, rendered in simple black ink. I'm in a business suit, heels planted, expression fierce. He's in full gear, shoulder bruised, mouth bloodied.

Behind us, the arena is in flames. The world is collapsing.

But we're standing side by side, holding hands.

The caption:

Let it burn. I've got you.

A sob punches out of me.

"I made this on the road," Maddox says. "Because I needed to remember what we looked like when we weren't scared. When we were just…us."

He looks straight up at the owner's suite again.

"I don't know how to fix everything. I can't give you back control or undo the things we lost. But I can tell the truth."

He drops the board. Tosses his gloves. Drops his stick.

And then he turns to face the owner's suite—face *me*—and sinks to one knee.

A roar detonates across the arena, but it sounds like static in my ears.

Because I can't breathe.

"Sloane Carrington," he says, without a mic now, just his voice carrying like thunder. "You're the only win that ever mattered."

My knees go weak.

He doesn't move.

The whole team stands behind him at the bench, silent and watching. Coach Holt nods once, arms crossed, eyes sharp but approving.

Tessa is crying.

So am I.

I push to my feet, trembling so hard I can barely stand, and move to the front of the glass. Hands braced. Heart pounding like it's trying to claw its way out.

Maddox stands. Picks up the drawing again. Skates forward until he's beneath me, face tipped up, haloed in light.

"I'm not asking for a second chance at the team," he says. "I'm asking for a second chance at *you*."

The silence is deafening.

And then it hits.

Applause. Screams. The crowd erupts, stomping, cheering, crying. Chants start again—my name this time, god help me— and all I can do is stare at him while my world shakes around me.

Because this man.

This gruff, guarded, maddening man—

Just laid his soul on the ice in front of thousands of people.

For me.

I don't remember walking out of the suite. Or running down the tunnel. Or bursting onto the ice in heels and a blazer like a lunatic.

All I remember is the sound Maddox makes when I reach him.

Like breaking and coming back together in the same breath.

I don't say a word.

I just throw my arms around him and kiss him like I've got nothing left to lose.

And maybe I don't.

But I've got him.

I don't know how long we stay like that—arms locked tight, mouths fused, the arena spinning around us like a dream we haven't earned.

When I finally pull back, it's not far.

My forehead presses to his, our breath shared between us, hearts pounding out a rhythm too big for words.

He cups my jaw, rough hands trembling. "You came down."

I nod, blinking hard. "You left me no choice."

That crooked, broken smile pulls at his mouth. "Good."

We just stand there.

The crowd still roars. The lights still burn. But all I see is him.

His hand is still wrapped around the comic, the edge bent now from his grip. I trace it with my fingers.

"You really drew this?"

"On the road. After that night in the suite."

I swallow, heat thick in my throat. "I look like a badass."

"You *are* a badass."

He exhales a soft laugh, vulnerable in a way that cracks something in me wide open.

"I'm not asking you to forgive me yet," he says, voice low so only I can hear it. "But I'll spend the rest of my life proving I was worth the risk."

I don't answer right away.

Because the truth is, I already have forgiven him.

He lifts our joined hands, kisses the back of mine in front of the whole damn arena, and for the first time in forever, I don't feel like I'm carrying this empire alone.

Because he's not just standing beside me.

He's *with* me.

We walk off the ice together—step for step—leaving the past where it belongs.

Behind us.

EPILOGUE

Maddox

Six Weeks Later – The Pit

IT'S QUIET TONIGHT.

No cameras. No crowds. Just the hum of the boards and the way her laugh echoes off the ice like it belongs here.

Sloane carves a perfect curve at center, scarf fluttering behind her, cheeks pink from the cold.

She's not rusty—she's lethal. Powerful. Beautiful. The kind of grace you don't lose, even after years behind a desk.

"If this is how you looked on Olympic ice, no wonder the world lost its mind."

She glances over her shoulder, eyes wicked.

"Careful, Lasker. You sound impressed."

"I'm trying not to look worshipful," I shoot back. "It's not going well."

She pivots with a flick of her blade—smooth and effortless—spraying a mist of ice in my direction. "Watch out, goalie," she says, voice teasing. "This isn't my first rink."

She shoots me a look, that deadly combination of boardroom steel and bedroom heat, and my blood sparks the way it always does with her.

No games. No secrets. Just this: her and me and everything we fought like hell to survive.

We haven't talked much about Boston. About Dean. About the board's vote or the press cycle that chewed us up and spit us back out.

She still lost part of her voting share for now. I still announced my retirement. But neither of us lost what mattered most.

We didn't lose us.

I skate toward her, slow and easy, like we've got nowhere to be. She watches me come, chest rising faster, pupils darkening even before I reach her.

She knows what I'm thinking.

"Here?" she murmurs, breathless.

"It's our ice," I rasp, taking her hand. "They just play on it."

Her scarf slips off. My fingers slide under her coat and brush the warm skin of her waist where her sweater's ridden up.

I feel her shiver—not from cold, but from the way I look at her. Like she's the only win that's ever mattered.

We kiss at center ice, slow and deep, the kind that doesn't end with mouths. My hand finds the back of her neck. Hers fists in my hoodie.

And yeah. We don't make it to the locker room.

She ends up on her back on my coat, legs wrapped around me, her soft moan swallowed by the rafters.

I fuck her slow, reverent, like I'm writing our names into the ice. Like every thrust, every kiss, every whispered promise is a contract the world doesn't get to void.

"I love you," she breathes against my mouth, shaking under me. "I'm never letting you go again."

"Good," I groan, buried to the hilt inside her. "Because I'm not giving you the chance."

We come undone together, bodies slick, hearts loud in the silence. After, I roll to my side, pulling her into my arms as we lie under the banners—our jerseys side by side up there now, hers stitched into the history she earned.

"I've got something for you," I murmur, reaching into my pocket.

It's the comic. The final one I sketched—the one I didn't give her until now. She sits up, unzipping the envelope, fingers gentle like she already knows what this means.

The panel is simple.

Me and her. Skates on. Backs to the boards. Facing the world, ready for the next period. Above us, in bold ink:

"Sudden Death's Got Nothing On Us."

Sloane presses her lips together, eyes shining. Then she curls into my side, tucking the comic to her chest.

"Think they'll let us back in the locker room?" she teases.

"Not if they see the ice."

She laughs again, full and easy, and damn if I don't feel lucky every time I hear it.

Because I almost lost this.

I almost lost her.

But now we've got overtime. A second chance. A new game.

And this time?

We play on the same team.

THE END

Thank you so much for reading **GAME MISCONDUCT**!

Want more Sloane & Maddox? Scan the QR Code below to subscribe to my mailing list or tap here and you'll receive access to the bonus scene!

Already a subscriber? Check out the latest newsletter for the link to the bonus content!

Ready for more in the Vipers World? Keep reading for chapter 1 of **HOLIDAY INTERFERENCE**, a holiday novella featuring Vipers Rookie, Cal Reid and event planner, Noelle Jennings!

HOLIDAY INTERFERENCE CH 1

Noelle

SNOW IN ATLANTA is like a bad one-night stand—brief, messy, and talked about for years.

Which is exactly why I didn't plan for one.

And why tonight's about to go sideways.

I tap my earpiece and dodge a tray of crab puffs. "Do we have confirmation on valet staging?"

"East entrance is backed up," Jules, my assistant, replies through a crackle of static. "Some guests already requested rideshares, but ETA's up to twenty minutes."

Of course it is.

The atrium at The Pit is warm and glittering, all golden lights and high ceilings and holiday sparkle so thick it practically hums.

We've got thirty-foot trees, a string quartet, and enough champagne to float a yacht.

On paper, it's perfection. On the ground?

It's barely holding.

I smile anyway, because that's what I do—smile, manage, adapt. I'm an event planner.

Stress is my cardio and disaster is my sidekick.

"This is Atlanta," someone laughs behind me. "We'll get a light dusting and everyone'll act like it's the apocalypse."

I don't turn around, but my left eye twitches with restraint.

We were supposed to get a flurry. Maybe two. Just enough to look cute on the event photographer's camera roll.

But now it's coming down in earnest, fat flakes slicking the windows and piling on the walkways like the universe had one too many eggnogs and decided to be dramatic.

Still, the sponsors are happy.

The quartet is plucking out some moody version of "Jingle Bell Rock." And no one's noticed the back end of the coat check is already soaked from guests shaking out faux-fur wraps like wet dogs.

I press a palm to my stomach and let out a slow breath.

Control. That's the word. If I keep the structure tight—timelines, tray passes, run-of-show—I can absorb the chaos before it shows.

And if I absorb it, it can't crack me.

A server swings by with a tray of bacon-wrapped figs, and I snag one before he disappears back into the crowd.

"Thank you," I murmur, taking a bite like it's communion. Warm, salty, grounding.

Overhead, fairy lights blink with a little too much sass.

The wind kicks again, harder this time. I glance at the front glass—snow slanting sideways, guests still smiling.

Atlanta doesn't believe in bad weather until it's already iced over Peachtree Street.

I press two fingers to my earpiece. "Jules, flag me if DOT updates the closure list. I don't want to wait until the news trucks show up to tell us we're stranded."

"Copy."

My phone buzzes. Another weather alert.

Another punch from Mother Nature in passive-aggressive font.

Inside, I walk the room like a slow orbit—checking corners, angles, guest clusters.

My heels click across marble, my dress swishes just right, and the smallest snag in a string of garland catches at the edge of my vision like a loose thread on a hand grenade.

I fix it before the photographer swings around.

Everything here is curated. Controlled.

Sparkling just enough to distract from the fact that I haven't had a real holiday in six years and my last date ditched me for a fitness coach with a ring light.

This? This is safer.

I adjust a centerpiece, tuck a stray napkin, and smile as a sponsor raises his glass toward me.

I don't do cozy. I do immaculate.

Until the wind knocks again, just a little harder.

And something in me flinches.

I'm halfway through texting the rideshare liaison when I feel it—that weird prickle at the base of my neck, like I've just stepped into the wrong scene in the right shoes.

Not panic. Not nerves.

Just… a shift. Like the room's holding its breath behind me.

I turn.

And there he is.

Leaning against a column near the back bar, sleeves pushed just far enough to show strong forearms and a watch that probably costs more than my car. Hair damp from snowmelt. Suit jacket open. Tie absent.

And a look on his face like he's already halfway checked out.

Cal Reid.

The Vipers' youngest rookie. Quiet. Massive. All sharp edges and no shine.

And absolutely not where he's supposed to be right now.

With Finn McCade on a tight leash from the front office, Cal's the one I worried about not falling in line.

Not because he's a troublemaker but because he's new at all of this and he already looks like the type of guy who barely tolerates the off ice things that come with being a major league athlete.

Instead of making rounds or smiling for the sponsor photo op like we discussed—like I *scheduled*—he's standing there like he's the only person in the building who knows how this story ends.

I exhale once through my nose, check my smile in the reflection of a glass ornament, and cross the floor.

The crowd parts easily, the way it always does when I walk through it like I belong—which I do.

I planned every second of this night down to the final strand of battery-powered garland.

But Cal Reid doesn't budge. Doesn't blink. Doesn't even pretend to be impressed.

He's not rude. Just… still.

Too still for a guy midway through his rookie season, wearing a suit like it's a punishment and watching the room like it owes him something.

"Reid." I soften the edges of my voice just enough to make it sound like I'm not annoyed.

Yet.

His eyes drag over to me slowly. Up close, they're hazel, reminding me of autumn leaves.

They're also unreadable and framed by dark lashes that don't match the expression underneath. They should belong to someone cocky, someone with too many selfies on his phone.

But there's no shine. No bite. Just calm. Heavy. A little broken, maybe, if you know what to look for. Like he's young but with an old soul.

"I'm guessing this isn't your kind of party," I say, half-smile in place as I stop in front of him.

He lifts one shoulder. "I was told to show up."

"You were also told to smile. And mingle. And maybe pretend you don't want to crawl out of your own skin."

"I'm here, aren't I?"

It's not the words. It's the tone—cool and even, like everything's on mute except for me.

"I'm going to go ahead and call that a no on the mingling," I say lightly, glancing past him toward the bar. "Unless brooding in formalwear is your personal outreach strategy."

A beat.

Then—barely, *barely*—the corner of his mouth twitches. Not quite a smile. More like a glitch.

Progress.

"You always this pushy?" he asks.

"I'm not pushy. I'm effective." I glance at my watch. "And currently twenty-two minutes behind schedule because someone decided to ice over the city."

His gaze slides toward the window. Snow streaks sideways across the glass like the sky's in a mood.

"I told the PR team you'd be a hit tonight," I add, turning my eyes back to him. "Tall, broody, no social skills? That's catnip for sponsors."

"I don't do fake charm."

"Good. Because I've had enough of that to last a lifetime." The words slip out before I can leash them, then hang there, sharp.

His eyes flick to mine again, more curious this time.

"I just need thirty seconds of you standing near a wreath and not looking like you want to murder someone," I say, smoothing the moment over with a practiced smile. "Think you can handle that?"

He looks me over—not in a way that lingers, not in a way that's rude. Just... observant. Like he sees everything and says nothing unless it's absolutely necessary.

"Depends," he says.

"On?"

"Is it a real wreath?"

My laugh slips out before I can stop it. "Why do I feel like that's the most you've said all night?"

"Because it is."

And there it is again—that flicker of a smile, or something close to it.

The rookie has a dry sense of humor buried under a solid wall of nope.

I shouldn't like that. I'm not even sure I *do*. But something low in my stomach tightens anyway.

"Come on, Reid. You give me thirty seconds, and I'll make sure no one drags you into a cookie-decorating station."

"Is that a real threat?"

"Only if you keep hiding in the corner like a surly Christmas statue."

He pushes off the wall, slow and loose, like he's not in a hurry to be anywhere. I don't move, don't step back. His body heat brushes mine on the way past, warm and solid and unbothered by the air between us.

For a rookie, he carries himself like he's already lived through a few battles.

I follow him toward the sponsor photo area, adjusting the fall of garland as we go. He stops where I point, turns to face the camera, and gives the most half-hearted, camera-unfriendly expression I've ever seen outside of a DMV.

"I said *not* murder," I mutter.

"I'm trying." He doesn't move, but there's the barest trace of amusement under his voice.

I step closer, adjust his lapel, and feel his breath when he exhales—slow and warm against my knuckles.

His eyes hold mine when I look up.

Just for a second.

But it's enough to make my brain fuzz and my pulse flicker, fast and low.

I step back. Quickly.

"Don't move," I say. "You almost look like a person."

"Careful," he says, deadpan. "That almost sounded like a compliment."

"I'll schedule you one for next year."

He holds still while the photographer snaps three frames, then turns to me like we've just completed a secret mission.

"Was that so hard?" I ask.

"I've had worse."

He pauses, then adds, "At least there were no cookies."

I blink.

And then I laugh. For real this time.

It's quick, and stupid, and warm in a way I didn't expect. But I feel it right down to my spine. And from the look in his eyes, he felt it too.

Just a flicker.

Just enough to mean something I don't have time to deal with.

PREORDER HOLIDAY INTERFERENCE **HERE**!

ALSO BY ELIZA PEAKE

The Atlanta Vipers Series

(Interconnected Standalone

Spicy, Hockey Romance)

Game Misconduct - AVAILABLE NOW

Holiday Interference - PREORDER NOW

November 2025

Power Play - WINTER 2026

Open Net - SPRING 2026

Line Change - LATE SUMMER 2026

Back Check - FALL 2026

Final Shift - WINTER 2027

The Cape Sands Series

(Interconnected Standalone

Spicy, Small Town Sports Romance)

Unexpected Forever

Mine Forever

The Madison Ridge Series: Homecoming

(Interconnected Standalone

Steamy, Small Town Romance)

Trouble Me

Remind Me

Wreck Me

Unexpected Christmas

Love's Kaleidoscope

A unique collection of love themed short stories.

NONFICTION

30 Days Until "The End": An Inspirational Guide to Finishing Your Novel in 30 Days

If you're looking for humor, positivity, and a swift kick to your flagging motivation, Eliza Peake's inspirational guide to completing a draft in thirty days is a must have.

GET A SNEAK PEAKE OF ALL THINGS ELIZA!

If you'd like exclusive content, first look at cover reveals, bonus material and other announcements first, join my newsletter, The Sneak Peake!

Want all the book fun in a drama free zone? Join my reader group, Eliza's Sassy Belles. We have a fun group going and growing all the time!

ACKNOWLEDGMENTS

I have many to thank for helping me with this book, because as always, it takes a village!

To my Queens, Melissa Ivers and Lilian Harris. I love you ladies beyond measure and treasure our friendship more than you know.

Silla at Masque of the Red Pen for keeping me straight with my edits; Canea at Concepts by Canea for making another beautiful cover that hit exactly the way I wanted; Ashley Estep for keeping my social media going when I don't want to be on there and for talking all the Taylor Swift with me when Ivers won't; Rose Lambson for all the amazing graphics you always help us with, I just love you and your talent; Richelle Emory for always being encouraging and for being my branding guru; My Sassy Belles, my ARC team, bookstagrammers, booktockers, and all the influencers who took a chance on me, and to my readers all over the world! You all had a profound impact on me at some point in this journey!

To Mr. P and Nat for supporting me always. I love you guys more than anything in the world. I hope you know that.

And to God, for blessing me with all of the people in my life supporting me and for bringing my dream to life.

XOXO 💋
Eliza

ABOUT THE AUTHOR

Hey y'all! I'm Eliza and I write spicy, all the feels romance full of heart, heat, and humor. My heroes are swoony alphas, my heroines are strong and audacious, and family is at the center of it all.

I'm a proud mom and a Southern girl who can bless a heart with the best of them. I live with my very own book boyfriend, a snoring dog, and a sassy cat.

In my downtime, I read all the panty-melting romances I can get my hands on, drink coffee by day, wine by night, and indulge my woo-woo side as often as possible. I'm also hopelessly addicted to tacos.

I dream of retiring to the beach someday where I'll continue writing sexy romance stories to my heart's content and taking sunrise and sunset walks in the sand, thinking of my next book!

Join my newsletter, The Sneak Peake, to get updates on all sorts of shenanigans, exclusive content, and news on books and appearances at http://elizapeake.com/subscribe/